PRAISE FOR BARRY MAITLAND'S BROCK AND KOLLA SERIES

'Riveting, intelligent crime writing from one of Australia's best.'—*Weekend West*

'No one drops so many wonderful threads to a story or ties them so satisfyingly together at the end.'—*The Australian*

'Maitland crafts a suspenseful whodunit with enough twists and turns to keep even the sharpest readers on their toes.' —*Publishers Weekly*, USA

'This Australian crime writer's popular Brock and Kolla series continues to do what it does best—intrigue and entertain. Verdict: tight suspense.' —*Herald Sun*

'There is no doubt about it, if you are a serious lover of crime fiction, ensure Maitland's Brock and Kolla series takes pride of place in your collection.'—*Weekend Australian*

'Barry Maitland is one of Australia's finest crime writers.'—*Sunday Tasmanian*

'Comparable to the psychological crime novelists, such as Ruth Rendell ... tight plots, great dialogue, very atmospheric.'—*Sydney Morning Herald*

'Maitland is a consummate plotter, steadily complicating an already complex narrative while artfully managing the relationships of his characters.'—*The Age*

'Perfect for a night at home severing red herrings from clues, sorting outright lies from half-truths and separating suspicious felons from felonious suspects.'—*Herald Sun*

'A leading practitioner of the detective writers' craft.'—*Canberra Times*

'Maitland is right up there with Ruth Rendell in my book.'—*Australian Book Review*

'Forget the stamps, start collecting Maitlands now.'—*Morning Star*

'Maitland gets better and better, and Brock and Kolla are an impressive team who deserve to become household names.'—*Publishing News*

'Maitland stacks his characters in interesting piles, and lets his mystery burn busily and bright.'—*Courier-Mail*

BARRY MAITLAND is the author of the acclaimed Brock and Kolla series of crime mystery novels set in London, where Barry grew up after his family moved there from Paisley in Scotland, where he was born. He studied architecture at Cambridge University and worked as an architect in the UK before taking a PhD in urban design at the University of Sheffield, where he also taught and wrote a number of books on architecture and urban design. In 1984 he moved to Australia to head the architecture school at the University of Newcastle in New South Wales, and he held that position until 2000.

The first Brock and Kolla novel, *The Marx Sisters*, was published in 1994, and was shortlisted for the UK Crime Writers' Association John Creasey Award for best new fiction. It featured the central two characters of the series, Detective Chief Inspector David Brock, and his younger colleague, Detective Sergeant Kathy Kolla. The sequel, *The Malcontenta*, was first published in 1995 and was joint winner of the inaugural Ned Kelly Award for best crime fiction by an Australian author. The books have been described as whydunnits as much as whodunnits, concerned with the devious histories and motivations of their characters. Barry's background in architecture drew him to the structured character of the mystery novel, and his books are notable for their ingenious plots as well as for their atmospheric settings, each in a different intriguing corner of London. In 2008 he published *Bright Air*, his first novel set in Australia, and later his Belltree Trilogy— *Crucifixion Creek*, *Ash Island* and *Slaughter Park*.

Barry Maitland now writes fiction full-time, and lives in the Hunter Valley. The full list of his Brock and Kolla novels follows: *The Marx Sisters*, *The Malcontenta*, *All My Enemies*, *The Chalon Heads*, *Silvermeadow*, *Babel*, *The Verge Practice*, *No Trace*, *Spider Trap*, *Bright Air*, *Dark Mirror*, *Chelsea Mansions* and *The Raven's Eye*.

BARRY MAITLAND

THE PROMISED LAND

WITHDRAWN

ALLEN&UNWIN

SYDNEY · MELBOURNE · AUCKLAND · LONDON

The characters in this book are fictitious. Any similarity to real persons, living or dead, is coincidental and not intended by the author.

Allen & Unwin
83 Alexander Street
Crows Nest NSW 2065
Australia
Phone: (61 2) 8425 0100
Email: info@allenandunwin.com
Web: www.allenandunwin.com

A catalogue record for this book is available from the National Library of Australia

ISBN 978 1 76063 267 0

Set in 13/17 pt Bembo by Midland Typesetters, Australia
Printed and bound in Australia by Griffin Press

10 9 8 7 6 5 4 3

The paper in this book is FSC® certified. FSC® promotes environmentally responsible, socially beneficial and economically viable management of the world's forests.

To Margaret

*With grateful thanks to all those who have helped me in the
writing of this novel, especially my wife, Margaret, Dr Tim Lyons,
Lyn and Kirsten Tranter, Annette Barlow, Angela Handley,
Christa Munns and Ali Lavau. Also to Mike and Sue Wright
who showed me a thing or two about Hampstead, and Mike and
Lily Cloughley who did the same for Godalming.*

'. . . the sofa cushions are soft underneath you, the fire is well alight, the air is warm and stagnant. In these blissful circumstances, what is it you want to read about?

'Naturally, about a murder.'

George Orwell, 'Decline of the English Murder', 1946

I

Charles Pettigrew shut down the computer on his desk and went out into the main office. It was deserted, both the women having left for the weekend. Angela, his senior (and only) editor, had taken the uncorrected Burdekin proofs home with her. He switched off the lights, locked the office and made his way down to the street door, where he glanced, as he always did, at the polished brass plate that declared *Golden Press*.

Autumn had come in earnest this week; dead leaves slippery underfoot, plucked by the swirling wind from the trees in Golden Square. He passed by the statue of George II or Charles II—he was uncertain which—and made his way to Leicester Square, where he caught the tube out to Hampstead and followed the same walk he took most evenings, down the high street. He'd lived here almost all his life, loved Hampstead and hated it. It was full of ghosts, of his parents and of the authors whom they had venerated—Keats, Lawrence, Wells, Fowles, Huxley, Milne, Waugh—now commemorated on the blue plaques that peppered the streets.

He walked on to Garden Gate, stopped for a whisky at the White Horse, bought a baguette at Le Pain Quotidien on the corner of South End Road, formerly a bookshop, Booklovers' Corner, where George Orwell once worked. Ghosts everywhere.

He reached home, 14 Parliament Hill Close, a late Victorian red-brick house his grandfather and father had both owned before him. A few letters waited in the wire basket behind the front door, and he carried them through to his study and poured himself a Scotch, sighed, loosened his tie, settled himself in the old leather armchair. In this room his grandfather and father had drunk whisky with the great authors of their day, many of whom they had published. Golden Press was truly golden then, a byword for contemporary British fiction of the highest order. No longer.

He flicked through the mail—bills, entreaties, flyers, and a large buff envelope addressed to him in printed felt-pen letters. Inside were a single photocopied page and a short covering note, handwritten:

Dear Mr Pettigrew, I believe this may be of interest to you. If so, you may contact me. Shari Mitra.

There was a mobile phone number.

He frowned, turning to what appeared to be a photocopy of the first page of a manuscript written on an old mechanical typewriter with a threadbare ribbon, a handwritten message scrawled across the top.

The manuscript read as follows:

THE PROMISED LAND
A novel by Eric Blair

The Strand Hotel, Rangoon, six in the evening. I was staying there for a few days in the course of business from the Viceroy's Office in Delhi. That evening I was sitting in the bar before going through to the restaurant. It was busy with traders, talking about their dealings in Burma and the latest news from home, and every table was taken. I noticed a tall, fair-haired man enter and look around in vain for a seat. He was different from the others, bearded, clothes rumpled, his skin weathered and discoloured by the sun, and on impulse I indicated the free seat at my table. He joined me and introduced himself as Ralph Halliday, an agent for one of the big timber exporters. He explained that he had just returned from an extended trip in eastern Burma, looking for new teak stands in the high country along the frontier with China. We went on to spend the evening together, during which he told me a remarkable story about a man he had encountered in the remote jungle, who had founded a unique community based upon radical utopian principles.

Pettigrew looked back to the note at the top of the page. The handwriting was shaky, and it took him a moment to decipher the words:

I hereby give this manuscript and all rights to its publication to my dear friend Amar Dasgupta. The novel 'The Promised Land' is not to form part of the GOP portfolio.

E. Blair, Cranham, 12 August 1949

Charles Pettigrew sat motionless, pondering, his forehead creased in a frown. It was a scam, of course. It had to be. And yet . . . In 1935 Eric Blair was living in a flat in Parliament Hill, not a hundred yards away. In June of that year he published a novel, *Burmese Days*, under the pseudonym George Orwell, and one warm evening in July, according to Pettigrew family legend, Charles's grandfather Mortimer had drunk whisky with the thirty-two-year-old budding author in this very room, quizzing him about his future plans, before they sat down to dinner.

Orwell sat in this chair that I'm sitting in now, Charles thought. It's like a message from the past, a lifeline from old Grandpa Mortimer. For, God knows, Golden Press needed a lifeline now. 'In business', Grandpa Mortimer had told him, 'you must be ruthless, boy. I let young Orwell slip through my fingers. He went with Victor Gollancz. Don't make that mistake. In business, you must go for the jugular.'

The more Pettigrew thought about it, the more he felt a strange and unfamiliar elation growing inside him. For so many years he had resigned himself to impotence and frustration as Golden Press slid downhill towards oblivion. Perhaps this, at last, was the coup that had always eluded him. You must be ruthless, he told himself. Go for the jugular.

2

A wedding. Detective Chief Inspector Kathy Kolla feel-ing uncomfortable—too much make-up, heels too high, music too loud, room too hot, too much else on her mind.

Her friend Nicole appeared at her elbow. 'She looks so happy, doesn't she?' Nicole took a big gulp from her cham-pagne glass. '*Radiant.* This is the only time we ever use that word, isn't it? "The bride looked *radiant.*" Like plutonium or something. That's what liposuction does for you.'

She was fairly pissed, Kathy saw, and was envious. Things being as they were, she was staying off the booze.

'Still,' Nicole went on, 'goes to show.' Another slurp.

Kathy, who wished she was somewhere else, said, 'What does it show, Nic?'

'That there's hope for us yet. She's *our* age, Kath! And this is her *first* marriage.'

'What's her secret?'

'She got him on the web of course. *Partners Perfect*. We should try it. We should.'

'Hm.'

'I will if you will. We could work as a team.'

Kathy's phone vibrated against her hip. 'Peter?'

'Guv. The Heath. We got another one.'

Kathy became very still. This was what she'd been fearing. The roar in the room died away. 'The same?'

'Exactly the same.'

'Where?'

'The Highgate side this time, Number One Pond.'

'See if you can get Tony Fenwick.'

'Right.'

'I'm on my way.'

'I'll have someone waiting for you on Millfield Lane.'

She rang off, told Nicole to apologise to the bride and groom for her, and hurried as fast as her heels would let her to the car.

~

When she reached the place, lights flashing, she found emergency vehicles cramming Millfield Lane to left and right along the wooded boundary of Hampstead Heath. No media yet. She changed her shoes for boots, pulled on a raincoat and ran to the police barrier, where a uniformed officer was waiting for her. She followed his flashlight into the dark shroud of the park around the glimmer of the large pond and stopped at the edge of a patch of thick shrubs where equipment was being prepared. Here she put on forensic overalls. As she was drawing on the gloves a man came stumbling towards her from the bushes and was sick. 'Sorry,' he mumbled. 'Sorry.'

She continued towards the circle of bright light where figures were clustered. They made room for her and she recognised Tony Fenwick, the pathologist who had attended the first case. She looked at the figure lying at his feet and saw that it was exactly like the other one. 'The hammer,' she said.

'Just so.' Fenwick nodded agreement. 'The hammer.'

Four days before, on the morning of Tuesday, 20 October, the body of Andrea Giannopoulos, twenty-eight-year-old wife of Valentin Giannopoulos, sixty-four, a Greek business-man, had been found by a dog-walker on the edge of Vale of Health Pond, a mile away across the Heath to the west and a few hundred yards from their home in Hampstead. She was fully dressed in her running gear, and her clothing and posses-sions had not been disturbed. Cause of death was multiple blows to the head by what was believed to be a heavy ball-pein hammer, so severe that her face was obliterated.

'How long ago?'

DI Peter Sidonis, barely recognisable in his crime-scene overalls, spoke up. 'Her husband found her around six thirty this evening. She'd gone for a walk on the Heath and he became alarmed when she didn't come home by dusk. Came in with a torch, calling her mobile, and eventually heard it ringing over here.'

Fenwick added, 'Yes, I'd say she hasn't been dead long. Rigor has hardly begun.'

'So who is she?'

Sidonis said, 'Mrs Caroline Jarvis, guv. Home in Highgate. Husband Selwyn Jarvis.'

'The judge?'

'The judge.'

Silence for a moment. Then Sidonis added, 'And her brother-in-law is Oliver Gowe, the Defence Secretary.'

Kathy drew a breath. 'Oh.'

'Over here, boss.' Sidonis led Kathy to a patch of grass on which lay a woman's shoulder bag, its contents spread out around it. 'Looks like he may have had a look this time.'

This was encouraging, Kathy thought, since he must surely have left traces. The lack of prints or DNA at Vale of Health Pond had been particularly frustrating, not helped by heavy rain that had fallen between the time of the murder and the discovery of the body. 'What's the weather forecast?' she asked.

'Periodic showers. They're working as fast as they can to process and protect this scene.'

'And no CCTV, I suppose?'

'Right.'

That was another thing that had hampered the Giannopoulos investigation—within the whole eight hundred acres of Hampstead Heath there were only three CCTV cameras, clearly marked. It was like investigating a murder from fifty years ago, with no technology. Kathy had almost been tempted to call Brock to see if they were doing it right.

Sidonis's phone rang. He listened. 'The dog's found something.'

The handler and her black labrador were waiting further along the main path, the dog almost invisible in the dark. The woman pointed her torch beam at stains in the dirt. 'Blood, we think.'

'Yes.' Kathy looked around her. 'He was probably waiting in those bushes for the right victim to come along, incapacitated her with a blow, then dragged or carried her to the pond.'

'That's what we reckon.'

'We?'

'Bonnie and me.' The handler nodded at the dog. 'She followed the trail back out here from the body.'

'Didn't find the weapon, did she?'

'No, but she was working the woman's scent, not the man's.'

Standing well back, Kathy peered at the trampled ground, several broken branches. 'Looks like there was a struggle.'

A police helicopter passed overhead, followed shortly by another chopper that slowed and hovered directly above them, searchlight beaming down.

'TV,' Sidonis muttered. His phone rang again. He turned to Kathy. 'They're outside on Highgate Road too, boss. Big media contingent just arrived.'

'Where's the husband now?'

'Ambulance took him home. Very shaken up. An officer's with him.' He gave Kathy the address in Highgate village.

She said, 'I'll go and talk to him. You know what to do here, Peter. Call me if you need anything.'

'Right, guv. This is going to be big, isn't it?'

When she reached the entrance to the Heath, she found the area solid with vehicles and media. She slipped through the clamouring reporters, hurried to her car and waited inside for uniforms to clear a way through for her. While she waited she made a couple of calls, then sat, tapping the steering wheel, thinking how right Peter was. This was her first big case as a chief inspector, the first as head of one of the Met's twenty-four Murder Investigation Teams, and the pressure was going to be huge.

A way finally opened and she followed a patrol car out into the village.

~

With its Georgian shops, old pubs and green spaces, Highgate still felt much like a village, though hemmed in by the London boroughs of Islington and Haringey. Judge Jarvis lived in a back lane in a mellow-brick eighteenth-century house that would have looked at home somewhere out in the shires. A woman police officer answered Kathy's knock.

'The doctor offered him pills, but he's refused to take anything. He changed his shoes and washed his hands—he got muddy on the Heath—and made one phone call to his sister-in-law, who's on her way over.'

'Have you got his shoes?'

'Yes, ma'am.'

She led Kathy to a sitting room in which the elderly man sat stiffly in an armchair on one side of the fireplace, staring at its empty partner on the other side.

He looked up at Kathy. 'Yes?'

'I'm Detective Chief Inspector Kathy Kolla, sir, in charge of the unit that's handling this case. I'm very sorry for your loss.'

'Yes, yes. Anything? Any developments?'

'A senior pathologist and the forensic unit are there now.

We're deploying a large team and will do everything we can to find those responsible as rapidly as possible. I'll give you my details and you can contact me at any time, day or night.'

As she spoke she was struck suddenly by a memory—Selwyn Jarvis not as a High Court judge, but as a criminal prosecutor, relentlessly grilling a witness in a case she'd been involved in with Brock. Which one was it? Maybe ten, fifteen years ago.

He said abruptly, 'Sit down,' and she pulled over a chair from a side table rather than take his wife's armchair. 'I don't want to be soft-soaped, understand? Treated as a *victim*, with kid gloves. None of that. I want to be *informed*.'

'I understand.' She could see that he was holding himself tightly together, determined to keep a grip, but his left hand was betraying him, tapping ceaselessly on his knee.

'Can you tell me your wife's movements this afternoon?'

'We had a cold lunch in the kitchen, then a quiet couple of hours in this room. Caroline sat there, in that armchair, reading a novel—that's it open on the stool—while I went through some court documents. At about three thirty she put down her book and said she needed some fresh air, a walk on the Heath. I . . .' His voice faltered and he tried to cover it up with a cough. 'I said I wanted to finish the document I was reading, if she would wait half an hour, but she was impatient and said she would go. We were aware of the terrible business with the Giannopoulos woman earlier in the week, of course, but she insisted she wasn't going to let a thing like that stop her walks. She loved them, her walks on the Heath. I foolishly let her go.'

He paused for a moment, face set. Then, 'We didn't know all the details of the other case. Is this . . . similar?'

'Yes. Very similar.'

He whispered, 'Dear God.'

'Do you have any idea where on the Heath she would have gone?'

'Well . . . she loved walking up to Parliament Hill. The sun was out between showers, a fine autumn afternoon, and she loved that wonderful view across London, the distant towers of the City . . . Yes, I think she would have gone up there. Not sure where else.

'But when dusk fell I tried to phone her. Went to messages, couldn't understand why. Then it was dark, and I tried again, same thing, and I began to worry. I thought she might have stopped in the village for something, so I went out to see. When I couldn't find her there, I went on to Merton Lane— knew she would have got onto the Heath that way. I kept calling her number and hadn't gone too far in when I thought I heard her ringtone, from among the bushes over by the pond. That's where I found her. I had a torch. I saw . . .'

And then he lowered his head and his hand stopped tapping.

Kathy waited while he pulled out a large handkerchief, coughed, wiped his eyes.

She said, 'I'm sorry to put you through this.'

'No, no. Go on.'

'Did you see anyone else?'

'Um . . . there were other people around, but I didn't pay them any attention. I was just looking for her.'

'No one you recognised?'

He thought, shook his head.

'Anyone carrying a bag or backpack of some kind?'

He looked puzzled. 'No. I'm sorry, I really can't recollect anyone. Actually . . . I only remember seeing people in the village, not on the Heath itself.'

'Her bag was lying to one side, opened.'

'Yes . . . Yes, I do remember that.'

'Did you touch it?'

'No. I didn't touch anything, except . . . I crouched down beside her and put my hand on her arm, called her name. Then I saw her face and realised there was nothing to be done. I called 999 immediately.'

He swallowed and Kathy asked if they could get him anything—a glass of water, a cup of tea—but he shook his head. The front doorbell rang and the constable went to answer it.

'That'll be Audrey.' Jarvis sighed. 'They were very close. Two beautiful sisters married to two difficult old men.'

She burst into the room as Jarvis got to his feet, enveloped him in her arms. 'Selwyn, is it true?'

'I'm afraid so, Audrey.' He stood awkwardly in her embrace, and finally eased away. 'I must speak to the detective here without delay. Be a darling and get yourself a drink and I'll be with you shortly.'

Audrey wiped her eyes, took a deep breath. 'I'm staying right here, Selwyn. I need to know everything.'

She turned to Kathy, 'I'm Audrey Gowe, Caroline's sister.'

Kathy introduced herself and they shook hands.

'Is it as bad as the other one?'

'I'm afraid it looks similar, Mrs Gowe.'

'Oh my . . . poor Caroline. Would she have suffered?'

'No. I believe it would have been over very quickly.'

She nodded. 'Have you contacted the boys, Selwyn?'

'Not yet.'

'Do you want me to do it?'

'No, they should hear it from me. Please, Chief Inspector, go on.'

Kathy said, 'Judge, at the moment we're assuming these are random attacks, but I have to ask: do you think it's possible that Caroline could have been deliberately targeted?'

Jarvis began shaking his head, but his sister-in-law said quietly, 'Of course she was deliberately targeted.'

They both turned to her. Jarvis said, 'What are you talking about, Audrey?'

'She was white, relatively wealthy and living in Highgate-Hampstead. You wait, that's what everyone will be saying tomorrow. They've been whispering it ever since that billion-aire Greek's wife was murdered. There have been several brazen attacks—four thugs on two scooters rode up to that Chinese tycoon who bought Byron House and mugged him in broad daylight outside his home, ripped off his gold jewel-lery and watch and disappeared.' She turned to Kathy. 'You check it out. The watch cost sixty thousand pounds. Obscene, isn't it? The watch, I mean. But people are saying it's a class war. The poor have had enough of the excesses of the rich and they're on the warpath.'

Jarvis broke in, 'Audrey, that's nonsense. Please, Chief Inspector Kolla needs to talk quietly to me. There's a bottle of brandy in the kitchen. Why don't you get us both a glass.'

She got to her feet reluctantly and went out, and Jarvis said heavily, 'Mind you, she's probably right. No doubt that is what they'll be saying tomorrow, the locals and the right-wing press.

But no, to answer your question, Caroline had no enemies. Everyone loved her. But I, on the other hand, am a judge. Is it possible that she was killed to punish me? If it weren't for the Giannopoulos case I might have thought so.' He hesitated, then said, 'Kathy . . .'

Kathy looked at him in surprise.

'Kathy, we are professionals in the same line of business. I was a Crown prosecutor for many years. We understand each other. I want you to feel free to share your thoughts with me, and I with you. We may be able to help each other.'

'Thank you, Judge.' Kathy was thinking that was the last thing she wanted—that and having a cabinet minister as the victim's brother-in-law. 'So can I confirm that you've had no threats made against you recently?'

'Absolutely none.'

'There will be formalities. We'd like you to check whether anything was taken from Caroline's bag. We'll need your finger-prints and DNA and the clothes you were wearing when you found Caroline, and we'll want to borrow Caroline's computer.'

'Of course. I suppose there were no CCTV cameras in the area?'

'No, I'm afraid not.'

'Caroline was dead set against them. She belonged to a group that protested vehemently against the installation of the first ones on the Heath, said they were against the spirit and history of the place. I told her she was wrong, but she wouldn't have it. To her, cameras on the hills where Keats once wandered and Constable sketched were an abomination.' He stared bleakly at the other armchair.

'Are your sons nearby?'

'Chris is an academic in California, presently at a conference somewhere I can't recall. Teddy's somewhere on a boat
in the Pacific. Caroline kept track of all that. Dear God, how
will I manage without her? I'm helpless.'

'No you're not, Selwyn.' Audrey came striding back in
with two large tumblers. 'You have a million friends and relatives to help you. But first we need quiet time to come to
terms with what's happened.'

The judge frowned at his sister-in-law. 'That I will never
be able to do.'

Kathy checked her watch and told them she must go. She
gave them her contact details and drove back to Hammersmith,
where her team was based. Around Shepherd's Bush the traffic
slowed to a crawl, and she tapped impatiently on the wheel,
seeing her destination in the distance up ahead, the squat glass
building they called the Box, glowing in the night. Efficient
and unlovely, its stack of open-plan office floors could hardly
be more different from the warren of rooms in Queen Anne's
Gate where she used to work with Brock's team, and she felt
a small pang of regret.

Finally the traffic began moving again and she drove into the
basement car park of the Box and took the lift up to the fourth
floor, where the area occupied by the Giannopoulos investigators was being rapidly expanded to cater for a multiple victim
inquiry. Zack, the computer suite manager, was directing the
placing of equipment over in one corner, while whiteboards,
graphic screens and work tables were being set up nearby. Kathy
called Phil, the action manager, into a small office in the corner
and began to get to grips with the logistics of it all.

~

Brock settled down on the couch with a glass of Scotch and switched on the TV. He'd been spending more and more time at Suzanne's place in Battle, near the Sussex coast, since he retired, and was feeling distinctly ambivalent about it. Of her two grandchildren who lived with her, Miranda, fifteen, had happily accepted his presence and was good company, with a quirky sense of humour and a passion for horses. Stewart, two years older, was another matter. He said little and sullenly resisted all attempts to communicate. But it was comfortable here, sociable; the food was excellent, the village community agreeable. And yet ... Suzanne had a purpose, running her antiques business in the high street of the small town. By contrast, Brock was feeling bored, useless, a layabout.

Suzanne said that many people felt like that when they retired, and it was only to be expected that he'd be grieving for his old life after thirty-five years in the Met. He was still waking suddenly in the night, hearing his phantom phone ringing. And it was sad these days, going back to his house in London, which seemed more and more like a mausoleum, a relic of older, more exciting days with like-minded comrades.

Being a practical man, impatient of self-pity, he had tried to think of some kind of project to occupy himself. Not golf like Roy and his mates, or fishing like old Dick Sharpe, or growing roses like Peter White. And not the local wood-turning group that Suzanne had suggested, although that might still be a possibility. For a while he'd flirted with the idea of taking up gliding again, something he'd done long ago at a club in Kent, and had wondered about ever since the Verge case. There was an excellent gliding club not far away, over by Lewes; he'd paid them a visit, got enrolment forms and had a good look around. But when he told Suzanne she was alarmed at the idea and had put her foot down. There was volunteering, or further education—a degree with the Open University perhaps, but what should he study? Marking time, he'd thought about all those books lining the walls of the staircase in his old house, so many of which he'd never got around to reading, and with Suzanne's help had drawn up a list of all those he really should have tried.

So far it hadn't been a great success. With most of them his interest had died by page fifty, and that was that. *The Name of the Rose* had been a bright exception, although he'd found himself, around page 300, mentally yelling at Brother William to take a closer look at the bloody library.

The Ten O'Clock News came on, and his attention suddenly focused. Detective Chief Inspector Kathy Kolla was seen emerging from dark woods, her face caught in the dazzle of TV camera lights, as a reporter announced, in those urgent tones usually reserved for terrorist attacks and plane crashes, that a second gruesome murder had been discovered on Hampstead Heath. Abruptly the scene changed to the Palace of Westminster, where Oliver Gowe, Defence Secretary, was emerging from a late sitting of Parliament. Looking strained and irritated, he pushed past yelling reporters and said, 'No comment at this time,' and got into a waiting car.

'Suzanne,' Brock called, 'come and look at this.'

3

Soon after midnight, Kathy was sitting in her corner of the office with the crime scene manager from Forensic Services, a dour Scot, examining diagrams and video of blood spatter made to luminesce by the application of luminol spray.

'This is just a preliminary thought now,' the CSM murmured, 'but compare the spread around the head of the second victim, here, and this one around the first. Do you see the difference?'

Kathy studied the images. 'There's much less spread around Caroline Jarvis's head.'

'Aye, and yet the injuries were just as severe.'

'So . . . he's learning? Improving his technique?'

'Possibly, but how—'

He stopped in mid-sentence and Kathy turned to see what he was looking at. She was surprised to see her boss,

Commander Steven Torrens, head of Homicide and Serious Crime Command, accompanied by *his* boss, the assistant commissioner in charge of the Specialist Crimes and Operations directorate, both dressed as if for a banquet—he in black tie, she in a sleek cocktail dress and heels—approaching through the desks and computers, staff staring as they passed.

The CSM stood up hurriedly and muttered, 'I'll be off then, ma'am,' and made a run for it.

Torrens said, 'Ah, Kathy, do you know Assistant Commissioner Cameron?'

'No, sir. Ma'am.'

They shook hands. Sally Cameron, something of a legend, was shorter and older than Kathy had imagined, but her presence was as formidable.

'Sorry to interrupt, Kathy,' she said, 'but we were at a rather tedious function and I thought we should do something more important. Brief us, will you?'

So Kathy did, starting with an update on the essential facts of the case, then taking them to the large map and explaining the logistical difficulties of Hampstead Heath.

'We're concentrating on the main part of the Heath east of Spaniards Road, within which both murders took place. Although there are only three CCTV cameras within the Heath itself, there are at least fifty in the immediate perimeter area. There are twenty-six path entries and exits into the East Heath that they could have taken, and many more off-track ways of getting in and out. From first light we'll have teams doorknocking the perimeter roads and alerting passing traffic for any sightings of strangers on the two occasions. We'll be checking overflights and satellite images for parked vehicles in the vicinity.'

'What are you looking for?' Torrens barked.

'Any vehicle that was in the area at the time of both murders, and someone carrying a bag.'

The assistant commissioner asked why.

'The problem for the killer is that with the gross type of wounds inflicted he's bound to be covered in blood. We assume he won't want to emerge from the park like that, and that he would have been wearing some kind of protective clothing which he'd remove and carry out in a bag.'

They discussed this, then moved on to close-up maps of the two murder sites. Kathy showed them the preliminary forensic results. 'We've found one possible trace so far—a single hair, blonde.'

'DNA?' Torrens asked.

'Yes, but not human, they think. Probably a dog. There are a lot of dog-walkers on Hampstead Heath, so it may have nothing to do with the murderer.'

She expanded on her plans for the next day, outlining optimal manpower needs.

'Granted,' Torrens said. 'For three days you have carte blanche, all the resources you need. Then we'll review the situation.'

The assistant commissioner stayed for another five minutes before shaking Kathy's hand and wishing her good luck. When she'd gone, Torrens drew Kathy aside. He was a big, beefy man, not unlike Brock in build, Kathy thought, but much more aggressive in manner.

'You've kept abreast of the press coverage?' he demanded.

'Not really, sir. I've been concentrating on the investigation.'

'Get someone working full-time with the press bureau, and make sure we're covering all the media and responding immediately to misinformation. You realise the sensitivity of this case, don't you? We need it resolved damn fast. It's unfortunate you've been hit with this in your first month as a team commander; I'm considering whether you need additional help.'

'Well, so far we've got all the manpower—'

'I mean in a command role, Kathy. Another, more experienced team leader to come in and take over this new investigation, the Jarvis murder, and let you concentrate on the Giannopoulos inquiry. Double the intelligence, double our chances.'

Kathy felt a jolt as if she'd been slapped. 'And double the possibility of oversights and confusion. With respect, sir, these are one case, one killer. Splitting the command doubles the risks of mistakes. I may be new to my rank and my role, but I've had twenty years' experience of homicide investigations at the highest level. I assume when you appointed me to MIT team leader you thought me capable of this. I know I am.'

A moment's silence. Kathy wondered if she'd spoken too loudly, if other people around had heard. Then Torrens said, 'All right. Three days—five pm on Tuesday. Then we'll see.' He turned on his heel.

~

Kathy worked for another couple of hours, responding to the stream of questions and information that kept pouring in. By three thirty am it was clear that there would be no breakthrough before daybreak, so she went to the rest room on the floor below and tried to get some sleep.

By dawn she was up, showered and back drinking coffee in the command suite in the task-force office. Around her sleepy figures were getting to work on CCTV downloads and phone records from the neighbouring towers, looking for numbers that had been operating in the area at the times of both murders. Two technical officers were busy adapting the HOLMES major inquiry system for their use, while others were combing records from across the UK and Europe for similar styles of assault.

Kathy talked to them all, then checked on the deployment of uniforms and detectives across the Hampstead and Highgate area. When she was satisfied that everything was working properly, she called Peter Sidonis, who arranged a car to take them to the Air Support Unit. There they boarded one of the EC145 Eurocopters for a flight over the crime scene area.

They approached from the east on a clear, crisp morning, flying over morning traffic on Archway Road. Looking down, Kathy made out the green area of Highgate Cemetery, and thought of her first murder case with Brock all those years ago, which began when Peg Blythe and her sister Eleanor returned home from their visit to Karl Marx's grave to find their sister, Meredith Winterbottom, dead.

Not far away, she saw a crowd gathered outside the Jarvises' house. The media, she assumed, hoping for a quote from the judge. She imagined him under siege inside, impatient and frustrated, and wondered how long he'd delay his current trial. Not long, she guessed.

The chopper swung to the south to make a sweep across the Heath. Below them now was the high point of Parliament

Hill, tiny figures pausing on their morning walk to look up. Then they were over Hampstead and banking north along Spaniards Road. Out to the right Kathy saw the whole sweep of the Heath, its woods and meadows, its necklace of ponds that long ago served as London's water supply gleaming in the reflected morning sunlight. Now, at the north end of the Heath, she saw the white block of Kenwood House, the stately home where Julia Roberts was seen filming a costume drama in the movie *Notting Hill*.

They began to lose height, coming down over the clearing of the old duelling ground in South Wood and dropping towards South Meadow and Number One Pond, where white-clad figures could be made out among the surrounding trees.

Kathy handed her headphones to the pilot and stepped down onto solid ground. As she and Peter Sidonis hurried towards the tree line a voice called out, 'Chief Inspector Kolla!' She turned as two men in dark anoraks ran towards her, assuming they were detectives until they were up close and she saw the microphone and camera.

'Any progress, Chief Inspector?'

Kathy shook her head, annoyed, and made to move on, but the man said, 'I suppose you'll be giving this case top priority, eh? Gotta keep the toffs happy.'

Kathy turned. 'We treat all homicide cases as top priority,' she said. 'We'll be treating this case like any other.' And she marched away. She was annoyed with herself for having risen to the bait, and her tone hadn't sounded quite right, but there wasn't time to worry about that. She moved in among the trees to get an update from the field team.

Nearby a car was waiting to take her and Sidonis to Westminster for the post-mortem. Things had changed a lot since Meredith Winterbottom was on the mortuary slab. Kathy vividly remembered the smells, the howl of the bone saw as she stood with Brock in an ancient basement next to the pathologist Sundeep Mehta as he worked on the old woman's body. Now the post-mortem examinations of suspicious deaths were carried out in a new facility across the road from the Home Office, and observers watched by CCTV link to avoid contamination.

They were shown to Fenwick's office and he took them through a virtual autopsy of CT scan imagery on his large computer screen. Caroline Jarvis's body had been scanned from head to foot and could now be rotated and digitally peeled away, layer by layer, in graphic three-dimensional colour, without the use of any scalpel or saw.

'Fifty-eight years old, in good health,' Fenwick said. 'A childhood fracture in the right ulna, here, and a partial mastectomy in the left breast ... here, for breast cancer five years ago. Otherwise fine. So, the damage ...'

The image swept up to Caroline's head, and Kathy gasped. The whole front of the skull had been crushed and shattered into small bone and teeth fragments.

'Very thorough,' Fenwick said. 'A methodical, workman-like job.'

'Not frenzied then?' Kathy asked.

'Oh, I couldn't say that. It certainly looks obsessive to me. I'd never seen anything like it until last Tuesday. There is one area that may be helpful.'

He manoeuvred the view around to enlarge the left side of the head.

'There. When the left temporal bone was struck, it broke up around a circular piece corresponding to the shape of the hammer head.'

He overlaid a cursor on the piece.

'Thirty-four-millimetre diameter. I'd say that's the size of the hammer head you're looking for. When we reassemble the fragments elsewhere we'll be able to confirm that, I'm sure.'

Kathy nodded. 'Good.'

'One other thing,' Fenwick said. He touched the controls so that the image seemed to withdraw from the skull, focusing instead on the flesh layer above. 'You see brown filaments here, and here, caught up in the pulped flesh?'

He zoomed in and Kathy said, 'They're everywhere.'

'Yes. We've collected and cleaned some and examined them under the microscope.' He brought up an image on the screen.

'Furry threads,' Kathy said. 'Green?'

'Right, green cotton threads. I think he laid a green cloth or towel over her head before he started hitting her.'

'Why?'

'To reduce the blood spatter, I'm guessing. Protect himself and his clothes. I'd say he was learning from the Giannopoulos murder, modifying his technique.'

Kathy said, 'There's a raw mark on her neck. Was he trying to strangle her?'

'No, it's only on the left side of the neck. I think she was wearing a necklace and he tugged it off.'

Kathy turned to Peter Sidonis, who shook his head. 'There was no sign of a necklace.'

'A trophy,' Kathy said, her heart sinking. This was looking

worse and worse: a killer who was developing his technique and now taking trophies—a true serial killer. He wasn't going to stop now.

~

As they were leaving the mortuary Kathy called the judge's mobile number and asked if they could meet to follow up a few points. He explained that he'd spent the night at the Gowes' home in Belgravia and would be spending the day there. He'd heard that his own house was under siege from the press.

Audrey Gowe answered the door and led Kathy to a sitting room. 'He's very withdrawn. Insists he's going back to work tomorrow, but I've tried to make him see sense—told him people will say his judgement is impaired and overrule his decisions . . . Ah, darling.'

Kathy turned to the doorway to see a man she recognised from TV, Her Majesty's Principal Secretary of State for Defence, Oliver Gowe, dressed in a dark suit, a coat over his arm.

Audrey Gowe introduced Kathy.

'So you're in charge, are you?' he said. Kathy had the impression of an exhausted man, for whom this was one problem too many.

'Yes, sir,' she said.

'I'm told you're throwing everything at this case. Is that true? You have all the resources you need? Because if you don't I can pull strings.'

'I have all I need at the moment, sir. We have over a hundred detectives and uniformed officers on the ground . . .'

He cut her off with a nod. 'Yes, yes. Well, keep my wife up to date, will you?' He turned to her. 'I must go, Audrey. Car's waiting. You'll cope?'

'Of course, darling.' She went out with her husband to the hall and Kathy heard the front door close. Audrey returned and said, 'Important meeting in Washington. Bit of a crisis. Selwyn is in the sunroom.'

She led the way to a conservatory overlooking a beautifully groomed garden. This house was much grander and more formal than the Jarvis home, and the judge seemed diminished in this setting. He put down the newspaper he was reading and got to his feet.

'Any news?'

Kathy described a little of what was happening and he asked about having his wife's body released for her funeral and said he would like to visit her to say goodbye properly beforehand. Kathy told him she would make arrangements, then took an envelope of photographs from her bag and showed them to him.

'These are the items of jewellery that Caroline was wearing, Judge. The watch, rings, bracelet. Can you tell me if anything is missing?'

'Oh . . . I'm not sure if I can. That's certainly her wedding and engagement rings, but whether she could have worn any others I couldn't be sure.'

'What about a necklace? Could she have been wearing one?'

'Oh yes, I think she would have been, wouldn't she, Audrey?'

'Definitely. What about the gold chain you gave her for her birthday? She was wearing that a lot. I'll look when we go back to Highgate, shall I?'

'Would you?' Jarvis sank back onto his chair.

Audrey gave Kathy a description of the necklace and the judge agreed to search through old receipts for details.

'One other thing,' Kathy said. 'Would Caroline have taken some green cloth with her?'

'Cloth?'

'Yes, a cotton towel or facecloth, perhaps?'

'No, certainly not.'

~

Later that afternoon Kathy received an urgent summons from Commander Torrens to his office in New Scotland Yard. There was something about his secretary's manner that made Kathy uneasy, as if she were aware of some disaster that was about to strike. After a delay, during which Kathy could hear Torrens's raised voice through the door, it opened abruptly and he waved her in. Without a word, he shut the door behind her and pointed a remote at a large screen on the wall. It came to life with a clip from a news broadcast. Over pictures of emergency vehicles, the commentator's voice said: '*Police continue to investigate the brutal murder yesterday evening of a second woman on Hampstead Heath. According to an unverified source, both women's bodies were savagely mutilated in a ritualistic manner. Residents of the high-value London district are said to be traumatised by this latest atrocity, but despite this the police are insisting on a low-profile approach.*'

The image switched to a clip of Kathy, her name and rank printed at the bottom of the screen, talking to camera: '*We'll be treating this case like any other.*' She looked indifferent, Kathy thought, almost bored.

'What the hell did you think you were doing?' Torrens exploded.

'They've edited it to change the inference, sir. I'd just said that we treat all homicides as top priority.'

'But that's what they do! That's why we don't make comments off the cuff! That's why we have a bloody press bureau!'

'I'm sorry, sir. He ambushed me.'

Torrens turned away, exasperated. 'I warned you about handling the media on this case, didn't I? Now our whole strategy has been thrown into chaos. Instead of trying to avoid panic, we've been made to look like we couldn't give a damn. I'm about to call a totally unnecessary press briefing to try to repair the damage. Is there anything, anything at all, that I can tell them to show we're on top of this?'

'We're following every lead . . .'

'Don't tell me, tell them. The media unit's waiting for you downstairs. Give them everything you can think of so they can write my statement.'

'Sir.'

'A shaky start, Kolla. Get your act together.'

~

Night fell, shifts changed over, no sign of a breakthrough. A DNA trace was found on Caroline Jarvis's purse which wasn't hers or her husband's, but there was no match on file and they had no idea whose it might be. At ten Kathy realised she'd been staring at the same screenshot for some minutes without taking it in. She got to her feet and told the duty officer she was calling it a night, heading home.

Home was new, an apartment on the south bank of the river at Vauxhall, on the twelfth floor, the same level as her old flat in Finchley. But so much grander—the view across the Thames to Pimlico and Westminster and beyond was breathtaking. She could still hardly believe it was hers, made possible by an unexpectedly large legacy from her working-class Aunt Mary and Uncle Tom in Sheffield, who had apparently been nurturing all these years a secret deposit of dubious money left them by Kathy's father before he killed himself. She saw it as a measure of how far she'd moved on that she could now find it funny that she was profiting from the old crook's crimes.

She poured herself a wine and sat at the big window, trying to unwind before bed. Two brightly illuminated boats passed by on the dark river below, a helicopter drifted across the sky, and she thought about Torrens's words: *A shaky start.* She'd made a mistake, but she refused to doubt her ability to do the job. She just couldn't think what else she should be doing. She needed a break, a little bit of luck. And she thought of Brock, wondering if he'd have done anything differently. She remembered him now as unruffled, taking it all in his stride, but perhaps it had never been like that.

As if it could read her thoughts, her phone rang and his name was on the screen.

'Kathy, how are you?' That familiar voice.

'I was just thinking about you,' she said. 'I suppose you've seen my stellar performance on TV.'

He chuckled. 'Don't give it a thought, Kathy. There's always some bastard trying to trip you up.'

'My boss thinks it's more serious than that. He's on the point of taking me off the case.'

'Torrens? No finesse. Believes in crashing through. Thinks he can make things happen by shouting loud enough. Murder investigations aren't like that. Sometimes it just takes time. Well, you know that. We've been in that situation often enough.'

'Yes, but then you always protected me from the heavy mob upstairs.'

'You sound tired, Kathy. Where are you now?'

'Just got home. I'm going to bed. When are you and Suzanne coming to see my new flat?'

'Soon—she's desperate to see the luxury penthouse.'

'It's not quite that. Come up to town for lunch or a show or something, when I get some time off.'

'Absolutely. In the meantime, don't let them rush you.'

After she'd rung off, Kathy finished her wine and went to bed, but found it impossible to sleep.

~

The next morning she started by going through an update on leads received from the public. All would be investigated, but in the meantime they'd been given priority ratings, A, B, C or D. One of the As caught her attention: a man who'd phoned in about something he and his girlfriend had noticed on the evening Caroline Jarvis was murdered. He had turned off Spaniards Road into the car park of the Spaniards Inn for a drink and found it full. As he was turning the car to leave they saw a man crossing from the other side of the road and going to a white van parked in the inn's car park. He remembered it because he'd complained to his companion that people shouldn't park there if they weren't customers of the pub. There was a light near the van and he could see the man quite clearly; he had been dressed in overalls and carrying a holdall. One of Kathy's team, Judy Birch, had spoken to the caller. The times seemed to fit and they were now searching CCTV for a sighting of the van.

By mid-morning they had tracked the van through Highgate and on to Crouch End, where the trail ran cold. They did, however, have one clear image of the number plate, registered to a plumbing contractor in Hornsey. Kathy called for backup to accompany herself and DS Birch.

The unit was in a quiet street, between a tyre shop and a monumental mason's yard. Two uniforms went around the back while Kathy and Judy Birch entered the front office, where a woman was working at a computer.

'Morning,' she said cheerfully, then frowned. 'You look like coppers.'

'You got it,' Kathy said and showed her ID. 'Boss in?'

'Mr Bell? Sure.' She lifted a phone. 'Teddy? Two cops to see you.'

Teddy Bell was a small, round man with a cheery smile. He took them through to his tiny office, invoices and dockets piled on his desk. They squeezed in, sat down, and Kathy explained what they were after.

'Saturday afternoon?' Bell tapped at his computer. 'Hampstead, yes, that would be Jabbar. Not in trouble, is he?'

'Full name?'

'Jabbar Chaudri.' He provided an address in Stoke Newington.

Judy Birch pulled out her phone.

'What was he doing over there?' Kathy asked.

'A problem with a leaking pipe in the old tollhouse opposite the inn. The property manager called us.'

'What time was that?'

Bell checked the computer again. 'Call came in three-oh-three pm, Jabbar attended at five thirty-six.'

Giving him enough time to call in at Number One Pond on the way, Kathy thought.

'Guv.' Birch showed her phone, on which was displayed Jabbar Chaudri's criminal record—four months' jail for aggravated assault on his girlfriend, twelve years previously.

Bell said, 'What's this about anyway? Jabbar's a good worker, a family man. Is he in some kind of trouble?'

'What about last Tuesday? What was Jabbar doing then?'

Bell checked. 'He had the day off.'

'And where is he now?'

Another tap on the computer. 'He's on a job near here, Harringay Avenue. Want me to call him?'

'No, thanks, I'd prefer you keep this to yourself for the moment, Mr Bell. It's probably nothing. Just something we need to check with him.'

Ten minutes later they saw the white van standing outside the address Bell had given them, and as they drew up behind it a man came out of the house, dressed in overalls and carrying a bag. He opened the van door and put the bag inside.

Kathy and Judy got out of the car. 'Mr Chaudri? We're police officers. We'd like a word, please.'

He looked alarmed. 'What's the problem? Is it Trudy? The kids?'

'No, nothing like that.'

'Hang on.' He frowned, peering at Kathy. 'Haven't I seen

you on TV? You're looking into the Hampstead Heath murders, aren't you?'

'That's right. We're speaking to everyone we can trace who was in the area on Saturday evening. We believe you were there—is that right?'

'How did you know that? Oh ... cameras, is that it? They're everywhere now, ain't they? Yeah, I was called out to the old tollhouse on Spaniards Road—leaking pipe.'

Kathy got him to describe his movements there and back, with times. Then she said, 'I don't suppose you were in the area last Tuesday morning, were you?'

'Tuesday? Oh, the first murder, right? No, I was at home, Stoke Newington, day off.'

'You didn't go out that day?'

'No, I'd got things to do at home.'

Kathy pointed to the bag Chaudri had put in the back of the van. 'I'd like to take a look in that bag, sir.'

Chaudri stiffened abruptly, and Kathy was aware of Judy Birch tensing at her side. The two uniforms from the backup car moved closer. Then Chaudri shrugged. 'Sure, why not?' He stepped away and Kathy went over and unzipped the top. It was full of tools, including two hammers.

'I'm going to have to ask you to accompany us to a police station to make a statement, Mr Chaudri, and give us permission to carry out forensic tests on your van and belongings.'

'I've got a busy schedule. What if I don't agree?'

'Then I shall arrest you on suspicion of involvement in the murder of Caroline Jarvis. I should also advise you that you do not have to say anything, but it may harm your defence if you do not mention when questioned something—'

'Yes, yes, I know.' Chaudri shook his head in disgust.

'—which you later rely on in court. Anything you do say may be given in evidence.'

They took him to Hornsey police station, where Kathy briefed a forensic team for a search of the van and tests of his tools and boots, and for the DNA from Chaudri's earlier arrest to be checked against the trace found on Caroline's purse. Then she and Judy began the interview.

They started by focusing on his movements on the morning of Tuesday, 20 October, when Andrea Giannopoulos was murdered. Chaudri appeared calm, almost resigned. He had left the house at six that morning, he said, and while his wife took the children to school and then went on to work, he went to a hardware store for paint and other materials he would need for the jobs around the house he planned to do that day. He spent the rest of the day at home.

The first results began to come in at twelve thirty and Kathy broke for lunch, arranging sandwiches and drinks for Chaudri and themselves. The hardware store confirmed that Chaudri's credit card had been used at eight twenty-three am on the twentieth to buy items that matched the list he'd given Kathy. That left enough time for him to have killed Andrea at around seven am.

The next result was less encouraging—Chaudri's DNA didn't match the trace on Caroline's purse. Kathy bit her lip with impatience and they returned to the interview room.

What had Chaudri been doing between six and eight twenty-three?

His answer was unconvincing. The hardware store hadn't opened when he first arrived and he had gone off somewhere—he couldn't remember exactly where—for a coffee and a roll. He gave a vague description of the café and detectives were sent out with Chaudri's picture to try to find it.

They moved on to Saturday afternoon. What exactly was Chaudri's route to the Spaniards Inn? He repeated what he'd told them earlier about coming into Hampstead from the opposite direction to Highgate, and Kathy ordered an urgent search of CCTV to check.

At four pm she called another break and Chaudri said he wanted to get a solicitor.

At four fifteen Kathy sat down with the forensics team leader. The results from the van and tool bag were disappointing. They had been unable to find any traces of either Andrea's or Caroline's DNA, and Chaudri's hammers didn't appear to match the post-mortem evidence for the two murders.

Chaudri's solicitor arrived at four fifty, and Kathy and Judy sat down with them soon after. Kathy told them that Chaudri was free to go, but that she wanted to retain his van and tools for further tests, and carry out a search of his home. Chaudri didn't object, although the solicitor demanded search warrants.

Kathy checked her watch and realised she was late for a meeting she'd arranged with a criminal profiler. She left Judy to follow up with Chaudri and returned to the Box feeling tired and frustrated.

~

She'd first met Dr Alex Nicholson—now Professor Nicholson—a decade or more before. Then the criminal profiler had seemed improbably young and pretty, and her analysis hadn't been much help. Now she had matured, acquired gravitas, and her manner was more cautious.

She stared around at the activity in the office and accepted a coffee from Phil. 'This is an informal meeting I take it, Chief Inspector? I've barely had time to read your notes. Haven't we met before?'

'Yes, with DCI Brock.'

'Oh, David!' Nicholson brightened. 'Of course. How is he?'

'Good. Just recently retired.'

'Ah. Give him my best if you see him. So, you've been landed with a big one.'

'You could say that.'

'Lots of pressure for results?'

'Very much so. I know this is early days for you, but with this second murder we're seeing a pattern emerge and I'm hoping you can give us a few ideas. Please think freely.'

The psychologist hesitated, tapped the file Kathy had given her, then finally spoke. 'Okay. First the location—why Hampstead Heath? Pragmatic reasons—potential victims, plenty of cover? That's practical, but two murders so close together does suggest something more personal to the killer, something specific. Or, as people are speculating, perhaps a socio-economic reason, because wealthy people live around there? Yet there's no theft involved. So maybe a personal reason, a personal association with the place. Somewhere the killer was taken as a child? Or maybe where he lost someone close—have there ever been drownings in those ponds? Whatever the reason, I'd assume that he knows the Heath well, either because he's lived around there or else has scouted out the locations recently.'

Kathy said, 'There have been two accidental drownings in those ponds in recent years, but we haven't been able to make a connection to our cases. I'll send you our notes.'

'Well, second, the type of assault: very violent, very specific and very unusual, like an attempt to obliterate the identity of the victims, or perhaps their intelligence.

'Third, the victims, both women, wealthy, the wives of powerful men. Have you found anything else to connect them?'

'No. They didn't know each other, nor did their husbands, and as far as we've been able to establish they had nothing else in common.'

'Well, there have been plenty of theories to explain male violence against women, if that's what this is. Assuming it is, we could speculate about a man who was abandoned by his mother, or wife; someone who feels inadequate in the presence of women, impotent perhaps; someone who's been saturated in a misogynistic culture of some kind.'

Kathy nodded, unimpressed. This was routine stuff.

'Look,' Nicholson said, 'you've already thought of all these things, and I'm sure you're looking into past crimes on the Heath—stalking incidents, assaults—but there's one thing screaming out at me here, Kathy.'

'What's that?'

'Two identical murders within just five days. That is not a normal pattern for a serial killer. Usually they build up to it, developing over time with weeks or months between attacks, but here we have the fully formed act bursting onto the scene—the same scene—twice in rapid succession. Why?'

Kathy nodded. 'Yes, why?'

Professor Nicholson frowned. 'This has been stewing inside his head for a long time, and in great detail, but he's been prevented from implementing his fantasies until now. Has he been overseas, or held in prison or some other institution? Now, suddenly, he's free to do it. And why should he stop now?'

'Yes, that's what I'm afraid of. Let's talk about the killer then. Male?'

'I couldn't say. Statistically likely, but this case is different. Was physical strength involved?'

'The hammer used would have been fairly weighty, maybe one and a half or two kilograms.'

'Quite possible for a woman to swing.'

'Both bodies were dragged a short distance into cover, but they weren't heavy. Could it have been two killers, or more?'

'Again, I can't say. It would have been muddy, wouldn't it? Didn't the footprints tell you?'

Kathy explained that the footprint analysis was ambiguous. Heavy rain at the first site had hampered forensics, but recovered prints suggested a match with prints of an Adidas Swift Run sneaker at the second. However, the ground had been much more disturbed at the second scene, possibly as a result of a struggle, and there were many more prints, some of which might have been made by another shoe of the same make, by a heavier assailant. They just weren't sure.

Kathy thanked Nicholson and they agreed to meet again in a couple of days, then Kathy returned to her computer and the endless stream of incoming reports.

4

Early morning drizzle, Brock shrugged on his raincoat, took up an umbrella and kissed Suzanne goodbye. He made his way up the high street, past the Abbey School and the long stone wall alongside the abbey and the fields on which, in 1066, the invading Norman army won the battle after which the town was named and changed the course of English history. The road continued down Lower Lake to the turning to the station, where he caught the London train. He enjoyed this weekly journey, an hour and a half across the Sussex and Kent countryside and through South London, then the local train to Dulwich and the walk to the archway into the courtyard where the leaves of the big chestnut tree lay thick on the cobbles, and into Warren Lane.

He opened his front door and climbed the stairs to his living room on the first floor, switching on the lights and the central heating, and settled down to the ongoing chore of culling the filing cabinets and box files, as ever amazed at how much stuff he'd accumulated over the years.

At midday he abandoned the chore, picked out several novels from the staircase on his way down and caught a train up to Blackfriars. Three stops on the Circle line took him to Westminster and the Two Chairmen, the small eighteenth-century pub at the end of Queen Anne's Gate. It was a gesture to the past, a visit to their local when they all worked together in the homicide annexe nearby. It was quiet inside and he ordered two pints and took a seat at a corner table.

After five minutes a familiar figure strode in and Brock got to his feet. Bren Gurney grinned when he saw him and came over, hand outstretched. Formerly a key member of Brock's team, Bren was now based at New Scotland Yard, a few blocks away, part of a specialist planning and research unit of Homicide and Serious Crime. They ordered lunch and talked, exchanging news. The youngest of Bren's three daughters had just started at Exeter University, and he talked about their trip down to see her, and his feelings about returning to the county from which his family originated.

Then, inevitably, the conversation turned to the past, to great times. They bemoaned the loss of their old base, that warren of offices at 9 Queen Anne's Gate and its well-kept secret, the Bride of Denmark, the snug bar in the basement made up of furniture and fittings salvaged at the end of the war from old bombed-out London pubs by the previous owners, an architectural publisher. And they recalled old murders and their triumphant conclusions, celebrated here in the Two Chairmen.

Their glasses were empty, and Bren rose to refill them and order lunch. Brock looked around him at the ancient beams, the original fireplace and the painting on the wall of the two 'chair men', the sedan chair porters who once frequented the tavern. All so familiar, and yet now somehow remote. And he was seized by a sudden resolution—no more nostalgia, no more grieving for the past. Only the future existed.

5

Tuesday, 27 October: D-Day. Kathy woke with a headache, convinced now that she wasn't going to be able to give Torrens what he wanted by the end of the day. It just wasn't that kind of a case—there had been no forensic breakthrough, no witnesses, no panicky phone calls from women confessing the ugly truth about their partners. In the end, it would be solved by patiently grinding down the data until something emerged. But what would happen in the meantime? And how could they prevent it? Blanket the Heath with patrols and cameras? He might just move away to another killing ground: Holland Park, Richmond Park, Dulwich Park—there were dozens of parks across London where he might start up again. All the same, they had introduced frequent patrols, together with the City of London Police who, by a quirk of history, were the body responsible for policing Hampstead Heath. They had also mounted extra CCTV cameras on the Heath and were experimenting with regular drone over-flights. Sensible precautions, but hardly investigative policing. She felt as if they were just covering their backs.

She began the day with a big briefing session, hoping that something new might emerge. She was disappointed. Jabbar Chaudri had now definitely been eliminated and no other suspect stood out. It seemed they had thought of everything and achieved nothing. The meeting broke up and she returned to her computer.

At midday she was still there, eyes glazed, sipping a coffee and eating a sandwich, when her phone rang.

'Detective Chief Inspector Kolla? I'm the duty inspector at Kentish Town police station, ma'am. I think we've got something you need to look at. Sounds like one of yours.'

She couldn't understand why this was coming from Kentish Town and not the City of London Police. 'On Hampstead Heath?'

'Not on the Heath, ma'am. In a house nearby, in Hampstead.'

In a house? Kathy shook her head. This didn't sound right. 'Go on.'

'Parliament Hill Close, number fourteen. Looks like someone was murdered with a hammer. Bloody mess, apparently.'

Kathy hurriedly wrote down the details and got to her feet, shouting instructions, the office erupting around her. She took the lift downstairs, jumped into the waiting car and they set off, siren blaring. Checking her tablet, she saw that the address was almost exactly midway between the two earlier murder sites.

She listened on her phone to an update. Two constables had attended a call from a woman at a house in one of the streets on the southern edge of the Heath. In a bedroom upstairs they had found what looked like a scene from an abattoir. Detectives had arrived, found a woman's body among the blood-soaked bedding and called for backup.

They arrived at the house, a red-brick Victorian villa outside which several emergency vehicles were double-parked. The Kentish Town detective waiting at the door gave Kathy a quick rundown.

'Crime scene are here, ma'am. They don't want anyone upstairs at present. Ms Nadia Gruszka made the call, and is in the sitting room with a constable. She comes here every Tuesday morning to clean for the owner, a Mr Charles Pettigrew. She arrived at eight, by which time Pettigrew had left—gone to work, she assumed, to his office in the West End. Her account got a bit confusing after that, but what it seems to amount to is that she didn't get to the upstairs rooms till about eleven, when she discovered the mess in the spare bedroom at the back. I've been up there and it's a bloodbath. God knows who's underneath it all, but I thought it might be connected to the Heath murders and asked our inspector to get on to you.'

'Has anyone tried to contact Pettigrew?'

'No, not yet.'

'Okay, thanks. We'll take over now.'

Kathy took plastic gloves and overshoes from her shoulder bag and made for the stairs. A figure in forensic overalls and a mask came out onto the landing ahead of her and she introduced herself.

'We'll be at least another hour before you can come in,' he said. 'But the victim is a youngish female, slender build, brown skin, with long wavy hair, very black. Probably South Asian ethnicity. Like the others, no possibility of facial identification. She's lying in the bed fully clothed in jeans and shirt. The killer covered her with the sheet before attacking her. Massive trauma to the head. No other visible wounds apart from the head. No identification on her person or in this room. She wore glasses—there's a pair lying on the floor.'

'Time of death?'

'Within the last twenty-four hours. Can't say better than that at the moment.'

'I need to take a look,' Kathy said.

The man stepped back and Kathy moved to the doorway of the bedroom. The sheet had been pulled back and a photographer was taking pictures of the body.

'Yes,' she said. 'It's the same. The hammer.'

'Yep, it's lying there beside the bed.'

'Really? It's here?'

'Yes.'

'Is that money on the floor?'

'About ten thousand in fifty-pound notes. Now everyone apart from CSI personnel should leave the building so we can do our job.'

'Okay. You've checked the other rooms up here?'

'Two other bedrooms and a bathroom. No immediate signs of disturbance.'

'Priority,' Kathy said. 'This is top priority.'

She went back downstairs, took a swift look at the other ground-floor rooms, and went to the sitting room, where a uniform was sitting with a woman, maybe late twenties, stocky build, alert intelligent eyes.

'Ms Gruszka? Is that right?'

'Yes.' She seemed quite calm.

'I'm Detective Chief Inspector Kathy Kolla. I'd like to talk with you if you feel up to it.'

'Of course. There is a body in the bed?'

'Yes.'

'Is it Mr Pettigrew?'

'No. It's a young woman, maybe Indian or Pakistani. Have you any idea who she might be?'

'No. Mr Pettigrew doesn't have any lady friends that I know of. But . . .'

'Yes?'

'There was a woman here last night, I think. There were two wineglasses in the kitchen, and one had lipstick on it. That is most unusual. What happened to her?'

'That's what we've got to find out. First of all, do you have identification, please?'

The woman unzipped a pouch on her waist and produced a Polish EU passport. Kathy opened it to the name, Nadia Gruszka. 'Where are you from, Nadia?'

'Katowice in Poland.'

'How long have you been in London?'

'Almost four years.' She gave an address in Holloway.

'How did you come to be working for Mr Pettigrew?'

'The recruitment agency.' She gave the name of the company, also in Holloway. 'I have been coming here for one year and a half.'

'Okay, now tell me what you did this morning.'

'I arrived here at eight o'clock, as I always do, and started on the downstairs rooms—this room, the dining room, the study, the kitchen, the bathroom—vacuuming and cleaning.'

'Was there anything unusual?'

'Only the two wineglasses. I put them in the dishwasher, along with Mr Pettigrew's breakfast things.'

'So he had breakfast here? Just him?'

'Yes, same as always—toast, marmalade and tea for one.'

'And did you start the dishwasher?'

'Yes, of course.'

'So there was nothing else unusual downstairs? No breakages, things out of place?'

'No.'

'Then what?'

'I went upstairs to Mr Pettigrew's bedroom, stripped the bed and put the linen in the washing machine.'

'Could you tell how many people had slept in the bed?'

'Only the one. Mr Pettigrew always sleeps on the left side. There was no sign anyone else had been in there. Oh . . .' She frowned.

'Yes?'

'I just remembered something: a bloodstain on his shirt in the laundry basket. I sprayed it with stain remover before I put it with all the other stuff in the washing machine.'

'You've washed everything?'

'Everything I could find, yes.'

'You didn't strip the other beds?'

'No, he would have left me a note if he wanted the sheets changed. I started vacuuming upstairs, and that was when I opened the door to the back bedroom and saw the mess, the blood. I didn't want to touch it. I tried to ring Mr Pettigrew at his office, but his secretary said he was out at a meeting and his phone was turned off. So then I called the police.'

'That bedroom door was closed—you're quite sure?'

'Yes.'

'What about the house windows?'

'All closed and locked, as usual, and the back door was locked—I had to unlock it to take the rubbish out to the bin.'

'How do you get into the house?'

'Mr Pettigrew leaves a key tied behind the front door. I get it through the letterbox, and I untie it and drop it inside when I leave.'

'Show me.'

They went to the front door and Nadia demonstrated.

'Okay. What about the back door?'

'It's a Yale lock. I don't have the key.'

'How about the alarm? Do you know the combination?'

'No. Mr Pettigrew doesn't switch it on when he leaves on Tuesday morning, and when I leave I press the activate switch.'

This all seemed very odd. If Pettigrew knew there was a body in the bedroom, why didn't he cancel the cleaner?

Nadia said, 'Please, can I go now?'

'I'm afraid not. We'll need you to go with an officer to a police station to give samples of your fingerprints and DNA and to make a statement.'

'But I've told you everything. I just want to go to my next job.'

'Sorry, Nadia. I'll tell them to be as quick as possible.'

~

The driver took Kathy into Central London, through Oxford Circus and down Regent Street, navigating the narrow lanes of Soho and arriving at Golden Square, an ambitious seventeenth-century speculation laid out by Christopher Wren when this part of the city was largely hovels and fields. Kathy got out at one of the four- and five-storey brick office buildings lining the west side of the square and looked at the names of the occupants— an advertising company, an independent filmmaker, publicity agents—and rang the bell beside the brass plate for Golden Press. The door buzzed and she went inside, climbed to the first floor and opened the door to the publisher's offices. She asked the receptionist behind the front desk if Mr Pettigrew was in.

'Do you have an appointment?'

'It's a police matter,' Kathy said, and showed her ID. 'Rather urgent. Is he here?'

The woman looked startled. 'Oh, um, no. He went out for a meeting a couple of hours ago. But he's due back any minute.'

'What about his phone?'

'He's turned it off. He does that often.' She smiled apologetically.

'Give me the number anyway, will you?'

The woman wrote it down and handed it to Kathy. 'Can I get you a coffee or something?'

'No, thanks.'

Kathy looked around, taking in the worn flooring, the old office furniture, the outdated equipment. It didn't look as if Golden Press was a flourishing business.

There was a sound of footsteps in the corridor outside and the door opened. A man appeared and glanced at Kathy, smiled, then said, 'Any messages, Penny?'

'This police officer is here to see you, Mr Pettigrew.'

'Really?' Pettigrew looked puzzled. 'How can I help you?'

'Do you have somewhere private we can talk, Mr Pettigrew?'

He led the way to his office, closed the door and invited her to sit down on one of a pair of ancient tubular steel chairs in front of his desk. He didn't seem in the least alarmed by her visit. 'So, how can I help, Inspector?'

'Would you mind telling me your movements this morning, from when you woke up?'

'Why? What's this about?'

'It concerns an incident in your street.'

'Ah, I see. Another robbery, is it? Well, I'm afraid I didn't see anything suspicious. My alarm went off as usual at six. I got up, had a shower, dressed, made my usual breakfast and left the house at seven forty, walked up to Hampstead tube station and came in to work. Didn't see anything out of the ordinary.'

'How about yesterday evening?'

'Um ...' He shrugged. 'Nothing really. Got home about six thirty. Uneventful evening, bit of TV, heard nothing unusual outside.'

'You were on your own all yesterday evening?'

'Yes ... oh, hang on.' He frowned. 'No, that's right. I did have a visitor.'

'Who was that?'

'A young woman called in, about eight.'

'Can you tell me about her?'

'Is it relevant?'

'I think it may be, yes.'

'Well, her name was ... let me see, I have trouble remembering.' He reached into his pocket for his glasses and took out a small notebook. 'I'm antiquated, you see. I use a paper diary. Where are we . . .? Yes, Shari Mitra. Do you want me to spell it?'

'Please.' Kathy wrote in her notepad. 'Indian?'

'Yes, from West Bengal, Calcutta—Kolkata, I should say.'

'Do you have her contact details?'

'No, 'fraid not. I've no idea where she lives.'

'A phone number?'

'Oh yes, I do have that.' He thumbed through his diary and read the number to Kathy. 'Do you want to contact her?'

'Why did she come to your house?'

'Business. She wanted to see if we would be interested in publishing a manuscript she had.'

'Why didn't she come here, to your office?'

'She was rather secretive. It's an unusual manuscript and she didn't want anyone else to know about it.'

'Had you met her before yesterday?'

'Once, yes.'

'In your house?'

'No, on Hampstead Heath, on the Saturday morning before last. That's—' he consulted his diary '—the seventeenth. We had a chat then and I told her I needed more information. She phoned me last Friday to say she had it and we arranged for her to call in last night.'

'Would you say she was an attractive woman?'

'I must say I'm puzzled by all these questions, Inspector . . . May I see your credentials again?'

Kathy showed him her ID and gave him a card. She couldn't make him out. His speech was articulate, yet his manner seemed distracted, as if his mind was far away. He studied her card closely, then shut his eyes and rubbed his temple.

'Are you all right, sir?'

'Just a headache. Don't know why—I never get headaches.'

'I have to get some background here, Mr Pettigrew. So she came to your house about eight, and then what?'

'We talked, she showed me more material she'd brought . . . then she left.'

'What time?'

Pettigrew opened his mouth, closed it again, wrinkled his brow. 'Not sure exactly. Um, actually, I did open a bottle of wine and we had a glass or two. I suppose she left around nine? Nine thirty?'

'You distinctly remember showing her to the door?'

'Well . . . not really, no, to be honest, but I must have done, mustn't I? I went to bed and got up this morning as usual—with a bit of a hangover, if the truth be told. Why? Has something happened to her?'

'Her body was found in your spare bedroom this morning by your cleaner. She'd been murdered.'

He rocked back as if he'd been punched. 'What? No! That's not possible.'

'Mr Pettigrew, I'm not satisfied with your account. I'm going to caution you now and ask you to accompany me to a police station to answer further questions. There's a police car waiting outside.'

As she got to her feet Kathy noticed a dog's basket with a blanket in the corner of the room behind the desk. 'You have a dog, Mr Pettigrew?'

'Eh?' He blinked in confusion, then saw where she was

looking. 'Oh . . . yes, I had a dog I used to bring to work. She died a couple of months ago.'

~

They took him to Kentish Town police station, where he was examined by a doctor and had blood, DNA and fingerprints taken. His clothes were exchanged for a pair of overalls and he was led to an interview room, given a cup of tea and told his solicitor was on his way.

Kathy meanwhile spoke to the doctor, who said, 'He sounds quite confused. It'll be interesting to see what the blood tests tell us. He says his GP's been treating him for depression and acute insomnia with Temazepam. He says he can't remember when he last took it or how much he took. Admits to being a "fairly" heavy drinker, which would exaggerate the effects of the drug, so his claims of gaps in his memory of last night may well be genuine.'

Pettigrew's solicitor had now arrived, and Kathy decided to conduct the formal interview immediately, before Pettigrew had any more time to gather his thoughts. For the next hour she listened while he went through it all again, trying with little success to flesh out the details. Regarding Shari Mitra, Kathy was able to establish only that she was aged about thirty and appeared well educated, said her home was in Kolkata and that she had arrived in England a few weeks before and was in possession of some kind of manuscript she wanted published. Pettigrew said he had no idea where she was staying in London.

Kathy then asked him what he was doing during the late afternoon of the previous Saturday, 24 October.

'Last Saturday?' He thought. 'Nothing much. I was at home, trying to catch up on some reading.'

'Alone?'

'Yes.'

'Did you see anyone, or speak to anyone on the phone, say between five and six thirty?'

He thought about it, then shook his head. 'Don't think so, no. Why?'

'How about the morning of the Tuesday before that, the twentieth?'

Pettigrew shrugged. 'The usual—work, the office. Like this morning, I would have left home by seven thirty and been in the office by around eight thirty, I suppose.'

Kathy finished the interview, explaining that they would have to ask him to remain at the station until further inquiries had been made.

When she returned to her car, she checked new information that had come in. A trace of Shari's phone showed that it had been used to make calls to only two numbers: Pettigrew's and that of a Steven Weiner, listed as a literary agent. Kathy tried the number. It went to voicemail and she left a message asking him to contact her urgently.

Then she phoned Pettigrew's office and got through to Penny.

'Oh, I'm glad you've called.' The secretary sounded flustered. 'Can you tell me what's going on? We've had reporters here from two different papers, asking questions about Charlie—Mr Pettigrew. Is he all right?'

'He's helping us with our inquiries about a case, Penny. I'd suggest you close the office if the press are being a nuisance, or direct them to us. I wanted to check something with you. Do you have an office diary there? Could you tell me if Mr Pettigrew had any appointments on the morning of last Tuesday, the twentieth?'

'Tuesday? Um ... he had one, with a rep from one of the distributors at ten. Oh yes, I remember now, he was late getting in and the rep had to wait. I made him coffee.'

'Um, about half an hour.'

'So Mr Pettigrew got in about ten thirty?'

'Did that happen often?'

Kathy thanked her and rang off. Plenty of time then to clean himself up and settle down after murdering Andrea Giannopoulos at around seven am. Meaning Pettigrew had no alibi for either of the previous murder times.

One of her team, DS Alfarsi, rang in with an update on the search of 14 Parliament Hill Close. At the back of a drawer in Pettigrew's bedroom a woman's necklace with a damaged clasp had been found, closely resembling the one ripped from Caroline Jarvis's throat.

Kathy took a deep breath, finally allowing the swell of excitement to burst inside her. This is it, she thought. He's the one.

~

At noon the following day Kathy stepped out of the conference room in New Scotland Yard filled with an enormous feeling of release. The mood had been positive—no, damn it, the mood had been bloody euphoric. The people from the Crown prosecutor's office could hardly contain themselves, saying they'd never seen such a watertight case. Sally Cameron was about as enthusiastic as anyone had ever seen her and Torrens looked like a man reprieved from the gallows. Kathy was surprised in a way—she'd thought that she was the only one on trial over the Hampstead murders, but it seemed everyone had been. There were cheers when Sally read out a note received from the office of the Home Secretary via the commissioner's office, expressing his congratulations on a brilliant piece of police work.

It hadn't been that, of course. It had been pure luck. Pettigrew had blown a gasket and ended his brief campaign of horror in a confused mental blur. If anyone deserved credit it was Nadia Gruszka, the cleaning lady, but no one was going to admit that. No one except Kathy. Beneath her great relief she felt an itch of dissatisfaction. She'd passed her first big test with flying colours, but it had been pure luck. She knew it and she thought of Brock and knew that he would know it too.

And there was the inconvenient fact that they didn't know who the third victim was. According to the UK Border Agency there was no record of anyone by the name of Shari Mitra entering the country within the past twelve months. Her fingerprints and DNA produced no matches, and information was being urgently sought from the Indian Central Bureau of Investigation.

Kathy had also tracked down the other person the victim was known to have made contact with in the UK, the literary agent Steve Weiner. He had an eye-catching website with links to his social media pages and email and phone contacts, but no physical address. There were also a large number of web references to him, and in particular to a spectacular bidding war he had conducted between publishers in 2012 for a novel by one of his authors. When Kathy phoned him, he had already seen the news item on Pettigrew's arrest and the police appeal for information on Shari Mitra. He explained that Shari had phoned him out of the blue on the morning of the previous Thursday, but hadn't got around to explaining what it was about.

'She was on the phone to you for eight minutes,' Kathy objected.

'Um, yeah,' Weiner said, sounding a little surprised that she knew. 'But she was kind of incoherent and I couldn't understand what she was saying. You know, the accent? And I was in the middle of a meeting at the time and I asked her to hold on, but when I got back to her she'd rung off.'

'You didn't ring her back?'

'No. I get lots of unsolicited calls from authors wanting me to read their stuff. I assumed she'd try again, but she never did. Look, I've got to rush, earn a crust. Anything else?'

Kathy let him go, thinking that he was the sort of man—condescending, full of himself—who would lie without hesitation if it suited him.

When she got back to the office, she found an email from the psychologist, Alex Nicholson:

Re: Hampstead homicides
Hi Kathy,
    I hear it's all over bar the formalities. Congratulations.
Probably irrelevant now, but I attach my preliminary thoughts

following our discussion on Monday and in the light of Pettigrew's arrest. Please let me know if I can help further.
All best,
Alex

Kathy scanned the attached report, most of it a repetition of salient facts. She focused on a list of points towards the end:

- #1 and #2 had distinctive settings, on the public Heath, in the open air, and next to pools of water. By contrast #3 took place indoors in a private house. I think this could be very significant and needs further study.
- There was a personal relationship between P and victim #3. Did he know the other two women?
- Victimology: obvious similarities between #1 & #2 (ethnic, socio-economic, domicile), which are very different from #3.

Yes, Kathy thought, all true, but it didn't alter the overwhelming forensic evidence proving that all three murders were carried out by the same man, Charles Pettigrew.

~

Brock rang her that evening. He told her he'd heard about her success from Bren Gurney, and was calling to congratulate her. He was interested in all the details, and Kathy thought it was a little sad, as if he couldn't let go of the job, wanting to savour it by proxy. He asked if she had plans for Christmas, two months away, but she hadn't thought about it, although she'd been vaguely aware of the first decorations appearing in shop windows. He said he hoped they could catch up.

6

Six weeks later, 14 December, towards one pm, Brock came into the shop to see if Suzanne wanted lunch. He saw her assistant Ginny showing a customer a case of Georgian silverware, and he went on through to the back office where he found Suzanne working on her books.

'I was going to call you,' she said. 'A woman rang, wanting to speak to you.'

'She rang here?'

'Yes . . .' Suzanne searched among her papers for the note. 'Maggie Ferguson.'

'The barrister?'

'No idea. She didn't say what it was about. I said I'd give you the message.' She handed Brock the note with the number.

He shrugged. 'Lunch?'

They had a sandwich at a café further down the high street while Brock searched the name on his phone. 'She used to be a prosecutor in the CPS. Handled a number of our cases, very smart. I got to know her quite well. But then she went over to the dark side—went into practice as a criminal defence lawyer. The enemy. Last I heard she'd got silk. Yes, here we are . . . became a QC in 2010. Defended the Khalol brothers, remember them? Got the bastards off. So what the hell does she want?'

'Ask her.'

He growled doubtfully. 'Maybe she's appealing one of my old convictions. Best to steer clear.'

He munched his sandwich in silence for a while, frowning. Eventually Suzanne said, 'Go on, ask her. Can't hurt. You can always say no.'

He didn't reply, got up to pay the bill. As they walked back he muttered, 'Oh damn it,' and tapped the number into his phone.

'Brock, thanks so much for getting back to me. How are you?' The barrister's voice, confident, forceful, brought back memories of when she'd been part of the team.

'Fine thanks, Maggie. What can I do for you?'

'Can you spare me half an hour?'

'Oh, I don't get up to town much.'

'I can be there by five. Battle, isn't it?'

'Today? Must be urgent. Not raking over one of my old cases, are you?'

'No, nothing like that. I have a puzzle that I think will interest you. Don't worry, there's no conflict of interest. What's your local?'

'The Abbey Hotel.'

'Who's the brewer?'

'Shepherd Neame.'

'Excellent. Mine's a half of Spitfire. See you at five.'

Brock rang off and raised an eyebrow at Suzanne.

'Pushy, is she?'

'Very.'

'Well, you never know, might be interesting. Something to get your brain working again.'

~

He arrived exactly at five and found her already there, seated in a quiet corner with two glasses on the table in front of her, a pint and a half-pint. They shook hands and she said, 'I got the Spitfire Gold, hope that's all right. I haven't tried it before. Yours is the pint. I have to drive back.'

Brock sat down. 'You're looking well, Maggie. Defence must be agreeing with you.'

'I always wanted to be a barrister, Brock, a real lawyer fighting it out in open court. The CPS was terrific training.'

'Our loss,' he said, and picked up the glass of ale. 'Cheers.'

'Cheers.' She took a sip. 'I'm defending Charles Pettigrew.'

'Are you indeed? I hope you haven't come to talk to me about that.'

She nodded. 'I understand. It's DCI Kolla's case and you and she were close. But as I said on the phone, there's no conflict of interest. The police case is overwhelming. There's no doubt that Pettigrew killed those women. We won't be challenging that.'

'What's your defence then?'

'He refuses to plead guilty; seems to genuinely believe he didn't do it. So the question of his sanity is bound to come up. Pettigrew won't hear of an insanity defence but it'll be raised, if not by us then by the judge or jury. And it will be an interesting one, because if he was suffering from a "disease of the mind" under the M'Naghten rules, then that disease is probably dissociative identity disorder, DID, which has rarely been accepted in British courts. This could be a landmark trial, Brock.'

'DID,' Brock said. 'Jekyll and Hyde.'

'Exactly. My belief is that he suffered some kind of break-down in early October, after which he coexisted as two completely contradictory personalities—on the one hand a respectable West End publisher, and on the other a brutal serial murderer of women.'

'Wouldn't it be simpler to assume that he's lying through his teeth?'

'I'd be very interested to hear your view on that after you've met and talked to him.'

'But that's not going to happen, Maggie.'

'Just hear me out. There's a subplot that doesn't affect the facts of the case or the final outcome, but which is annoying both the police and myself because it's unresolved. The first two murders are pretty clearly opportunistic random attacks on two women walking on Hampstead Heath who were unknown to Pettigrew, but the third was different. He says he knew the victim and admits he invited her to his house on the evening she was killed there. But we still don't know who she was. Neither the police nor a private detective we've hired have been able to establish her identity. Pettigrew has given us a name and said she was an Indian national from Kolkata who came to London expressly to see him, but there's no record of her ever having entered this country. We have her fingerprints and DNA, but no matches for them. We don't even know what the poor woman looked like because the damage to her skull was too great to make a reliable reconstruction. We have a CCTV image from a camera in Hampstead of a woman wearing similar clothes, who may or may not have been her, but the face is too blurred to be useful, even with enhancement.'

'So?'

'Pettigrew has an elaborate story about his dealings with the woman, which may be pure fantasy. The only pieces of evidence he's been able to produce to support it is an entry in his diary and a single sheet of paper.'

Ferguson reached into her briefcase and pulled out a thick file from which she retrieved a page and handed it to Brock. He studied it, frowning.

THE PROMISED LAND
A novel by Eric Blair

The Strand Hotel, Rangoon, six in the evening . . .

He read to the end, peered at the handwritten paragraph at the top, then set it down. 'Eric Blair rings a bell.'

'That was George Orwell's real name. Pettigrew says this woman was trying to sell him a previously unknown novel by one of the greatest authors of the twentieth century.'

'Sounds like a scam.'

'Yes, that's exactly what he thought at first, but then he wasn't sure. He claims that she gave him other material that was very convincing, but he's been unable to produce any of it. And he told no one else about it, neither the other people in his office nor anyone else.'

'Intriguing.'

'Yes, it is, isn't it? If it's a delusion, then it might have a bearing on his DID condition. But whatever it is, it's a missing piece of the jigsaw, and neither I nor the police like going to trial with that.

'So here's my pitch, Brock. You are the most experienced and expert person I know at interviewing and assessing suspects' stories. I don't want you involved with the police investigation in any way. You would not be called as a witness, and you would not appear anywhere in the court documents. All you would do is sit and chat with Pettigrew, listen and assess. If you discovered some hopeless contradiction in his account that might persuade him that his brain really has been playing tricks, that might be useful to me in persuading him to let me prepare an insanity defence. But that's not the main thing. I just want to know that there isn't some nasty surprise lurking in there that might upset the apple cart later on.'

'I'm not a private detective, Maggie.'

'No, I've got one of those on hand who can follow up any leads you give me. You would be paid on a time basis at top consultants' rates, and you would give me a report for my eyes only.'

Brock didn't reply. He picked up his pint and took a slow drink.

'I think the best thing to help you decide,' Ferguson said, 'would be for you to have a preliminary chat with Pettigrew, without commitment, just to get a feel for the man.'

'Where is he?'

'HMP Belmarsh.'

'And Kathy wouldn't know about this?'

'Absolutely not. Only you and me.'

'All right,' he said at last. 'A preliminary chat, no commitment.'

~

In her team's suite in the Box, Kathy finished the Monday morning briefing with a feeling of quiet satisfaction. The mood of these meetings had relaxed noticeably over the past weeks, the success of the Heath murders investigation lifting their confidence in themselves and in her, and she now felt securely in command. She also knew them all individually much better; their quirks, their private lives, their nicknames—'Wiss' (Wow I'm So Sexy) for carefully groomed Andy Alfarsi, and 'Pop' for Peter Sidonis, her number two, father of many children, who had emerged as a strongly supportive element in the group. Self-possessed and softly spoken, he reminded her of Bren Gurney, another family man, with whom she'd worked for so long in Brock's team. And then there was the other woman on the team, DS Judy Birch. Her reports were always the most meticulous, her follow-ups the most rigorous, but she was hard to read, reserved and rarely smiled. She was also a taekwondo black belt, fourth dan. Kathy had seen the video clips of bricks and slabs of timber being shattered by Judy's toes.

She returned to her office to type up her comments on the defence statement from Pettigrew's lawyers, passed on to her by Virginia Ashe from the Crown Prosecution Service with the note, *Is this a sad concoction of bluster and desperation or what?* And it was true—the matters of fact *on which the accused takes issue with the prosecution* were trivial, the *evidence in support of an alibi* practically non-existent. Kathy would almost have felt sorry for Maggie Ferguson if she hadn't suffered under her cross-examination in the Crown Court several times before.

She looked up at the picture of Charles Pettigrew tacked to the pinboard on the wall, feeling the familiar sense of revulsion at the bland, vaguely bemused mask behind which lurked the poisoned mind of the killer. Others were astonished at the contrast between the physical savagery of the murders and the mild gentlemanly appearance of the accused, but not Kathy. She'd seen it many times before. Didn't they remember the benign face of Dr Harold Shipman, who had killed at least two hundred and eighteen patients? If there was one thing she'd learned after dozens of homicide investigations, it was that murderers looked just like everyone else, and often hid behind a benevolent manner.

7

'I'm not sure this is a good idea.' Suzanne straightened Brock's tie, checked his suit. It was the first time he'd worn either in months.

'You're probably right. One meeting. If I don't like the smell of it, that's that.'

'She's a defence barrister, David. You know what they're like. And it's Kathy's big case, for goodness' sake.'

'I know, I know.'

She drove him to the station for the train to London Bridge, where Maggie Ferguson was waiting to collect him for the twenty-minute drive out to Belmarsh prison. Heading east, parallel to the river, through Greenwich and Woolwich in pouring rain, they came to Thamesmead. As they turned in from the highway, with Woolwich Crown Court over to the

right and Her Majesty's Prison Belmarsh up ahead, Brock
felt a sense of apprehension. There it lay, dull brown and as
discouraging as a bureaucrat's audit in the streaming rain.
What was he doing coming back here, impersonating a real
detective? He hoped he wouldn't meet anyone who'd recognise him.

Maggie led the way into reception and through the
security checks to one of the interview rooms set aside for
lawyers' meetings with clients. As they waited she said, 'I'll
introduce you to him, then leave you to it. I just want you to
have the chance to listen to him and form your own opinion.'

They got to their feet as Pettigrew was brought in.

'Hello, Charles,' Maggie said, sounding unnaturally cheery,
as one might for a hospital patient. Which was how he looked,
Brock thought—pale, withdrawn and passive.

'This is David Brock, the famous Scotland Yard detective
we discussed. Everyone just calls him Brock for some reason.'
She smiled encouragingly.

He nodded, offered his hand. 'Pettigrew.'

There's an intelligent brain in there, Brock thought,
looking at the eyes studying him. He shook the hand, which
was limp, offering no resistance.

'I'm going to leave you to talk with Brock, Charles. You
can be completely frank with him.'

The door closed behind Maggie, and Pettigrew sank into a
chair, regarding Brock with a weary expression. 'So . . . Brock.
I'm very glad that you were willing to come to see me. I have
been interviewed by a great many people recently, but none
of them seem interested in hearing the truth. What would
you like to know?'

'I'd like to hear about your dealings with Shari Mitra. From your first contact with her.'

'Ah, yes . . . therein lies the mystery.'

He spoke softly, rather slowly, and Brock had a sense of all his reactions, his speech, his movements, having slowed down as if to give him time to prepare for any new shock.

'Friday, the sixteenth of October, I left my office in Soho and returned home as usual. There was a hand-delivered A4 envelope waiting in my letterbox.' He sounded exhausted to be going over it all again. 'I opened it and found the note from Shari and the accompanying photocopied page. Have you seen those?'

'Yes,' Brock said. 'Maggie showed me. What was your reaction?'

'Oh . . . I was mildly intrigued, I suppose.'

'You didn't take it seriously?'

'Not at first. I certainly spent some time thinking about it, and after a bit I decided I would have to take a closer look. Eric Blair was George Orwell, of course—you know that?'

'Yes.'

'Yes, well, it so happened that when I read that page I was sitting in an armchair that George Orwell had once sat in. My grandfather, who founded Golden Press, was a friend of his in the thirties when Orwell was living in Hampstead—in Pond Street, near the station, then in Parliament Hill, near our house. So, yes, certainly it got my attention.'

'Did you think it might be a forgery?'

'Yes, of course. But then I thought about the date on the note at the top of the sheet, the twelfth of August 1949, right towards the end of Orwell's life, just five months before he died.

He was quite ill at that point, in a clinic in the Cotswolds—at Cranham, as it says in the note—and we know that he did have ideas at that time for a new book about Burma that never transpired. It seemed to me conceivable that he might have typed a page or two of an idea for a novel called *The Promised Land*, which I'd never heard of. The style seemed right, and the concept of a novel on the same theme as Thomas More's famous book *Utopia* and, by the sound of it, with a similar beginning—a man meets a traveller from a far country who tells of an idealistic community in the wilderness—yes, I could imagine Orwell playing with an idea like that. So I thought it might possibly be authentic, a literary curiosity that had got lost along the way.'

Pettigrew had become more animated now, leaning forward across the table between them, nodding at each point he made.

Brock asked, 'Did the name Amar Dasgupta mean anything to you?'

'No, not a thing. I checked a biography of Orwell I had and I couldn't find any mention of him.'

'What about GOP? What was that?'

'Yes, that was quite interesting. In 1947, for tax reasons, Orwell set up a company, George Orwell Productions Ltd—GOP—to own the copyright on his work and receive his royalties. So it seemed that here he was deliberately excluding this new novel from that arrangement, and intended writing it under his own name, Eric Blair, rather than George Orwell, so that he could give the copyright to Amar Dasgupta. That was rather intriguing. I wondered why he would have done such a thing.'

'So what did you do?'

Pettigrew shrugged, sighed. 'I suppose a decent cup of coffee is beyond the realms of possibility? I have this dream of a creamy cappuccino.'

Brock took out his phone and called Maggie. She said she'd see what she could do.

'So,' Pettigrew went on, 'what I did was to call Shari on the number she'd given me, to try to get some impression of who I was dealing with. And, I have to say, I was quite impressed. She sounded like an intelligent, well-educated young woman. She explained that she was seeking a publisher for a manuscript that had been in her family for many years, of which she had given me a copy of the first page. I said, fine, come to my office and we can discuss it, but she wouldn't do that. She insisted that she would meet only myself, and the project must remain confidential between us until we had signed an agreement. She said she would meet me some-where neutral and show me other material she had, but if I refused to do this she would go elsewhere. So I agreed. She told me to meet her the next morning at the Pergola on West Heath. Do you know it?'

Brock shook his head.

'It's one of Hampstead Heath's hidden treasures, a long pergola structure in the Hill Gardens, with a rotunda and belvedere. We met at ten, and we had the place to ourselves. Again, I was impressed. She seemed respectable, sensible, rather studious. She told me she had only arrived in the UK a few days ago from Kolkata, and I asked her if she was involved in publishing over there. She said no, but she was very interested in literature, and mentioned some authors she particularly admired—Naipaul, Ghosh, Arundhati Roy, McEwan and, of course, Orwell. Then she told me the story of how she came to have this manuscript, and why she was bringing it to me.

'She said that she came from a family of merchants from West Bengal, and Amar Dasgupta was her great-grandfather. They dealt in precious stones, and in 1927 Amar was sent to Burma to buy rubies and sapphires. On his way to the fabled Valley of Rubies at Mogok in Upper Burma, he fell ill and stopped in the small town of Katha to recover. There, in a hospital on the bank of the Irrawaddy River, he met the local police superintendent, a young Englishman of his own age, who was recuperating from a bout of dengue fever. His name was Eric Blair.

'According to Shari, the two men became friends, and to pass the time discussed a book that Blair was thinking about writing, based on his experiences in the Indian Imperial Police in Burma, in which he'd been serving for the past five years. Blair was thoroughly disillusioned with the role of the British in India and Burma, and the whole idea of the British Empire, and he wanted to expose it in a novel. Dasgupta, on the other hand, had been brought up to believe the opposite, and together they worked out a story in which two of the main characters—Flory, an Englishman, and Dr Veraswami, an Indian—would debate this. According to Shari, the character of Dr Veraswami was based on an uncle of Dasgupta who was a doctor in Calcutta, and who strongly supported British rule as having brought peace and progress to the subcontinent. Seven years later that novel was finally published as *Burmese Days*, Blair using the pseudonym George Orwell to avoid libel suits from his former colleagues in Burma. There was no acknowledgement of Amar Dasgupta's contribution then or later.'

He paused as the door opened and a prison officer came in with two cappuccinos. 'Here we are, gents.'

'Thank you, Kevin,' Pettigrew said. 'Much appreciated.'

When the officer had gone, Brock asked, 'You're getting on all right with the staff then?'

'I try to be respectful. But of course they think I'm a murderous maniac, and they don't turn their backs on me.' He stared down at the coffee cup. 'Is there any point in this? I've been over it so many times. The police think it's all irrelevant nonsense, this story, and they're probably right. I've become a character in a terrifying work of fiction, guilty of a horrendous crime I didn't commit. Sometimes, for a minute or two, I might be distracted and forget, but then I blink and the feeling of nausea swells up inside me again. I can't escape. The fact that everyone who's ever known me seems as shocked as I am doesn't really help. It just makes me feel more helpless.'

'Let's finish the story,' Brock said quietly. He was thinking that Pettigrew was one of the most articulate suspects he'd ever interviewed, but that would probably count against him in court, magnifying the horror of his crime.

Pettigrew sighed, then after a moment continued. 'Shari's story moved on twenty years. After Independence in 1947, things were very turbulent in Bengal as elsewhere in India. East Bengal separated to become East Pakistan, with many Muslims from Calcutta fleeing there, and many Hindus from the east pouring in to take their place. The Dasgupta family, as Hindus, were secure enough in Calcutta, but their business was very volatile. Many refugees needed to raise money and were trying to sell their jewels cheaply, but there were few buyers. Eventually, in 1949, in an attempt to find a new market, Amar sailed to London to try to drum up some business in Hatton Garden. While he was there, he made inquiries about his old friend Eric Blair, whose progress as a famous author Amar had been following. By this time Orwell had published most of his great works—*Animal Farm*, most recently—and had finished writing *Nineteen Eighty-Four*, his final published novel.

'Amar learned that Blair was seriously ill with tuberculosis, staying in the Cranham sanatorium in the Cotswolds, and he decided to go and visit him.'

Pettigrew paused to sip his coffee. 'Ah,' he said wistfully, 'that is very nice. I'm learning how to appreciate the small luxuries, like a few minutes of solitude, or a sleep without nightmares.'

'Were you persuaded by Shari's story?'

'I think by this stage I was almost inclined to believe it, yes. I wasn't an Orwell specialist by any means, but what she'd told me did fit with all the facts I knew. And I suppose I was rather touched by the thought of these two men, who had first met in a hospital on the other side of the world, meeting again now, twenty years later, in another clinic, one of them close to death.

'Shari said that Amar was shocked by Blair's appearance; he was very sickly, confined to bed. He felt the cold keenly, and his handkerchief was spotted with the blood that he was coughing up. But his brain was as sharp as ever, and he was desperate to tell one last great story that would "complete the arc", as he put it, by returning to Burma with the themes that he'd begun all those years ago in Katha. He had started the project, calling it *A Smoking Room Story*, but it wasn't right and he had abandoned it. But now, just when the doctors had insisted on total rest and taken away his typewriter to stop him working, the form of the novel had become clear in his mind.

'So he and Amar devised a scheme. Each day Amar would visit the hospital and sit with Blair, who would quietly dictate to him the chapter that he had mentally composed during the previous night. Amar would then return to the Black Horse Inn, where he was staying in the town, and type up the chapter while Blair rested, working on the next. They did this for a month, and at the end of that time they had a completed work, *The Promised Land*.

'Well, I was stunned at that—a complete Orwell novel that no one had ever heard of? Was that really possible? And did it still exist? That's what I asked Shari, of course. She told me that in the final year of his life, 1990, Amar Dasgupta came to stay with Shari and her widowed mother, who looked after the old man. Shari was a little girl at the time but remembered him clearly, and the box of beautiful coloured precious stones that he brought with him. She knew nothing about the Orwell manuscript until earlier this year, however, when her mother finally told her Amar's story. According to Amar, when the novel was finished Blair told him that he was going to repay the debt he owed Amar for making first *Burmese Days* and now *The Promised Land* possible, by giving him the novel, to have it published as he pleased and to own the copyright and royalties. Amar was overwhelmed, of course, but Blair insisted and signed the declaration on the first page of the manuscript.

'Amar had already stayed too long in England, and his family were demanding that he return to India, which he did soon after, taking the novel with him. He told Shari's mother that he had never done anything with it, other business being always more pressing, but now he wished to give it to her, to secure the future of herself and her daughter Shari. The old man died, Shari's mother put the package away and forgot about it until early this year, when she was told that she had breast cancer. Thinking of all the loose ends she should tie up in her life, she remembered Amar's legacy and told Shari about it. Shari was now a graduate of the University of Calcutta, where she had studied English literature, and was thrilled by these revelations. According to her mother, Blair had told Amar not to go to his regular Orwell publishers, Secker and Warburg, as it might create complications, but instead to approach another excellent London publisher, Mortimer Pettigrew of Golden Press, who was a personal friend. And so, finally, three generations later, here she was, talking to me.'

'It is a good story,' Brock said. 'And then I suppose she asked for money.'

Pettigrew gave a tight smile, drained the last of the coffee and nodded. 'You're a cynic, Brock. Yes, she asked for money. She said she was almost broke and she wanted to bring her mother to London for treatment. She thought that the manuscript would be worth hundreds of thousands of pounds on the open market, and an initial advance of ten thousand would be reasonable to secure sole access to test the authenticity of the work. I replied that so far all I had seen was one sheet of paper, and I'd need to see more before I agreed to pay anything. And what was this "other material" she had mentioned on the phone?

'She reached into the bag she was carrying and produced another envelope like the one she had put through my door. From it she took a photograph—black-and-white, old, creased, a bit fuzzy, but still quite legible, of two men sitting side by side. I recognised Orwell straight away, that funny little moustache. I always wondered about that moustache—he hated the Empire, and yet he insisted on wearing that trademark of a 1920s colonial officer until the end of his life, even when he was down and out in Paris and washing dishes and the management wanted him to shave it off. Anyway, it certainly looked like him, sitting in an armchair with a blanket wrapped around him, and next to him a middle-aged Indian man beaming at the camera.

'Okay, I said. Anything else? And she produced an old envelope bearing a George VI penny red postage stamp post-marked Cranham, 30 August 1949, and addressed with the same shaky handwriting to A. Dasgupta Esq. at the Savoy Hotel, The Strand, London. From inside she pulled out the single page of a letter from Blair to Amar, thanking him for his visit, telling him they were increasing his streptomycin injections and reassuring him that he would be alive and well to attend "your publication party for *The Promised Land*".

'And what about the manuscript itself? I asked. Did you bring that? But she shook her head. She said she would put that in my hands when I had ten thousand pounds, in cash, ready for her. I told her I would think about it and let her know, and we parted.'

Pettigrew raised an eyebrow at Brock. 'What would you have done if you'd been in my position?'

'Some research?'

'Yes, exactly. I went home and reread Orwell's biography, checking the details of her story, and everything seemed to fit—the dates, the places, the circumstances. Then I got on the internet and found that the Orwell archive is held by University College London and much of the material can be viewed on the web. I found they had the notebook in which Orwell had started to write that abortive last novel Shari mentioned, *A Smoking Room Story*, just a couple of handwritten pages. You can call up photos of the pages on the computer and I compared the writing to the note at the top of that first page of *The Promised Land*, and to my eye it looked identical. I just couldn't fault anything she'd told me. I would have liked to speak to the scholars at UCL to see what they thought, but I was afraid that if I involved anyone else word would get out and there would be a bidding war for the manuscript.

'So I waited, and thought about it, and finally phoned her on the following Monday, the nineteenth. I said I agreed to her terms, and we arranged to meet at the Pergola on Wednesday morning, when we would exchange the manuscript for the ten thousand and a preliminary contract that I would draw up and we would both sign.

'She never showed up. I waited an hour, tried her phone but it went to messages. I had a horrible feeling that she'd approached someone else and got a better deal, but I tried to convince myself it was for the best. Then, that evening, she phoned me and said that she'd read about the murder on Hampstead Heath the previous day on her way to the meeting and it had frightened her and she'd turned back. Also, she'd phoned her mother in Calcutta, who was angry because she'd only asked for ten thousand up front and should have demanded twenty. She explained to her mother that, if all went well, this would be only a preliminary payment and there would be much more later, but her mother said she didn't have time to spare.

'I decided to put my foot down at that point. I said no, we'd made a deal, take it or leave it. She got upset and rang off, and I didn't hear from her again until the following Monday morning. She said she'd stick with our original agreement and would come to my house that evening with the manuscript. She asked that I tell no one about our arrangement, and I agreed.'

'So this was the evening before her body was discovered.'

'Yes.'

'Was it your suggestion she come to your house?'

'No, it was she who insisted on it.'

Brock noticed a change in Pettigrew's manner, the man becoming more hesitant, a slightly puzzled expression on his face as he described what happened.

'She arrived at eight pm as arranged.'

'Had you had anything to eat or drink at that stage?'

'I had a biscuit and cheese while I waited for her, and a whisky. Well, a couple of whiskies, actually. She seemed nervous, and cold—it was a chilly night and she had only a light jacket. I took her into the living room, in front of the fire. She was carrying a plastic carrier bag—Sainsbury's, I think. I asked if I could get her anything and she said a glass of wine would be nice, so I fetched a bottle and glasses. She apologised for the delay and said her mother had been difficult, understandably in view of her illness. She said it would help matters if I could give her some idea of how much she might expect as an advance against royalties if I was satisfied with the manuscript, and we talked about that.'

Brock said, 'What was the atmosphere like? Was she excited? Flirtatious?'

'No, nothing like that. It was a bit strained, in fact. I tried to put her at ease by telling her how Orwell had been there in that room and so on, but the conversation was awkward. She drank her wine quickly, and I poured her another glass, and then she said that she had the manuscript in her bag and if I fetched her money she would let me look at it. So I went to my study and got the envelope of cash I'd collected from the bank earlier in the day and we made the exchange.

'The manuscript was maybe an inch thick, about two hundred pages, and I immediately began checking to make sure there were no blank pages. It looked very convincing. As I thumbed through I saw places where Orwell had made alterations with a pencil and I became quite excited to feel it there in my hands, an amazing piece of literary history.' He looked at Brock with a rueful smile. 'A once-in-a-lifetime publishing scoop, that's what I was thinking.'

'Go on.'

'Well ... she counted the cash, and I became engrossed in the manuscript, and she left and eventually I went to bed.'

'You remember her leaving?'

'Um ... not really, no. I was so engrossed in the book, you see. I don't remember much else about the evening, to be honest. I know that sounds a bit weak—the police quizzed me about it over and over—but I was just so taken up with the book.'

'Can you remember it now, what you read?'

'Well, sort of . . . I couldn't write it down.'

'The gist, the story?'

'It's a bit vague. Possibly I'd had a bit too much to drink, and I was tired . . . I know it doesn't sound convincing, but it's like . . . trying to remember a beautiful dream that's elusive and always just out of reach. There was a very strong scene with a beheading, I remember, and an evil man, powerful and corrupt, hovering in the background of the story like a dark shadow. It haunts me.' He rubbed his eyes in frustration.

'And the next morning?'

'My alarm went off as usual. I got up and went to work.'

'What about the manuscript? Did you look at it again?'

'No . . . I thought I must have locked it up in the safe in the study, and I decided to leave it till I returned that evening. I know, the police say they couldn't find any manuscript, and I can't explain that. Or, rather, there's only one explanation— someone broke into my house and murdered Shari and stole the manuscript.'

Pettigrew let out another long sigh, shook his head. 'I know, I know. Maggie tells me that the police are saying the forensic evidence doesn't support that theory, but if they'd just get their noses out of their microscopes they'd realise it must be true. No one who has known me can believe I could have murdered those women. And that manuscript was authentic, I'd swear to it. Some people would commit murder for a thing like that, a unique treasure.'

'Maggie tells me you don't have an alibi for the times of the first two Heath murders.'

'Yes, that's true. I was feeling unwell on the Tuesday morning of the first one and was late getting into work, and

I was alone at home on the Saturday afternoon of the second one, probably asleep at the time it happened. But isn't that supportive, in a way? If I was the Heath killer, surely I would have made up some kind of alibi for myself. The fact that I didn't shows my innocence!'

He looked desperately at Brock, then, seeing the expression on his face, slumped. 'Dear God, what have I done to deserve this? If I were brave enough, and had the means, I'd put an end to it and save us all the trouble. Maggie seemed to agree that it would be a good idea to involve you, but I've never really been sure what she believes.'

'She believes that there are aspects of the case that haven't been made clear. She wants me to try to throw some light on them.'

Pettigrew gave a bitter laugh. 'I notice you don't say she believes I'm innocent.'

'She's a very good lawyer. She'll do everything in her power to prove you are. But she's worried that no one's been able to find out anything about Shari.'

'Yes, the police have been going on at me about that, but she never told me anything about her situation. There was her phone. Maggie said they traced where it was bought to a shop somewhere south of the river ... Elephant and Castle? But Shari never mentioned where she was living. All I could say was that I didn't think she was staying at the Savoy like her great-grandfather had done—I noticed her shoes were very worn and her jacket was a bit shabby.'

'Did the police get you to re-create her face?'

'Yes, I worked with someone on a computer. It wasn't easy. I felt we got some things right—her hair, the shape of her face, the style of her glasses—but overall it didn't really capture her. It just looked like any young Indian woman. Maggie says they haven't had any luck with it.'

'No.' Brock checked his watch, consulted his notes. 'You lost your wife Fran a year and a half ago. How long had you been married?'

'We celebrated our fortieth anniversary two months before she died.'

'Hard for you. Maggie said a stroke?'

'Yes, totally unexpected. Everything normal then bang.'

'How have you coped?'

'How? Work, friends, pills, drink.' He shrugged. 'You try to carry on.'

'What kind of pills?'

'Oh, nothing illegal, just stuff the doc gave me. Helped a little, maybe. Made me sleepy, but I didn't mind that.'

'So you were clinically depressed.'

'Yes, of course I bloody was. Half my life had been gouged out of me in an instant.' He drew a breath, lowered his head, whispered, 'Sorry. Mustn't feel sorry for myself. Fatal.'

'Are you seeing somebody in here? A psychiatrist?'

'Yes, yes. Everybody wants to talk to me. But what's the point? I say to them, "All you have to do is tell them that I'm incapable of doing what I'm accused of", and they give an awkward smile, because they all believe I must have done it, otherwise I wouldn't be here, would I? Pure Kafka.'

There was a tap on the door and Maggie came in. 'How are we doing?'

'Fine,' Brock said. 'We've had a good chat.'

He and Pettigrew got to their feet.

Pettigrew said, 'I've seen you before, you know.'

'Have you?'

'At the Old Bailey, giving evidence at a trial. Long time ago, the Causley boys.'

'Ah yes. Nasty.'

'Yes, I was there, and I saw you in the witness box. Very impressive. That's why I told Maggie you might be a good person to advise us. They claimed they were innocent too, so now I know how they felt. Except, unlike them, I really am innocent.' He looked bewildered. 'I am, you know. I really am. Please . . . please help me.'

When they got back to the car, Maggie said, 'What do you think?'

Brock said, 'Old hands say they can spot a liar by little signs that give them away, but they've done scientific experiments and it isn't so. Even the most experienced interrogators perform poorly with good liars. I certainly wouldn't have picked him as a good liar, or as a psychopath, but I could be quite wrong. What fascinates me is the elaborate Orwell story. You say there's no corroboration for it?'

'Apart from that single sheet of paper, nothing. No manuscript, no photograph, no letter to the Savoy, nothing. Just a very elaborate, vaguely plausible story that Pettigrew could have dreamed up himself.'

'He told me he's convinced that someone broke in to steal the manuscript.'

'What, the Heath serial killer just happened to be a collector of literary manuscripts? Even I would blush trying to present that defence, not to mention the fact that the thief took the manuscript but left ten thousand quid scattered on the floor. And that he got in without any sign of a forced entry and left without leaving a trace.

'No, the DID explanation is the only one that makes sense to me, Brock. I agree with you; I wouldn't pick him as a good liar either—he lacks the self-confidence. I think he genuinely doesn't know what he's done. The lack of an alibi for the times of the first two killings supports that—Dr Jekyll has no idea what Mr Hyde has done, so he hasn't prepared an alibi for him. You don't agree?'

'Hmm. I'd like to talk to someone who knows him well. What about someone at his office?'

'There's really only his editor, Angela. She's worked with him for years. Want to try her?'

She put a call through to Golden Press and Angela answered. She said she'd be happy to talk to Mr Brock.

Mister, Brock thought. By the time he retired he'd forgotten what a powerful weapon the title of *Detective Chief Inspector* was.

~

The front office was deserted when Brock stepped in, and he looked around before ringing the bell on the counter. He had expected the Golden Press offices to be a bit more impressive, but the air of genteel decrepitude didn't disappoint him. This was exactly what he thought a small independent London publisher's offices should be like: musty and reeking of past encounters between the great and the good.

A middle-aged woman appeared and asked if she could help him.

'I'm hoping to speak to Angela,' he said. 'My name's Brock, David Brock.'

'Oh, Mr Brock, hello,' the woman replied. 'I'm Angela. Maggie Ferguson said you might call in. Let's go through to Mr Pettigrew's office and we won't be disturbed. Can I get you a coffee or anything?'

'No, thank you. I just wanted to speak to someone who knows him, to get a better picture of the man.'

She showed him into the office and said, 'The police searched this room and took away several things, including Sophie's basket, I can't imagine why.'

'Sophie?'

'Charlie's dog, a retriever. After his wife died he sometimes used to bring Sophie to work with him and she'd lie quietly in her basket all day. He was heartbroken when she died and couldn't bear to get rid of her basket. He loved his dog.'

So did Adolf Hitler, Brock thought.

Examining some framed photographs hanging on the wall, he pointed to one and asked, 'Isn't that Ernest Hemingway?'

'Yes, with Mr Adrian Pettigrew, Charlie's father.'

'In a bar, naturally.'

Angela smiled. 'Yes, in Kingston, Jamaica.'

'And this one, in uniform?'

'On the Western Front, Wilfred Owen with Mr Mortimer Pettigrew, Charlie's grandfather, who founded the firm. In six years it'll be a hundred years old.'

'Is that right? And that one at the end is the present Mr Pettigrew?'

Brock could see the family resemblance, but whereas the earlier publishers had smiled triumphantly at the camera,

Charles Pettigrew looked diffident and vaguely worried. 'When was it taken?'

'About ten years ago. He was at the Edinburgh Festival with one of our authors, Bartholomew Jowitt.'

'I don't think I've heard of him.'

'No, I'm afraid he never amounted to much. He was a crime writer. Most of our present authors are.' She indicated a display of books on a shelf, and Brock noted the lurid cover images, mostly featuring knives, pistols and other deadly weapons.

'So Charlie specialises in crime, does he?' He picked up one of the volumes, *Killers*, by D.C. Priest, with a cover image of a pair of hands gripping a woman's throat.

'Not really by choice. That's just the way things have turned out.'

'How long have you worked for him?'

'Sixteen years.'

'Has he been a good boss?'

'Very fair, and generous.' She seemed to be struggling a little to find positive adjectives. 'A very nice man.'

'But?'

'Well, sometimes I wished he had a bit more fire in his belly—about the business, I mean. When I joined the firm, we had eight staff. Now, even our receptionist has gone and there's just me left. Charlie's father was alive when I started, and at eighty he was still the real power, although Charlie was supposed to have taken over. Adrian—AP—was the one who decided what to publish and what not, and his judgement was always spot on. Do you remember Oliver Smart's *Summer in Seville*?'

'Vaguely. It was a bestseller, wasn't it?'

'Huge. It carried the firm for years. AP picked it. Charlie's never had a success like that. He's ended up with mainly crime writers by default, but they're not the kind of author he really wanted to publish.'

'How do you mean?'

'Not proper literature, in his opinion. He'd love to publish more literary fiction, but somehow he's never been very lucky with those. Jonathan Gratz?'

'No, I don't think I've heard of him.'

'Nobody has. Sold less than five hundred copies, but Charlie was convinced he was the next James Joyce. That author in your hand, Donna Priest, sells fairly well, but Charlie thinks her books trashy, catering to ghoulish voyeurism—those were his words to me, in private. He'd never say that to his authors, of course. He's the most polite man I've ever met. Kind of ironic now—Donna writes true crime and she'll probably end up writing a book about Charlie. Though I just cannot believe he did what they say.'

'But if the police are right, can you imagine how it might have happened?'

'That's what I've been struggling to do. How could dear old Charlie be capable of something so horrible?'

'Something to do with his wife's death?' Brock suggested.

'Yes, that's the only thing I can think of. He hasn't been the same since she died. It's as if she'd been holding him together.'

'How did he change?'

'Well, he didn't look after himself, and he was drinking.' She frowned, looking down at her hands.

'Go on,' Brock said quietly.

'One Friday evening, about three months ago, I came back from a meeting with an agent and the office door was locked. I assumed everyone had gone home, but when I came in I saw a light in Charlie's office. I put my head round the door and saw him sitting here, at the desk, holding a tumbler of Scotch, staring at nothing. He looked up and waved me in, told me to join him for a chat. I could tell from his voice that he'd already drunk quite a lot, and when I sat down and looked more closely at him I was alarmed to see tears on his cheeks. He poured me a glass and told me that Penny, our secretary, had just asked for a reference. Apparently she was looking for a job elsewhere as an editorial assistant. I said not to worry, we'd soon get someone else, but he waved his hand and said no, no, I should do the same thing, look for a job elsewhere. He said I was wasted here and he'd let me down, let everyone down; he'd been a failure, let down the family tradition. It was pretty embarrassing and I tried to break in, but he just went on. He said, "You know, Angela, I really hate this place, Golden Press, always have, it's been a millstone around my neck. I've lived a lie, out of funk, out of guilt." And then he told me this rather unpleasant story.

'When he was a small boy, six or seven, he came home early from primary school one day. There had been a sex education lesson, and the headmaster had described how babies were made. It had made him feel dizzy and sick, and he'd been sent home. When he got there, he went up to his room. The door was open, and inside he saw his mother and a man, both naked, on his bed. He wasn't sure at first what they were doing, because he recognised the man as his Uncle Bob, his mother's brother. Then he remembered the school lesson and he realised. He watched them for a minute, then quietly went away. That evening, at dinner with his parents, his father, AP, asked him how school was. He said he'd felt ill and came home early and saw his mother and Uncle Bob having sexual intercourse—that was the term he used, like in the school lesson. His father sent him to his room, and he heard them rowing downstairs. He never saw or heard of his uncle again, and a week later he was sent to a boarding school, where he was bullied for five years until he tried to hang himself. Then AP sent him to another school, which wasn't so bad.'

'Oh dear.' Brock frowned.

'I probably shouldn't have told you, should I? I didn't tell the police. But you're on his side, aren't you? It probably isn't relevant. But the fact he'd tell me a story like that just shows how depressed he's been without Fran, his wife. She was strong, kept him going.'

~

At the station, waiting for the Hastings train, Brock phoned Maggie.

'How did it go?' she asked. 'Find out anything useful?'

'Not sure. Have you spoken to Pettigrew's cleaner?'

'Yes. She's on the witness list. She didn't tell me anything we didn't already know.'

'Could you arrange for me to speak to her?'

'Okay. Any particular time?'

'I'll fit in.'

8

Kathy pulled up outside the Holy Emmanuel Apostolic Church of Christ, formerly the Three Crowns public house. Next to it was the Polski 777 Crazy Grocery and beyond that the burnt-out ruin of what had been the Sitar Indian Restaurant, beneath two floors of share accommodation in which three people had died the previous night. The fire investigators had detected accelerant in the remains of the restaurant kitchen and suspected foul play, making this a case for Homicide and Serious Crime.

DS Alfarsi was with her, and they pulled on overalls, boots and hard hats and walked over to the fire scene, where one of the investigators was waiting for them. He took them inside, interpreting the debris as they picked their way through the mess.

Kathy's phone rang and she checked the name. Selwyn Jarvis. 'I'd better take this,' she said and turned away. 'Hello, Judge.'

'Kathy, I hope I'm not interrupting, but I wonder if you could spare me a little time to discuss a matter that's come up.'

'Of course. Concerning your wife's death?'

'Possibly. Could we meet? Perhaps after work, if that suits.'

They arranged for her to go to his house in Highgate that evening.

~

He opened the door as soon as she rang the bell and ushered her into the living room.

'Can I get you anything—a drink?

'No, thanks.' Kathy looked around for signs of decay. An old man abandoned. Would he go off the rails like Charles Pettigrew? Brock was lucky to have Suzanne, but Bren had told her that he'd seemed restless and bored when they'd last met.

Jarvis indicated his wife's armchair for her to sit. 'So how are things going?'

'With the case? Very well. I'm hoping we can get to trial early in the New Year. The defence is very weak.'

He nodded thoughtfully. 'I still find it incredible that a man like that ... I would have said, one of us. Quite incredible that he should have been capable of such acts. Insanity defence, of course?'

'Not yet. He's still pleading innocent. But I assume it'll come to that.'

'Yes, yes. Have you by any chance heard about the sad case of Roger Walcott?'

The sudden change of subject surprised her. 'Only what I've seen in the news.'

It had been a lead item a few weeks before—the suicide of a High Court judge in a Central London hotel room.

Jarvis nodded, frowning. 'Mm. Shocking business. And utterly out of character. Roger was very well known to all of us, full of energy and optimism, happily married. His wife had taken off to Switzerland for a week with the children and grandchildren and he'd booked into a hotel in town convenient for work. Then this. Unbelievable. There was no note, and it was so out of character that a few of his friends wondered if it really could have been suicide, and so I offered to have a word with you, off the record. We just want to be reassured that every possibility has been examined.'

'I see. I haven't seen anything about it in-house. It was a hanging, wasn't it?'

'Yes.'

'Hangings are such a common form of suicide that they're rarely referred to us, but I'm sure that in the case of a High Court judge it would have been investigated very thoroughly. If you like, I'll make inquiries. Is there anything particular you're doubtful about?'

'Only what I said, that he was the last person we would have expected to do a thing like that. And I suppose . . . well, two judicial tragedies so close together makes people wonder.'

'Well, you can be assured that this had absolutely nothing to do with Caroline's murder. I'll see what I can find out.'

'Thank you. I'd be most grateful.'

~

Brock was already sitting at a table in the Castle, around the corner from Holland Park tube station, when the girl walked in. Outside the evening traffic was sluicing through the freezing rain and she looked soaked and miserable. He got to his feet as she looked around, then came towards him. They shook hands.

'Hello, Nadia,' he said. 'I'm David. Can I get you something? Vodka?'

She looked at his whisky and gave a cautious smile. 'Okay.'

'With tonic?'

'Sure.'

He got her a double. She shook her wet headscarf, looking tired, glad to sit down.

'Finished for the day?'

'Yes.' She nodded towards the tall white stuccoed houses on the far side of Holland Park Avenue. 'Two doctors. Very untidy.' She tasted her drink. 'You're a policeman, yes?'

'I used to be. I'm retired now. I'm just doing this to help Mr Pettigrew's lawyer find out who the woman was that you found in his house. It's sad that no one knows, don't you think?'

She shrugged, indifferent. 'She said you would pay for my time.'

'Yes.' Brock took out his wallet and placed it on the table between them. 'Tell me about Mr Pettigrew.'

She made a face. 'I didn't really know him. For eighteen months I was working for Hannibal Lecter and I had no idea. I only met him a couple of times, when I arrived before he left for work. I was very lucky to escape, yes? All I knew was his house.'

'Yes, but an experienced cleaner like you can tell a lot from your clients' houses. How many clients do you have at the moment?'

'Fifteen.'

'And I bet you know all about them—their drug habits, their infidelities, their problem children—without ever meeting them, just from cleaning their houses.'

Nadia granted him a little smile. 'Maybe.'

'So what about Charlie Pettigrew? Off the record.'

'Like I say, I didn't know him. I thought he was a bit sad. He didn't seem to have many friends. The only drugs I saw were medicines from the doctor. He drank quite a lot, that's all I can say, but so do most of my clients. They have parties and leave piles of bottles. But Mr Pettigrew had plenty of bottles on his own, no parties. No visitors. He made no trouble for me, and he left me a nice tip in an envelope last Christmas. I was hoping for the same this year too. Bad luck for me.'

'Did he have many lady visitors?'

'No. That's why I was surprised when I saw two wine-glasses that morning, one with lipstick.'

'No condoms in the house?'

'No.'

Brock frowned, toyed with his wallet, Nadia's eyes following.

'I'm sorry,' she said. 'But what can I tell you? No pornography, no whips or handcuffs, nothing. He was just . . . nothing.'

'So who was the lady in the bedroom?'

'I've no idea.'

Brock's eyes were still on his wallet, but his ears picked up something, a change of tone, a note of defiance.

She drained her glass. 'Thanks for the drink. I'll go now, if you can give me my fee.'

Brock opened the wallet and slid out two twenty-pound notes, which she quickly picked up and stuffed into her coat pocket.

Then he slid out two more notes. 'Yes, you do know, Nadia. You know something about her. Something you didn't mention to the police.'

She was motionless for a moment, then said quietly, 'When I came to London, I cleaned hospital toilets for two years before the agency decided to trust me to clean for private clients. They won't like it if I'm involved with police. I don't want to be a witness or appear in court. When I found the body, I very nearly ran away without calling the police, but I knew they would find out I'd been there and then I'd be in worse trouble.'

'I understand. I'll speak to Mr Pettigrew's lawyer to see if she can agree with the police for you not to appear in court.'

'Thank you.'

He pushed the notes towards her. 'So what do you know about her?'

'The week before the murder, I was taking the recycling wheelie bin—the one with all the bottles—out to the street and I noticed a young woman standing there, looking at the house. She looked like an Indian or a Pakistani. I said hello and she asked if I lived there. I said I cleaned for the owner and she asked if he was a nice man. I said, "He's okay. Why, you looking for a job?" She laughed and said the last thing she wanted was to be a cleaner. That made me annoyed, like she thought she was too good to soil her hands. I said,

"We all got to work," and she told me about her friend, a Romanian girl, who was a cleaner too, vacuuming the offices in the Shard all night. She said her friend came home each morning worn out with just a few pounds in her hand after the agency took their cut. The Indian said she wanted better. So I asked her how she was going to do that—marry a rich man or something? And she laughed and said she'd already tried that and it didn't work. Then she left.

'The thing is, I don't know that she was the woman in the bedroom. The woman in the street's clothes were shabby, and she wasn't wearing glasses like the woman in the police picture. She looked Indian, that's the only connection, so I decided they weren't the same and I didn't mention it to the police. I didn't want more complications.'

'Fair enough,' Brock said. 'What about her build?'

'I don't know what the woman on the bed was like. She was mostly covered up.'

'She weighed fifty-six kilograms, slim build, one hundred and sixty centimetres tall.'

Nadia nodded. 'Yes, that's the same.'

'Did she mention the name of her Romanian friend?'

'No.'

'But it was a woman?'

'Yes.'

'And they were living together?'

Nadia thought about it. 'Yes, I think so. At least, she talked about her coming home tired each morning, so I assumed they lived together.'

'Do you know the name of the agency she was working for?'

'No.'

When he was sure she had nothing more to tell him, Brock let her go, watching her disappear into the streaming rain. He wondered if her family in Katowice knew she was here, cleaning houses in London.

He phoned Maggie Ferguson and asked her to find out whether the police had checked the lenses of the glasses found with the murdered woman's body. 'And I may have a lead on the victim. It's possible that she was living with a Romanian woman who has a night job cleaning offices in the Shard.'

Maggie said she'd get her detective to look into it.

'Let me know if he gets anywhere,' Brock said. 'I'd like to speak to her myself.'

'You sure, Brock?'

'I'm intrigued, Maggie. I admit it. Humour me.'

~

When he got home, Suzanne was already in her dressing-gown, ready for bed. Feeling tired he sank onto a chair in the kitchen and told her the story of the Polish girl while she heated up some soup for him. Finally she said, 'It was a scam gone horribly wrong, wasn't it? That Indian girl trying to sell him a fake manuscript, not realising she was talking to the Hampstead Ripper. That poor girl—imagine, when she finally realised what she'd got herself into.'

'Yes, you're probably right.'

'You don't sound convinced.'

'Oh ... it's just that I've met him, and I find it hard to picture.' He shrugged. 'But human nature never ceases to amaze.'

'There's one way to find out. Send that page to John. He'll tell you if it's a fake.'

'Yes, I thought of that.' In fact, he'd been thinking about John Greenslade quite a lot recently—the son he didn't know he had until the Chelsea Mansions case a few years before. He was an Associate Professor of Renaissance Philology of all things, at McGill University in Montreal, an expert in authenticating texts, and had worked as a consultant in forensic linguistics for the Montreal police on several cases— and once, on the Chelsea murders, for himself and the Met. 'It probably wouldn't do any harm to ask him if he'd take a look.'

'Well, go on, give him a ring.' And Suzanne handed him the phone.

~

Kathy was finally put through to a Detective Inspector O'Hare at West End Central. When she explained why she was calling, he suggested they meet to talk it over. She was pushed for time but agreed anyway, so here she was, back in the neigh- bourhood of Golden Square, drinking coffee.

'Have you discussed this with anyone else?' O'Hare asked. 'Your boss?'

'Commander Torrens? No. Should I?'

'Might be wise.'

'I just want to be able to reassure Judge Jarvis and his mates that Walcott's death was thoroughly investigated and suspicious circumstances ruled out.'

'Jarvis, eh? Interesting. Yeah, they stick together, these bloody judges. Thick as thieves. I'll be glad when I've seen the last of them.' He sounded bitter. 'Anyway, you can reassure him all right. Sir Roger Walcott, High Court judge? 'Course it was thoroughly investigated.'

'It's just that these other judges are bothered because they say it was so out of character.'

'Well, let's say they maybe didn't know him as well as they thought.'

'Oh? What does that mean? Come on, why are you being so cagey? Why do I need to discuss this with my boss?'

O'Hare made a face as if he'd tasted something sour. He glanced around at the other people in the café then leaned across the table to Kathy, spoke in a low growl. 'Just between you and me, right?'

'Okay.'

'He was found in the bathroom of his hotel suite, throttled by his dressing-gown cord tied to the shower head, naked and lying next to a teddy bear.'

'A what?'

'A teddy bear. And on the floor nearby was his laptop. There was stuff on it that shouldn't have been there.'

'What kind of stuff?' She stared at his blank face. 'What . . . children?'

'You said it, I didn't. Really disgusting filth. Turn your stomach. It's assumed that he didn't mean to kill himself, but slipped on the tile floor and choked to death. There was bruising consistent with a fall and a struggle to release himself.'

'Bloody hell.'

'So what do you do? The bastard had tried several paedophile cases . . . well, you can imagine.'

'Unsafe verdicts, retrials.'

'Yeah. It went to the top, the Lord Chief Justice, the Home Secretary, and they decided to close the book on it. We weren't able to identify the children in the pictures and there was no evidence he'd committed any offence other than possession of illicit material. He was dead and beyond prosecution. He had a lovely wife and a perfect family—two children, both surgeons. What good would it do to go public?'

Kathy nodded. 'You think my boss would know about it?'

'Maybe not, but if he talks to his boss he'll soon be told to back off.'

'Right, thanks. I'll tell Jarvis that no stones were left unturned.'

'Good idea. Just don't tell him what slithered out from underneath them.'

~

She waited twenty-four hours before contacting Jarvis, just to let him think that her inquiries had been exhaustive.

'I'm afraid there's no doubt,' she said. 'Sir Roger must have been under tremendous stress. It was very thoroughly investigated and we're satisfied there was no third party involved.'

'But . . . it just doesn't make sense, Kathy. I saw him the evening before and he was in the best of spirits, talking about his plans for Christmas. His wife Amelia was expecting him to come over to Geneva to see his new grandson. She'd spoken on the phone to him less than two hours before he must have died. It makes no sense.'

'Yes, that does make it hard for everyone,' she said, hearing the treacherous hollowness in her voice. 'But we never really know what's going on inside another person's head, do we?'

'Bollocks. I always knew exactly what was going on inside Roger's head—ambition and the pursuit of the good life. He'd as soon have topped himself as farted in front of the Queen.'

'It went as high as the Lord Chief Justice, sir. He was satisfied.'

'Lord Chief Justice The Right Honourable The Lord Wilfred Prendergast of Southend on Sea is always satisfied, Kathy. He's bloated with satisfaction. It means nothing.'

'Sir, I can only tell you what I've discovered.'

'Was there something seamy, Kathy? Is that what they're covering up? Was there a woman in that hotel room with him? Or a man? Was he being blackmailed? Is that it? You can tell me. Amelia will never know. I'll put a quiet word out to the others and they'll understand. They'll keep shtum.'

Kathy took a deep breath. 'I'm sorry, sir, all I can say is—' she thought desperately, What the hell *can* I say? '—there's nothing untoward.'

After she put the phone down those weasel words echoed in her head. *Nothing untoward*. Like hell there wasn't.

9

Brock parked his car in the multi-storey and made his way onto St Thomas Street. Above him glowed the ninety-five-storey glass pinnacle of the Shard, erupting like a vast luminous icicle out of the jumble of the London Bridge neighbourhood. A gust of cold wind caught him as he turned the corner and propelled him under the legs of the tower and into the shelter of the reception foyer. He looked around for a green cap, and caught sight of a woman standing checking her phone. Maggie Ferguson's PI was a slight, unobtrusive figure whom he could imagine melting into a crowd.

'You're looking for a haystack in a needle.' She grinned. 'Who knows how many Romanians there are working in here? Half the cleaners are employed through third-party agencies who pay cash and don't know and don't care what their clients' nationalities or immigration status really are.'

'But you think you've found someone?'

'I spent last night up at the office reception area on level two, talking to the girls. There are twenty-six floors of offices above that with seventy-three tenants of varying size, serviced by half-a-dozen cleaning contractors, who come and go during the night. I spoke to all the supervisors I could find, and some of the cleaners. Only one admitted he knew of a Romanian girl. This was a driver for a company called CCC Services, an Aussie. I managed to have a few words with him on his way out. He goes around in a van and collects his cleaners from various locations in East and South London, brings them here, where they work till about midnight, then he takes them on to other locations, sometimes in the City, sometimes at Canary Wharf, before driving them back to the drop-off points at about seven am—all round a twelve-hour-plus shift.

'When he's driving the girls—they're all women—he listens to their chatter: Africans, Jamaicans, Pakis, various Europeans. No English, of course. One night he overheard two black girls getting into the van talking about "that Roma bitch", then they shut up sharp when a girl in a red anorak got in. When the newcomer took a seat at the other end of the van, the two girls carried on whispering and glancing back at her. He checked her name on his list—Elena Vasile. Tall, thin, black hair, pale complexion, mean look on her face, probably mid-twenties.

'She wasn't on last night, but I was waiting for the van this evening. They drop the girls off and pick them up on the other side of the block, London Bridge Street, and I watched them arrive half an hour ago.'

She pulled out her phone and showed Brock a sequence of photos she'd taken of a young woman in a red anorak. 'I'll send these to your phone.'

'I've just missed her then,' Brock said.

'Yes. If it's like last night, they'll be coming back down around midnight for the next place. Thing is, they don't dawdle. I don't think you'll get a chance to talk to her in transit, and unless you've got a police ID I doubt they'll let you into the office areas to try to find her there.'

'Any ideas?'

'You got wheels?'

'Yes.'

'Well, if it was me, I'd be waiting on London Bridge Street for the van—it's got the red CCC Services logo on the side— and I'd follow it to its next destination and try there.'

'Thanks.'

'Of course, it could all be a complete waste of time. I tried to track her down—driver's licence, national insurance, social media. Nothing, couldn't find a match. Even if Elena Vasile really is Romanian, there could be a dozen other Romanians up there right now. But then, that's what this is all about, yeah? You must have had that all the time when you were a copper, sitting around in cars, waiting for a break. I'll leave you to it. Good hunting.'

He watched her go, thinking, Yes, that is what I used to do, but it was a long time ago, and I had backup and resources.

He set off to explore. At one time he knew every brick and doorway of this crowded district of Southwark, but now he found himself experiencing sudden disorienting shifts and displacements where new developments around the London Bridge underground and overground stations shouldered into the old familiar fabric along with crisp new buildings on the Guy's Hospital site next door. Glass was gradually displacing soot-stained London brick. He drank several cups of coffee and rang Suzanne and told her he probably wouldn't be home that night.

~

Soon after midnight Brock's car, parked on London Bridge Street, was passed by a white van with the CCC logo on its side. It pulled in up ahead on the edge of the plaza in front of the Shard, its exhaust misting in the cold night air. After a few minutes eight women came hurrying out of the building and climbed in, one wearing a red anorak. Brock put his car into gear and eased out as the van drove off fast, circling back around the block and under the railway bridge. They passed Southwark Cathedral on the left then crossed over the Thames on London Bridge and into the City of London financial district on the far side. Traffic was light, and Brock stayed close as they turned into the narrow canyon of Fenchurch Street, heading towards the strange bulk of the 20 Fenchurch Street tower, dubbed the Walkie-Talkie, and Brock wondered if they were going to do a tour of London's new towers. But then the van pulled to an abrupt stop outside an older block, and as he drove slowly past he watched the women pile out and disappear inside. He came to a stop further down the street, waited, then followed the van again as it drove past and on into the maze of city streets.

It found a park near Liverpool Street station and Brock did likewise, watching the driver get out, lock his van and stride away. Brock followed, glad to stretch his legs, and watched the man cross Bishopsgate and go into an all-night café. Brock returned to the station, bought a packet of sandwiches and a coffee, and returned to his car to wait.

At three am he woke from a light doze to the sound of the door slamming on the van. He saw its lights come on and they moved off again, back to Fenchurch Street to pick up the cleaners and then out through the East End towards the towers of the Isle of Dogs and Canary Wharf. The same routine was repeated, Brock finding a parking spot within sight of the CCC van and settling down to wait. Perhaps he was overtired, mildly febrile, but he felt unexpectedly elated at being back on the job again, like in the old days. He told himself that he could still do this, and would soon have to bring it to a positive conclusion.

It was after seven am when the women filed out of the glass tower and made for the van. They were exhausted now, heads down, wearily climbing inside. They drove back into Stepney, where the van made a stop and two of the women got out. Then across the river to Deptford, where two more were dropped off. Light was beginning to glimmer in the east as they came to the Elephant and Castle, another old familiar area transformed by new towers and construction cranes. They turned down Walworth Road and came to a stop near the turning into the East Street Market. One woman got out, wearing a red anorak, and Brock quickly pulled in to the kerb and followed her.

She walked with long strides and he had to run to catch up with her as she turned into East Street, busy with vans and people unloading goods onto the pavements. She had her phone out now and was making a call as she wove around the obstacles. Past the Kyrenia Café and opposite the Halal Meat butchers she turned into a quiet side street, where he finally caught up with her.

'Elena.'

She stopped abruptly and turned to face him.

'I need a quick word with you.'

She stared at him, weighing him up, then said, 'I don't speak English,' and turned away.

'It's about your Indian roommate. Did you know she's dead?'

She took no notice, striding on towards a 1960s block of deck-access flats.

'Elena, please!'

She looked back over her shoulder and spat, 'Leave me alone or I call the police.'

'If you don't talk to me *I'll* call the police, Elena, and you don't want that.'

Up ahead Brock saw a man in a black leather jacket striding towards them. As he reached Elena she nodded back over her shoulder at Brock and he barely had time to react as the man hit him hard in the stomach, then again in the face. He fell to the ground, trying to protect his head as the man began kicking him, silently, methodically. Finally he stopped, knelt beside Brock and felt for his wallet.

Through the pain in his ribs and head Brock heard a yell. He looked up, feeling dizzy, and saw three people running towards him. One of them crouched down beside him, a big black face wrinkled in concern. 'You all right, mate?'

Brock groaned and tried to sit up as the man put a hand under his arm, heaving him upright. Looking around he saw that Elena and the man had disappeared.

'I'll call the coppers.' A woman's voice.

'No,' Brock said, grunting as pain shot through his knee when he put weight on it. 'It's okay. They left my wallet.'

One of the men stooped to pick it up for him. His three rescuers were all West Indian, and the woman seemed to be in charge. She said, 'Help the man back to the shop, boys, and we'll clean him up.'

He limped with them to East Street and the corner shop, Rosie's General Store, which the woman appeared to own. There she ordered the men to bring a chair for Brock, a bowl of warm water and a towel, and the first-aid kit. As she worked on his face she said, 'I think you're goin' to have a black eye, my dear. What were you doin' back there anyway? What happened?'

So he explained that he was working for a firm of lawyers trying to trace the family of a murdered Indian woman. 'I think she'd been living around here with a Romanian woman. That's who I was trying to talk to, but her friend didn't like it for some reason.'

'What was the Indian girl's name?'

'She called herself Shari Mitra, but that might not have been her real name. She was murdered on the twenty-sixth of October. The Romanian woman is called Elena Vasile.'

Rosie considered this for a moment, then said. 'I know that Elena and her friend, and I don't like them. But she did have another girl living with her for a time. Only she said she was a Paki, not an Indian, and she was called Uzma. She would have been about the same age. She used to come in here, but I haven't seen her in months. Have you, boys?'

The men shook their heads. Then one of them said, 'She worked at Enver's for a while, but she didn't last long. She thought she was too good to be a kebab girl.'

'Yes,' Rosie agreed. 'Very well spoken, she was. Quite posh. Who murdered her then? Her old man?'

'Why do you say that?' Brock winced as she dabbed iodine on the graze across his temple.

'She told me she'd run away from her husband.'

'Yes, she told someone she'd been married to a rich man and it didn't work out.'

Rosie chuckled. 'No, no, a man with a British passport who *said* he was rich—that old story. She was fed up at home in Pakistan and her family were desperate to get her married, so when she met this *rich London businessman* on the web they were all delighted, although he was quite a bit older. They got married over there and he brought her back to London, and that's when she discovered that he had a grubby little hardware shop in Stepney in which he expected her to work twenty-four seven, and when she objected he beat her. Eventually she ran away, crossed the river and ended up here.'

'I see. Do you know her husband's name?'

'No. But I'm sure a smart private eye like you will soon find him. You'd best take some judo lessons first, though.' And she burst out laughing.

~

Half an hour later, after a hot cup of tea and one too many jokes at his expense, Brock thanked them and limped back to his car. There was a yellow plastic packet stuck to the windscreen bearing the words PENALTY CHARGE NOTICE ENCLOSED. He peeled it off and eased himself into the driving seat, examined his battered face in the mirror with a shudder, then pulled out his wallet to see whether he had any money left. It seemed the man hadn't touched his cash or credit cards, and he thought everything was intact until he realised his driver's licence was gone.

His phone rang—Suzanne. 'David! Where are you?'

He cleared his throat. 'Um, Walworth . . . I'm following a lead. I was going to call you.'

'Are you all right? You sound odd.'

'No, no. Everything's fine.'

'Where did you sleep last night?'

'Um, in the car, on and off.'

'You're joking.'

'No, it's fine. I've got one more little job to do, then I'll go home. I thought I might stay at Warren Lane over the weekend.'

'What? No, you can't, David. Ginny and her husband are coming for dinner tonight, remember? And you promised to help Miranda with her project this weekend. Are you sure you're all right? You do sound quite . . . unsteady.'

'I'm fine. Okay, I'll try to get back by lunchtime. Maybe get some sleep this afternoon. Help Miranda tomorrow. Okay?'

'Fine. Are you sure you're fit to drive?'

'Yes, yes. See you.' He rang off, then realised he was parked outside a chemist. He went in and bought painkillers, then went next door for an energy drink, returned to his car and set off north again, back through Elephant and Castle towards the river. Half an hour later he was in Shadwell Road, lined with oriental food shops and travel agents with posters for cheap flights to Dhaka, Lahore and Mumbai. Another familiar hunting ground, this time unchanged from before. He came to the small police station in a row of shops and got out to look at the missing-persons posters in the window. And there she was, Uzma Jamali, a pretty, intelligent face, missing since last April. He went inside and said he might have news of her and wanted to speak to her husband. The duty constable looked doubtfully for a moment at the state of his face, then gave him the details—Mr Tariq Jamali at Jamali Hardware, 286 Shadwell Road, not a hundred yards away. Brock thanked him and returned to his car.

A short, fierce-looking man was standing in the doorway of number 286, arms folded across his apron, glaring at passers-by as if to dare them to come inside, then becoming distracted by the backsides of two girls in short skirts walking by.

'Mr Jamali?'

He turned to Brock and his face lit up. 'Yes, sir! Come inside, come inside!'

Brock went in, looking at the boxes of hinges and screws, the racks of tools and rows of stepladders.

'There's everything you might need in here, sir.'

'Mr Jamali, I'm an investigator working for a firm of lawyers.'

Jamali's expression switched abruptly to alarm.

'It's possible we may have some information about your wife.'

'Really? Have you found her? It's been so long, I'd almost given up hope.'

'It's a question of identity.'

'Ah, I understand.' Jamali went behind the counter and took a photograph album from a drawer. 'This is Uzma, my wife. You see how beautiful she is? These were taken at our wedding in Pakistan last year, and this one with her sisters in her parents' house. I have more. Take one if you want, to show your lawyers. I reported her missing to the police on the tenth of April, eight hours after she left. She would have been thirty-two this last July the sixteenth. You see how beautiful she is?'

'Yes, indeed. And intelligent?'

'Oh, very! And well educated. Look, look.' He pointed to a framed document hanging on the wall, a degree certificate for Uzma Dehwar, awarded a Master of Philosophy (English) from the University of the Punjab, Lahore. 'Dehwar was her family name,' Jamali explained. 'Now, of course, she is Uzma Jamali.'

'What do you think happened to her?'

Jamali shook his head. 'Alas, we had an argument that day and she ran out through that door and never returned. She was not happy here. London was a disappointment to her. It was not what she had imagined. I used to tell her: *Uzma, Uzma, London is not the promised land!* She had crazy ideas. She thought she might be a famous writer and dreamed of a life of luxury and idleness, but she did not understand that you must work hard for everything. I blame her parents for spoiling her. We had disagreements. All I wanted was for her to be like my mother, a good wife. So where is she now? You say you have information?'

'I'm not sure, Mr Jamali. I'll have to show her photograph to the lawyers. You say she left everything behind? All her personal things?'

'Yes, yes, they are all upstairs, undisturbed, waiting for her return.'

'Did she have any books?'

'Yes, over here. I put them in this box to take them to the second-hand shop to sell them.' He lifted it onto the counter and Brock looked at the covers. His head hurt and he found it difficult to focus. They all appeared to be by Pakistani authors, names unknown to him—Ishrat Afreen, Fatima Bhutto, Qaisra Shahraz, Sarwat Nazir.

'Women writers,' Jamali said with a dismissive wave of his hand. 'Not good for her. They turned her head.'

'And you say she wanted to be a writer. Do you have anything that she wrote?'

'No.' He spoke sharply. 'That's what our argument was about that day. I caught her upstairs scribbling away while I was down here running the shop single-handed, so I took her papers from her and burned them, every page and notebook that I could find. But if you see her, please tell her that I forgive her.'

Brock returned to his car and set off for Battle. Suzanne was busy with customers in her antiques shop and didn't see him as he went upstairs, ran a hot bath, pulled off his clothes, poured a large Scotch, lowered himself into the tub and promptly fell asleep.

~

An hour later Suzanne saw his coat lying on the stairs leading up to the flat. Puzzled, she picked it up and saw the dirt and the rip in the sleeve. She called his name, got no reply, then went up to the bathroom door and saw the top of his head, just visible over the rim of the bath, a glass of whisky untouched on the floor.

'David?'

No sound, no movement. She thought, *Oh God, he's dead*, and went over and put her hand into the water. It was cold.

'David . . .'

His arm jerked suddenly and he lifted his head. 'That you, Suzanne?' he mumbled.

She stared in horror at his face, the whole right side bloodied and bruised, the eye swollen shut. 'What happened to you, darling?'

'Nothing, nothing. Hell, it's cold.' He began to shiver.

She became all action, pulling the plug to drain the bath, grabbing a thick towel and wrapping it around him as he struggled to his feet. She saw the bruising down his side and the way he winced as she tried to hold him. She got him to stand by the radiator while she dried him, then found him fresh clothes and helped him dress. When she brought in his thick black coat, he looked confused and said, 'What? What are you doing?'

'Come on, we're going in the car.'

'I don't think I can manage dinner with Ginny. I just need to lie down.'

'We're not going to Ginny's.'

She got him downstairs and out to her car, him groaning with every step. When he was buckled in and she started the engine, he said, 'Well . . . where are we going?'

'The Conquest.'

'What's that, a pub?'

'It's a hospital, David, and when we get there you're going to have to tell them what happened to you. Did you have an accident? Were you knocked down?'

He took a deep breath and finally seemed to focus. 'In a way. I was knocked down by a thug who kicked the hell out of me. My own fault, should have seen it coming.'

'Dear God, where was this?'

'Walworth.'

'And you drove all the way back?'

'Felt all right till I fell asleep. Just need to rest, love. Don't seem to be able to see out of this eye.'

'You sound concussed. Hang on, it isn't far.'

When they got there, she helped him to limp in to Emergency, where a triage nurse brought him a wheelchair and tried to get some details out of him. When Suzanne explained that he'd been attacked, she said she'd have to call the police, but Brock said no and showed her his old police ID card which he still had in his wallet and told her he was on a case and just needed patching up.

While they waited Suzanne phoned Maggie Ferguson and told her what had happened. She wanted to speak to Brock, who took the phone and gave her a brief mumbled account. She said she'd come down to Hastings, but Suzanne persuaded her there was no point for now.

Later, Suzanne was taken in to see the doctor, a young registrar, who was studying an X-ray film.

'The cheekbone, here, the zygomatic bone, has a hairline fracture, you see? He was lucky he didn't lose his eye. Also—' he held up another film '—two rib fractures, here and here. Indications of concussion. He should have complete rest for five days and then take it easy for a further four weeks. No driving, no lifting, no strenuous exercise. We've dressed the wounds and they shouldn't be touched for five days, then get his GP to look at them. We'll give you some painkillers and a prescription for more.'

Suzanne went in to see him, lying on a bed in the Emergency ward. Half the right side of his face was obscured by the thick dressing. 'You look like a zombie,' she said.

He gave her a rueful smile.

'I hope this has taught you a lesson,' she said.

10

Kathy finished the call from Maggie Ferguson with a frown. It was extremely annoying that Maggie's detective had apparently managed to do what she had not—discover the identity of Pettigrew's third victim. But it was also unsettling. What else did Maggie now know that she didn't? Was this the thread that she would use to unravel the prosecution case? Kathy now had to refocus on a job she had mentally closed almost two months before. She called to Alfarsi to get a car to take them to Stepney.

~

Tariq Jamali looked more irritated than concerned. 'I don't understand. Do you know where my wife is or not?'

Kathy said, 'I'm afraid you must prepare yourself for bad news, Mr Jamali. It seems possible that the body of a woman found in Hampstead last October is Uzma.'

'What? A body?'

'Yes, sir. We'll need to run more tests, but it does seem very likely that it's her.'

'But . . . let me see her. I will tell you if it is her.'

'I'm afraid she was too badly injured for that to be possible.'

'She was run over?'

'She was murdered.'

His eyes widened and he sank onto a chair beside the counter. 'The Hampstead murders! Is it possible?'

'She was found on the twenty-seventh of October, and until now we haven't been able to identify her. She was using the name Shari Mitra. Have you any idea where Uzma was at that time?'

He didn't seem to hear at first, and Kathy had to repeat the question.

'October? Six months after she left me? No, I have no idea.' His look of shock changed to a frown of anger. 'Why would she be in Hampstead? What was she up to there? Was she there to see a man? A wealthy man?'

'Why do you say that?'

'I know Uzma. Hampstead is rich people, yes?'

'Had she done this before, gone after rich men?'

'She thought I was a rich man, then when she discovered that I wasn't she left me. She was a whore.'

Kathy said carefully, 'Let me understand you, Mr Jamali. Are you saying that Uzma was working as a prostitute?'

'Working? Ha! Uzma didn't work. But she had the mind of a whore.'

Kathy changed tack. 'This detective who came to see you, did he tell you why he came here?'

'What do you mean? He came to find out about Uzma. I gave him a picture.'

'But how did he find you? Why did he think Uzma was the woman he was looking for?'

'He didn't say. Actually, I didn't like him. He had a dirty coat with a tear in it, and his face was bruised, like he'd been in a fight.'

'What was his name?'

Jamali shrugged. 'I don't know. He said he was working for a lawyer, that's all.'

When Kathy got back to the patrol car, she phoned Maggie Ferguson.

'Maggie? I want to talk to this detective of yours.'

'No, that's not possible, Kathy. I've told you all we know. He's been badly hurt. He can't see anyone.'

'I don't care if he's only got hours to live, I want to talk to him.'

'Give me ten minutes.'

Twenty minutes later Maggie called back. 'No, it's not possible for you to see him, Kathy. Doctor's orders. But he thinks it would be worth your while to talk to someone called Rosie, a West Indian lady who runs Rosie's General Store on East Street in Walworth. She put my bloke onto Mr Jamali, and he thinks she probably knows more than she told him. That's all I can tell you.'

Kathy and Alfarsi drove across the river to East Street and found Rosie in her shop, busy with customers. She left them to her boys and took the two detectives into the back room.

'Yes, he was a nice man—too old for what he was doing, mind you. He was trying to follow that Romanian girl who lives in the flats round the back there, and one of her friends set upon him, gave him a real beating. I tried to clean him up.'

'Hang on,' Kathy said. 'What Romanian girl?'

'Elena, her name is, Elena Vasile, and he was wanting to ask her about the girl sharing her flat, who he thought was an Indian, but we always assumed she was a Paki.'

Kathy got her to slow down and spell it all out.

'Okay, so how did this bloke know that the Indian or Pakistani girl was living with Elena?'

'Oh, I've no idea, and anyway we think she moved out some time ago. We haven't seen her for months.'

'And the Romanian man?'

'Marku, a bad boy. I'll bet your local people know about him. Constantin is his other name, I think. Yes, Marku Constantin. They say he's a pimp, runs a string of girls.'

'So this Pakistani girl was a prostitute?'

'I couldn't say that for a fact. I told the old man, she had airs, a posh voice for a Paki.'

Kathy showed her Uzma Jamali's picture and Rosie nodded. 'Yes, that's her, who called herself Uzma. I didn't know her other name.'

When they returned to their car, Kathy checked the names on the PNC, then rang CID at Southwark Borough Command. They confirmed that the Romanian Marku Constantin was suspected of running a prostitution ring using unregistered migrant girls, and had been investigated for welfare benefit fraud and extortion, but hadn't yet been charged.

Kathy rang off and she and Alfarsi went to the block of flats behind East Street where he lived. There was no reply to their knocks, and a neighbour came out and told them that both he and the girl Elena had left in a hurry hours before, taking luggage with them.

While they waited for a warrant to be issued to search the flat, they went down to the enclosure at the foot of the block that contained the garbage bins and began searching through them. It didn't take long to discover a plastic sack containing items of women's clothing and used toiletries, as well as torn sheets of paper and other stationery items. Thumbing through these, Kathy noticed what looked like scraps of photocopied typewriting similar to *The Promised Land* manuscript page. She also came upon a business card for Steve Weiner, literary agent. On the reverse was a hand-written note: *10.30, Sweet Pepper Café*. A check on Google told her the Sweet Pepper Café was in Putney High Street.

Kathy left Alfarsi to carry out the search and headed west. Traffic was congested in the South London streets and it took an age to reach Putney High Street and the café. She went inside and looked around. Judging by the menu chalked on a blackboard, it specialised in interesting pastries and coffees from exotic locations. She ordered an espresso from Papua New Guinea and asked about Steve Weiner.

'Yeah,' the Eurasian girl behind the counter said. 'That's his office over there, the table in the corner.'

'His office?'

'Yeah, where he meets his clients. He lives upstairs. Want me to call him?'

'Thanks, but first, do you remember seeing this woman?'
She showed the girl Shari's picture.

'Ye-es, I think I do remember someone like her. Because
of her bag.'

'Her bag?'

'Yeah, a big Indian carpet bag. Really lovely, it was.'

'This would be a couple of months ago?'

'Suppose so.'

'Was she alone?'

'Yes.'

Kathy thanked her, asked her to call Weiner and went to
sit at his table. After ten minutes a man appeared at the café
door and spoke to the girl behind the counter, who pointed
at Kathy. He came over to her, looking bored and weary, as if
he'd been woken after a boozy lunch. Kathy got to her feet.

'Mr Weiner, I'm Detective Chief Inspector Kolla of the
Metropolitan Police. We spoke a couple of months ago about
Shari Mitra. I'd like another word, please.'

'Oh. Do I have any choice?'

Kathy smiled. 'Not really. Take a seat.'

He called back to the Eurasian girl for an Algerian mocha
and sat down with a sigh. 'I told you, I know nothing about
her. I spoke to her briefly on the phone and that was that.'

'You'd swear to that in a court of law, would you,
Mr Weiner?'

'Sure.' He looked away, bored, to check out the other
customers.

'So you deny that you met her here the following morning?'

He turned slowly back to face her.

'Let's try again,' she said. 'With the truth.'

He took a deep breath, stared at the tabletop and began drawing a pattern with his fingertip. 'Look, when you contacted me I'd just heard the news about her being murdered. It didn't really surprise me, somehow. She had some kind of scam going on, trying to flog this dodgy manuscript, and I smelled trouble. I didn't want to get involved, so I just told you the short version.'

Kathy wondered if he'd ever been an actor; every gesture, every intonation seemed calculated for a camera. 'So what's the long version?'

'Okay, I agreed to meet her and told her to come here, and she gave me this shaggy-dog story about a great-uncle or grandfather or something who knew George Orwell, who'd given him this amazing unknown last novel worth a fortune.'

'You didn't believe it?'

'What, unknown Indian knocks on door bearing fabulous gifts? Come on. Ever since the Hitler Diaries scam it's every publisher and agent's worst nightmare.'

'Did you find out anything about her?'

'I asked her for proof of identification. Nope—no passport, no driver's licence, no credit card, nothing. That was good enough for me.'

'Did she show you the manuscript?'

'She tried to show me a page, but I told her not to bother. What good would it do? I assumed it was a passable forgery, and I'd be none the wiser. That's when she got narky and walked out.'

It might be the truth, Kathy thought, or not. It was hard to tell with Weiner. He was as plausible telling this version as the last, and as glib.

She returned to Walworth, where Alfarsi had now gained entry to the Romanians' flat and done a thorough search. There was nothing of interest.

~

Brock lowered himself gingerly onto the bed and lay back with a sigh. 'The wood-turning group is looking increasingly attractive,' he said.

The phone beside the bed rang and Suzanne reached across for it. 'It's Maggie,' she said, and gave her a summary of what the doctor had told them. Then, covering the mouthpiece, 'Can you talk to her?'

'Of course.' He took the phone. 'Maggie. No, I'm fine really. Just got to take it easy for a day or two.'

'I have a problem, Brock,' the lawyer said. 'Kathy Kolla is giving me a hard time. She says we're obstructing her investigation and if I don't get my detective to her for an interview she's going to get a court order. I'm not sure if I can hold her off.'

'Did you tell her about Rosie?'

'Yes, and she's talked to her, but now she wants to know how you came to know about the Romanian girl, Elena Vasile. Apparently she and the bloke who beat you up have done a runner, and she's blaming you for not reporting them right away. The only thing I can suggest is that we give her a full and detailed account of your investigation, without revealing your identity, but I don't think that's going to satisfy her now. She's really pissed off and wants to give you a grilling. I'll do what I can, okay? But I thought I should warn you.'

Brock rang off and told Suzanne what she'd said.

Suzanne winced. 'What are you going to do?'

~

Kathy put the phone down and stared glumly out the window at the night. Rain was spattering against the glass, distorting the glimmering lights below in strange fluid patterns.

Her mind turned back again to Maggie Ferguson. The bitch was playing games, deliberately frustrating her investigation. It was obvious why she wouldn't let Kathy talk to her detective—the bastard must have discovered something that Maggie was going to spring on them in court. Well, she wasn't going to get away with that.

The phone rang. A voice she barely recognised. 'Brock? Is that you?'

'Yes ... um, got a bit of a cold. Nothing serious. Look ... we wondered if you were going to be free at all tomorrow? Sunday? Suzanne's just dying to see your flat. Me too, of course.'

'Oh, that would be great. I am free actually.'

They arranged a time in the morning and she hung up feeling a bit more cheerful. Something to look forward to.

~

The intercom sounded and Kathy went to the screen. She saw Brock's face, or at least half of it, off to one side of the camera.

'Come on up,' she said. 'Twelfth floor.'

She got a shock when she opened the door and saw the other side of his face.

'My God, Brock, what happened to you?'

'It's nothing. A fall.'

'A hell of a fall. Come in, come in. Sit down. Have you seen a doctor?'

'Yes, yes. It looks worse than it is.' He gazed around. 'Kathy, this is magnificent! That view. What did you do, rob a bank?'

'Just lucky, a matter of timing. Where's Suzanne?'

'She stopped off to buy a couple of things. She won't be long. Gives us a chance for a chat.' He produced a bottle of champagne and bunch of flowers he'd been hiding behind his back.

'Oh, they're lovely.' And she laughed.

'What's funny?'

'I was just thinking about the other time you gave me flowers—our first case together, remember? Things went pear-shaped and you brought me some flowers to the flat in Finchley and I threw them at you.'

'Oh ... yes, of course. I'd forgotten.' He seemed to find the memory unsettling.

'I was really mad at you. We've come a long way since then, haven't we?'

He followed her to the kitchen bench and watched her fill a water jug and put them in.

'Coffee?' she said.

'No, I'm fine. Let's just sit down and talk.'

He seemed oddly subdued, or maybe troubled, and she had a horrible thought that he was going to tell her that he had something wrong with him. They sat by the windows and she said, 'How have you been, apart from the fall?'

'Good, good. I had lunch with Bren a while ago. He told me a bit about you, your new job. It sounds as if you're going really well.'

'It was a bit tricky at first, with the Hampstead murders, you know?'

'Big case to land you with at the start. But you got your man.'

'Yes, well, things have settled down since then. The team's working really well. There's the usual management bullshit, of course. We're all snowed under with work, just needing to get on with the jobs at hand, so what does management do? Insist that we drop everything to attend a two-day *wellness workshop*. Then, when we're more or less recovered from that, the team leaders have to go and waste another two days on a *change management course*, with a bloody exam at the end! Honestly, Brock, you're well out of it.'

'But you wouldn't change it for anything, would you?'

She smiled. 'Probably not. So, what have you been getting up to?'

'Well, not much until a few days ago. Then I had a strange approach from Maggie Ferguson.'

'Maggie! She's defending my Hampstead killer.'

'Yes, she told me. In fact, that's why she called me. She told me the police case against Pettigrew was overwhelming, but there was an aspect that bothered her.'

'You discussed my case with Maggie Ferguson?'

'Only in the broadest terms.'

'What aspect?'

'The business of the manuscript.'

'That's a red herring.'

'Yes, very possibly, but since no one had been able to identify the woman who brought it to him, and whom he killed, it was an unknown that bothered her. She asked for my opinion.'

'How were you going to do that?'

'I talked to Pettigrew.'

'You *interviewed* my suspect?'

'I listened to his story.'

She'd got it now—he wasn't ill, he was embarrassed. And so he bloody well should be. 'Didn't you think of speaking to me first?'

'Of course, but Maggie said there'd be no conflict of interest. It wouldn't have a bearing on the outcome of the case and I wouldn't give evidence. I insisted on that.'

'She's Maggie Ferguson, Brock! The defence counsel! Why would she approach you if it wasn't to help her defence? Against me.'

And then it dawned on her, the damaged face, the limp. 'Oh no . . . It wasn't you, was it? Who tracked down Uzma Jamali? Please tell me you weren't Maggie's bloody detective.'

He couldn't look her in the eye now. He stared down at his shoes, scratched at his beard, frowned, then finally nodded. 'Yes, I tracked her down.'

She stared at him, sitting there like a big shaggy damaged bear trying to look contrite. 'I can't believe it.'

He began to speak but she cut him off. 'Hang on. Go back to you interviewing Pettigrew. What did you make of him?'

'Frankly, I couldn't get a grip on him. If he's a psychopath, he's unlike any other I've met over the years. And that bizarre story of the lost Orwell manuscript, where had that come from? The only thing I could think was that he'd been the target of an elaborate hoax, for money. But how did that square with the Hampstead murders? Was it just an unfortunate coincidence that Uzma picked the killer as her victim? As you know, I don't like coincidences.'

'So you decided to solve the case your way.'

'No, no. I just wanted to get someone else's perspective on him, to try to make sense of him. I spoke to his editor at Golden Press, and that only made me more confused. There was the story about his mother when he was a little boy—you know about that?'

Kathy nodded.

'But he seems to have been an entirely passive and non-violent man. So then I spoke to his cleaner.'

'His cleaner?'

'Yes, Nadia from Poland, who found the body. She told me that when she was taking Pettigrew's bin out the week before Uzma was murdered she spoke to what she took to be an Indian woman who stopped outside the house. She asked questions about the owner and Nadia asked if she was looking for a cleaning job, but the woman said no, her housemate from Romania was a cleaner at the Shard and she wanted something better than that. She joked that she'd married a rich man, but that didn't work out. So, based on that and a bit of shoe leather, I tracked down Elena Vasile at the Shard, followed her to Walworth, met Rosie and ended up at Tariq Jamali's in Shadwell Road.'

'And got beaten up in the process.' Kathy shook her head, not sure whether to throw him out or feel sorry for him. 'You old bastard. You just wanted to prove that the Met couldn't do it without you—that *I* couldn't do it without you.'

'No, no, Kathy. Nothing like that.'

'Oh really? Why didn't Nadia tell *us* about the Indian woman?'

'Because the agency that employs her doesn't like their

girls getting involved with the police, and she was afraid they'd send her back to cleaning hospital toilets. Look, I know I've trodden on your toes, and I'm very sorry. I didn't mean that to happen. But I did at least identify your victim for you, and there's no harm done, is there?'

'Except to my pride. Is there anything else I should know?'

'Um, well, I've sent a copy of the manuscript page to John in Montreal for him to take a look.'

'Oh, so he's involved in my case too, is he?'

'I didn't mention the case or the name Pettigrew, but I thought he might be able to throw some light on the authenticity of the document. I'm sorry, Kathy. I was just trying to help. You are absolutely sure he's your Hampstead killer, are you?'

Exasperated, Kathy turned on him. 'Yes! Did Maggie show you the forensic report?'

'No. She just said the evidence against him was strong.'

'It was overwhelming, Brock. Hell, he even had Uzma Jamali's dried blood on his trouser legs when we arrested him the next day. And there's evidence tying him to the second murder too. The killer made a mistake and opened Caroline Jarvis's handbag, leaving a small DNA trace. We've now established that the trace belongs to Pettigrew. The killer also took a trophy, Caroline's necklace. We found it in a drawer in Pettigrew's bedroom. In addition, a hair was found on Caroline's body, a dog's hair, and the DNA matched that of the hairs of Pettigrew's dog. So yes, I am absolutely sure he's the Hampstead killer.'

'But why, Kathy? How could a man like that become such a monster?'

'Rage—rage at his mother, rage at women, rage at his own impotence and failure. He realised that Uzma was trying to make a fool of him, and he lost it. You should have seen that bedroom where he killed her. He slaughtered her in a blind rage.'

'I see. And the Orwell manuscript?'

'Uzma was running some kind of scam, trying to get an advance from publishers and agents for a fake Orwell novel—we know of at least one other person she approached. And yes, she was unlucky enough to choose the one who happened to be the Hampstead killer. Pettigrew mustn't have been able to believe his luck. Unfortunately—for him—he took too many sleeping pills with a bit too much wine, and passed out after he'd done the deed. The next morning he went off to work forgetting that he'd left the mess in the spare bedroom.'

'Is that possible?'

'He was taking Temazepam for insomnia. Traces were found in his blood the next morning. It's a benzodiazepine, with a possible side effect of anterograde amnesia. Of course it's possible. But the rest is fantasy—there was no Orwell photograph or letter or other manuscript pages in that house. He's either imagined it or made it up to make his story sound more plausible. So you can tell John not to waste his time.'

Brock nodded, but she could see he wasn't done yet.

'Uzma was living with the two Romanians, Elena Vasile and her boyfriend who beat me up, right?' he said. 'Suppose they were part of it. Seems likely they would be, doesn't it? So suppose the plan was for Uzma to put something in Pettigrew's drink—Rohypnol, for example, which is also a benzodiazepine. Something to knock him out, then let the

Romanian bloke into the house with the idea of robbing Pettigrew.'

'There were no traces of a third party in the house, Brock.'

'Still, with the right clothing, gloves and mask, we go onto crime scenes all the time without leaving traces. It could be done.'

'But they didn't rob Pettigrew! The ten thousand in cash he'd withdrawn from the bank to pay for the manuscript was left in the bedroom where we found Uzma. Are you saying Marku Constantin, the Romanian, killed her? Why?'

'Maybe *he's* the Hampstead killer.'

'What?' Kathy stared at him in disbelief.

'Maybe he wanted to frame Pettigrew so you'd stop looking for him. So he killed Uzma and planted Caroline Jarvis's necklace in Pettigrew's house.'

'And the dog hair? How did that come to be on Caroline's body?'

Brock sighed and shook his head. 'Right,' he said wearily. 'I didn't know about that.'

Kathy suddenly felt very sorry for him. Her closest friend, the mentor who had shaped her own career and helped her through its crises, was obviously now going through a major crisis of his own, of withdrawal from his old life.

'No,' he said finally. 'You're absolutely right, Kathy. It doesn't make sense.'

There was a buzz from the intercom. Kathy went over and saw Suzanne's face on the screen. 'Hello, Kathy.' The metallic voice sounded tentative. 'Is it all right for me to come up now?'

'Yes, I've cleaned up most of the blood. Twelfth floor.'

She opened the door, waited in the lobby for the lift to arrive.

Suzanne stepped out and said, 'Oh dear, is he in big trouble?'

Kathy said, 'I think we'd better open that bottle he brought.'

~

By the time they'd finished it and Brock had reluctantly elaborated on his attempt to be a private eye, they decided to go down to the pub on the waterfront nearby for lunch. They found a quiet corner, snug and warm, and they relaxed, talking about other things—Suzanne's business, her grand-children, plans for Christmas.

'Nothing much.' Kathy shrugged. 'I used to try to get to Sheffield to see my aunt and uncle up there. Remember them? But they both died early this year. It was their unex-pected legacy that made it possible for me to buy my new flat.'

Suzanne said, 'Well, if you're not doing anything special, come down and have Christmas dinner with us.'

'Yes!' Brock cried. 'Brilliant idea. Why not?'

Kathy looked at them and smiled, realising how much she'd missed them both, but Brock especially—the way they could read each other's thoughts without a word spoken. 'Actually, that would be really nice.'

'Good,' Suzanne said, like a diplomat pleased at having negotiated a tricky peace treaty. 'You know there's the spare room, Kathy. Stay as long as you can manage.'

And then, turning to Brock, Suzanne said, 'And no more working for Maggie Ferguson, right?'

Though he gave a rueful nod, Kathy recognised a certain nuance in his look. 'But?' she prompted.

He began to raise his eyebrows in feigned innocence, then smiled, realising he'd been caught out. 'It's just something that's been nagging at me, something that Tariq Jamali said to me: "I used to tell her: *Uzma, Uzma, London is not the promised land!*"'

Kathy nodded. 'Exactly. That's probably where she got the idea from. You've got to remember how desperate she was. All her hopes dashed and no one to turn to—her husband, her family back in Pakistan. She was living with people who were probably trying to force her into prostitution. *The Promised Land* was her dream of a way out.' Then Kathy reached across and took his hand. 'Forget it, Brock. It's my problem now.'

II

Christmas came and went, a great success. The weather stayed unseasonably mild—according to the weather reports, Kent was warmer than Athens—and Kathy stayed five nights. They ate and drank too much and went out for country walks, watching gulls flashing white against the dark clouds of passing showers above the ruins of Battle Abbey. The atmosphere in the house was warm and companionable, the Christmas spirit contagious, spoiled only by Suzanne's grandson Stewart's air of moody teenage truculence. At one point this had flared into a rage when Brock had scolded him for not helping his grandmother with chores and refusing to take part in the family activities. Stewart turned on him and told him he didn't belong there and had no right to criticise him, then stormed away and locked himself in his room for the rest of the day. Kathy remembered an incident from years before, when the two grandchildren, recently abandoned by their mother and with no one but Suzanne to depend on, had felt threatened by her friendship with Brock. She wondered if that insecurity still bothered Stewart, although Miranda now seemed untroubled by it. Apart from that, Kathy went home feeling refreshed and happy to have re-established contact with the people who had been such a large part of her life.

This positive mood didn't last long when she got back to work. People were clustered around a computer screen, reading the online edition of one of the tabloids. As she approached she caught sight of the headline, SUICIDE JUDGE COVER-UP. Alfarsi saw her and said, 'Justice Walcott, remember him? Seems he was a raving nonce.'

Kathy said, 'Oh yes? Who says?'

'They've got hold of an internal police report. Apparently the computer found in his hotel room was full of kiddie porn. They're saying we hushed it up.'

When she was alone at her desk, Kathy rang West End Central and asked for DI O'Hare.

'He's gone,' the desk sergeant said.

'Gone?'

'Retired.'

'When?'

'December twentieth. He had a hell of a leaving party.'

'Was this sudden?'

'No, no. He's been waiting for the day as long as I've known him. Forty years exactly since he signed on.'

'Do you have a contact number for him?'

'No. Made a point of it. He didn't want to know. He's on a ship somewhere in the Atlantic, on his way to family in New Zealand, I understand, via Miami, Rio and who knows where. Can anyone else help you?'

'No, thanks.' She rang off, wondering; she'd spoken to him just four days before his retirement and he hadn't mentioned leaving. No reason why he should, she told herself, but still.

The call she was dreading came in towards midday, a message left on her phone by Selwyn Jarvis in a low, urgent tone, demanding a meeting. She called him back later in the afternoon, and he insisted on seeing her that evening at his club in Mayfair.

~

The Harris Club occupied a small but well-proportioned Victorian palazzo, and had no identifying sign at the entrance; Kathy had to check the number to be sure she'd got the right place. Inside she found Jarvis buried in a deep leather armchair in a room bulging with dark oak features.

'So they let women in here, do they?' she asked him.

'Oh yes, but they're not so sure about lawyers. Too many of us have been joining and there are rumblings that our numbers should be restricted. What'll you have to drink?' He waved to a steward.

'Look, thanks for coming,' he went on. 'I didn't want to talk on the phone, and I don't want to embarrass you in any way, but you are the senior investigating officer for my wife's murder, and I felt I had to speak to you. You've read today's reports about Roger Walcott?'

'Yes.'

'It seems plain to me now that this is a campaign, a conspiracy. Roger heard a number of paedophile trials and always came down hard on those found guilty. So did I. Now we are being punished. Someone is taking their revenge and attempting to undermine our verdicts.'

Kathy frowned. 'You think this has a bearing on Caroline's murder?'

'I'm sure of it. It's too much of a coincidence. What do you really know about the suspect, this Pettigrew character? Could he be a paedophile? Part of a ring?'

'There's been absolutely no indication of that.'

'Then perhaps he's a victim too, like Roger and me.'

Jarvis was leaning forward across the arm of his chair as if he might reach out and grab her, his eyes staring, willing her to believe. But it made little sense to Kathy; if Walcott was framed and murdered shouldn't Jarvis himself have been the victim rather than his wife? And how did Andrea Giannopoulos fit in? Trying to keep the doubt out of her voice she said, 'I could check his past associations, friends . . .'

'Yes! It's there, Kathy, something. And if not him, then the answer lies in one of the paedophile cases that Roger or I heard.'

~

Brock's New Year's resolution was to make more of an effort to sort out his papers and books at Warren Lane, to act ruthlessly to unclutter his life. After procrastinating for a few days, he pulled himself together and caught the 8.07 am up to town.

When he reached his front door, fumbling with his keys, he felt a cold drip run down the back of his neck. He looked up and saw that a section of the roof gutter was broken. In another place grass was growing out of the gutter. He groaned, trying to remember how long it was since he'd had anyone up there to check the roof. And now that he really looked, he saw how shabby the external paintwork was too. All the same, he loved the house, the oriel window jutting out over the lane like an elevated sentry box, the rumble of electric trains from the cutting on the other side of the lane. It had once been a shoe-maker's workshop with house above, and he was convinced that the smell of leather still seeped from its bricks and timber.

He stepped inside. The house felt cold, neglected. He sniffed for any hint of damp and thought he detected some-thing else, neither damp nor leather. As he picked up his mail and climbed the stairs he tried to work out what it was. A bit like peppermint. He switched on the central heating to try to dispel the chill, brewed a mug of coffee and sat at the kitchen table to open his mail. Then the phone rang.

'Hello?'

'Mr Brock?'

A female voice, foreign, and he was about to hang up when it added, 'I am Elena Vasile.'

'Are you indeed?' He felt an itch of excitement. He was still in the game.

'Yes. I would like to apologise for my friend. I hope you are not badly hurt.'

'I'll survive.'

'He wanted to protect me, after Uzma disappeared. I have seen her picture in the newspaper. Poor Uzma.'

'Yes, poor Uzma.'

'I have something of hers that you might be interested in, a document.'

'What kind of document?'

'Many pages, in a folder. Uzma said she brought it to England when she came from Pakistan. It is called *The Promised Land.*'

'I see.'

'I think you would be interested in it, yes?'

'I might be. If I could believe that you really had it.'

'You have seen the first page, I think?'

'Yes.'

'Then I will send you the second page. Wait . . .'

Brock waited, and after a moment his phone pinged and a document appeared. He scrolled through it:

This visionary's name was Ulisses Topaz, a big soldierly man of indeterminate age and powerful personality, who walked unaccompanied into Halliday's camp one afternoon. He accepted Halliday's hospitality and spent the evening talking about his adventurous life. He was of mixed Portuguese and native ancestry, his family being members of the Topass people of Batavia and Timor, and he had served as a sepoy in the Portuguese garrison of Goa, and later with distinction in the administration of the Portuguese State of India, and then in the service of several Indian princely states. From these experiences he determined to found a community based upon those principles of justice which he had identified as essential for the fulfilment of human society. For some years he wandered through South-East Asia searching for a suitable location for his experiment, until at last he came upon the remote village of Toruama on the Burmese–Chinese border.

Toruama was in a piteous state when he came upon it, the people racked by poverty, malnutrition and disease, and terrorised by a brutal overlord. However it was ideally located on an island, secure in the middle of a great lake, on which he believed that the inhabitants might build floating islands on reed mats to cultivate plentiful crops. Accordingly he led the people in a revolt against the overlord, and established his own ideal republic, A Terra Prometida, The Promised Land.

Brock spoke to Elena again. 'Yes, I've read it.'

'And now you believe me, yes?'

'Maybe.'

'Uzma told me it is precious, very valuable.'

'Where did she get it from?'

'It's a complicated story. It will take time to explain it. We should meet to talk.'

'I don't deal in books, Elena.'

'Uzma told me that many people would be interested in owning this document, but look what happened to her. I need a partner, someone I can trust, who will protect me. Will you be my partner, Mr Brock?'

'I would have to see the rest of it.'

'Of course. I can meet you tomorrow morning.'

'All right. Where?'

'On Hampstead Heath, the bridge on Viaduct Pond, at ten o'clock.'

'Very well. How did you get this numb—?' But she had hung up. He assumed her friend had traced it from the details on his driver's licence.

He took a note of the number from which she'd called him, then phoned Kathy. It went to messages and he asked her to ring him.

He was wading through documents from a box file labelled *Cases Jan–Jun 1984* when she rang back.

'Sorry, meeting.' She sounded rushed.

'Kathy, I've just had a phone call from Elena Vasile.'

'Elena? The Romanian girl?'

'Yes.' He described their conversation.

Silence, then Kathy said slowly, 'Sounds like what Uzma tried on Pettigrew.'

'It does, doesn't it? I assume you'd like to talk to her?'

'Yes, I would.'

'So you want me to go ahead?'

She hesitated, then said, 'If you're up to it.'

'Oh yes, very much so,' Brock growled. 'I've got a bone to pick with Elena Vasile and her friend.'

They made arrangements and then Brock tried to get back to his documents, but couldn't concentrate on them. He printed a copy of Elena's page, read it again, then emailed a copy to his son John in Montreal. The reply came back almost immediately.

That's great, Brock. The more pages the better. Without doing a lot more reading I didn't feel confident about identifying features of Orwell's writing style, so I've made contact with a colleague in the English department here who's an Orwell specialist. She was <u>very</u> interested in that first page, got quite excited in fact. Wants to know more of the context of course, but I had to tell her that was confidential at this stage. I'll show her this page and get back to you.

Love to Suzanne and Kathy,

John

Brock returned to culling his old files for another couple of hours before breaking for lunch, a pie and a pint at the nearby Bishop's Mitre. After lunch, more files until his eyes glazed over. He collected a few books to read and then, as he was about to leave, thought for a moment and went to a drawer of oddments in the spare room. From the back he drew out a brass knuckleduster. He smiled, tried it on for size, then slipped it into his pocket.

~

Kathy didn't have time to dwell on Brock's call because a new revelation in the Walcott case had just appeared on her screen. The newspaper reported that a key piece of incriminating evidence from the police investigation had come into their hands. This was an extract from the forensic analysis of Walcott's computer, which implicated another judge, as yet unnamed, as having been involved in a paedophile ring with Walcott.

Kathy phoned the office of her boss, Commander Torrens, requesting an urgent appointment. It was late afternoon when she got to see him. He seemed distracted, his mind elsewhere as he asked what she wanted to see him about.

'It's about Judge Jarvis, sir,' Kathy said, and watched his head snap up, attention focused.

'What about him?'

She explained about his preoccupation with Sir Roger Walcott's death, his suspicion of a conspiracy targeting judges.

Torrens groaned. 'You've read the newspaper reports about Walcott, I take it?'

'Yes.'

'And the latest report about another judge?'

Kathy nodded.

Torrens leaned forward, lowering his voice. 'What I'm about to say doesn't leave this room, Kathy.'

'Yes, sir.'

'We understand this second man is Jarvis.'

Kathy was startled. 'Really?'

'Yes. And between them, Walcott and Jarvis heard over a dozen paedophile cases. This is going to be ugly. You'd better set down everything Jarvis said to you about Walcott in a report for my eyes only.'

'Sir.'

Kathy left, thinking about Selwyn Jarvis. Could this possibly be right? He'd just lost his wife in the most shocking of circumstances, and here was this new disaster about to strike him. And she thought about the implications closer to home. Homicide had been involved with both men. Would the Command be implicated in accusations of a cover-up? Would she be dragged into it? She went over in her head the information she'd shared with him, the places they'd been seen together—his home, his club. She got to work on her report for Torrens.

12

Brock was giving a lecture to a class of young detectives at the Crime Academy. At some point both he and his audience realised that his material was completely out of date and irrelevant, and people began to murmur. He tried to improvise to hold their attention, but that only seemed to make things worse and they started to get up and leave. He began to sweat, fumbling for words. Eventually only one man was left, someone he knew but couldn't quite place. The man was staring at him with a look of utter contempt. Brock gulped for air and woke.

He turned to check that Suzanne was still there. Her dark hair, recently trimmed in a shorter style, spilled across the pillow, and he was filled with a sense of relief and gratitude. How could he have managed without her? He eased himself quietly out of bed and padded through to the kitchen to make tea, carrying the mugs back to the bedroom, watching her come awake.

'Morning,' she mumbled. 'What's the weather like?'

He went to the window and pulled aside the curtain. It was a sharp cold morning, frost riming the grass with white, and he wished he'd never agreed to this meeting. Enough was enough. He took his tea through to the bathroom and showered and shaved. His face was looking almost normal again.

After breakfast, when he'd procrastinated as long as he could, he kissed Suzanne goodbye and went out to his car. It refused to start. He swore to himself and stomped back to the house. He'd never make it by train and told Suzanne he'd have to cancel.

'Take Heidi,' she said.

He hesitated. Heidi was Suzanne's dearest possession, a brilliant red 1978 Mercedes-Benz 280SL two-door roadster. He'd only driven it a couple of times. 'Oh, I couldn't.'

''Course you can.' She handed him the keys. 'She could do with a long run.'

Despite the cold gloom of the day he drove with the top down, wearing a thick coat, a cap and a scarf wound around his neck, and began to feel more positive about the trip. He pulled over at one point to answer his phone, a call from Kathy to say that she was having to attend a crisis meeting at headquarters but DS Alfarsi would be at Hampstead Heath with other officers as arranged, to intercept and arrest Elena Vasile.

'Don't worry, Kathy,' Brock said, thinking how good it was to be no longer called to crisis meetings at headquarters. 'Everything will go smoothly.'

Parking around the Heath was always difficult, spaces in the narrow lanes and perimeter residential streets hard to find, but the dull weather seemed to have deterred visitors, and he found a spot in a small car park on the edge of the woods close to the path to Viaduct Pond. He was twenty minutes early and called Alfarsi to let him know he'd arrived. The detective replied that his team was in position, two officers in the woods on the west side of the pond and himself and another among the trees to the east. Brock was warm now and took off his heavy coat and put it in the boot, transferring the knuckleduster to his trouser pocket. He slammed the lid shut and set off down an avenue of skeletal sycamores and made his way to the meeting place without catching sight of anyone except a solitary elderly dog-walker.

He stopped at the centre of the viaduct and looked down at the turbid waters of the pond, then took out a guide to the Heath that he'd brought with him and leaned on the iron parapet, turning to the section on the viaduct. It was all that remained of a failed project in 1844 by a local landowner, Sir Thomas Wilson, to subdivide this southern area of the Heath as a residential park. The viaduct was to carry the access road across the boggy valley below, but proved so difficult to build that the scheme was abandoned and the viaduct came to be known as Wilson's Folly. While excavating the swamp to create the ornamental pond, some strange artefacts had been found, including deer antlers, bronze and stone axes, and a human skull with two holes in it. Brock hoped this wasn't an omen. He checked his watch—five to ten.

After fifteen more minutes he decided to call Elena, but as he took out his phone it buzzed and her number came up.

'Hello, Elena?'

'You are at the viaduct?'

'Yes. Where are you?'

'I cannot come. I am sorry. I will contact you again to make another arrangement.'

She sounded tense, panicky. He said, 'What's happened?' But the line went dead. He frowned with irritation and called Alfarsi, who seemed unfazed.

'Not to worry, boss. Next time, eh?'

Brock made his way back to his car, not as annoyed as he felt he had a right to be. The sun had broken out through the clouds and the air was fresh. He thought of delaying his return, exploring Hampstead and perhaps getting an early lunch at the Spaniards Inn.

At one point he became lost among the meandering paths and thick woodland, passing joggers and walkers with an endless variety of dogs. Finally he emerged onto the entry path he remembered and came to the car park, deserted. He went over to the Merc, unlocked the door and got in. As he swung the door closed he felt something sticky on his fingers. He looked at them and saw them covered with a red stain. His first thought was that somehow the paint on the car was coming off. He looked down and saw red on the cream-coloured driver's seat too. *What the hell?* He looked up, wondering if it could be something dripping from the trees overhead. Somewhere nearby he heard the urgent wail of a siren.

He got out of the car again and took out his handkerchief, wiping his hand, looking around. He could see dark stains on the sandy gravel beside the boot. Looking at his handkerchief he couldn't help thinking that the stains looked like blood.

Afterwards he wondered why it took him so long to work that out.

The siren abruptly cut out, and as he stood watching, a police car swung fast into the car park in a spray of gravel. Two uniforms jumped out and ran towards him, then came to a stop, their eyes fixed on the red-stained handkerchief in his hand. One of them stayed motionless in front of him while the other circled around to his left. The motionless one said, 'What's with the blood, sir?'

'Blood?' Brock looked down at his hands. 'Yes, it does look like that, doesn't it? But it can't be.'

The man on his left had moved in close, and Brock turned to him, recognising the look in his eyes. 'Hey, relax,' Brock said with a smile. 'I'm a DCI with Homicide, just retired.'

'Do you have ID, sir? I'll take that.' The copper reached forward with a gloved hand and took the handkerchief. The other man was talking into his radio in a low mumble that Brock couldn't make out. He reached into his pocket for his wallet and handed over his card.

'Driver's licence?'

'Oh ... I was robbed recently. They took my licence. I haven't got a replacement yet.'

'Can I have the car keys, please?'

Brock handed them over. As he did so he noticed movement along the path leading from the Heath and saw several men running fast towards them. The first to reach them panted, 'DS Alfarsi ...' and showed his ID to the uniforms. He turned to Brock. 'What happened, sir?'

'Ah, Alfarsi, I'm glad to see you. It's nothing. I came back to my car, and when I got in I noticed my hand had picked up some sort of pink stuff from the door. I don't know what it is.'

Alfarsi gave him an odd look, then drew out plastic gloves from his pocket, asked the uniform for the keys and walked around to the back of the car. Brock remembered putting his coat in there and called to him, 'I believe I left it unlocked.'

Alfarsi pressed the button and the boot sprang open. He stared at what was inside.

'What is it?' Brock said, and felt a hand grip his arm as he tried to step forward. Inside the dark hollow of the boot he caught a glimpse of a woman's body, curled up, her clothes and bare leg covered in wet blood. Alfarsi was leaning in, checking for signs of life. He turned to the others, face expressionless, and shook his head.

He looked at Brock. 'Can you identify this woman?'

They allowed him to move closer and he saw black hair, white skin, purple lipstick. 'It looks like Elena—Elena Vasile. The woman I was supposed to meet.'

'Did you have an argument?'

'No, no, we didn't make contact. I had no idea she was in there.'

Alfarsi hesitated a moment, then said, 'Mr Brock, I'd like you to accompany us to a police station to make a formal statement.'

'No, that isn't necessary and it's wasting time. Come on, man, whoever did this must still be nearby.'

Alfarsi stared at Brock, at the blood on his hands. 'Sir, I must insist that you accompany us. I am arresting you for the murder of Elena Vasile.'

Looking around at the scene, Brock barely listened while Alfarsi recited the familiar words of the caution and they bagged and cuffed his hands.

'Mr Brock? Can you hear me? I asked if you had anything to say.'

'Alfarsi, listen to me, you're making a mistake. You need to put a cordon around this area. Can you see a weapon?'

Alfarsi ignored him and gave instructions to the others to secure the scene, then led Brock to the patrol car.

They took him to Holmes Road, appropriately enough, in Kentish Town. It was the same police station they'd taken Pettigrew, housed in a yellow-brick building that reminded Brock of a Victorian workhouse. Inside he observed with detachment himself being processed. The only thing to disturb the calm routine was the knuckleduster they found in his pocket, which caused a few stares.

Stripped of his clothes, swabbed and fingerprinted, he was allowed a phone call. He rang Suzanne.

'You've been arrested for *what*?'

'I'm sorry,' he said. 'They've got everything mixed up. I'm sure they'll sort it out soon enough. I'm afraid you may have to do without Heidi for a while.'

'Never mind that. Are you hurt again?'

'No, no. I'm fine.'

'What can I do?'

'Ring Maggie Ferguson. Tell her I may need her help smartish. I'm at Kentish Town police station.'

'Right, yes, she got you into this mess. I'll never forgive her. What about Kathy, does she know?'

'I imagine they'll tell her, but I doubt if she'll be allowed to get involved. If I'm not free by this evening you could give her a ring when she's off-duty.'

'All right. You sound very calm, love.'

'Yes, it's all a stupid mistake, but it's interesting seeing it from the other side. I'd better go—they're threatening me with a cup of tea.'

'I'm coming up to see you.'

'I'm sure there's no need. See what Maggie says. And take extra care, you hear me? Keep the house locked, don't go out on your own.'

~

Kathy had heard. She was sitting in an anteroom outside one of the large conference rooms at headquarters, inside which a cluster of worried senior officers and lawyers were discussing the Walcott/Jarvis problem, when the call from Alfarsi came through. She listened in disbelief, getting him to go through it all again. Finally, when she was satisfied that he'd done everything by the book, she told him to stay at Kentish Town and await instructions. Then she sent a text to her boss inside the meeting room.

Sir, I've just been notified that ex DCI David Brock has been arrested at Hampstead Heath and charged with murder.

She counted sixteen seconds before Commander Torrens burst out of the room.

'Who the fuck did he murder, for God's sake?'

'The body of a woman was found in the boot of his parked car. It seems to be Elena Vasile, the Romanian woman who was involved in the Pettigrew case. She'd been stabbed.'

He listened, incredulous, as she gave him the background.

Finally he said, 'All right, but your team can't investigate this. You're all witnesses, too involved—you especially, Kathy. You've been close to Brock for years, right? I'll put Alun

Hughes's team onto it. You'll need to brief them and then keep clear.' He saw the frown on her face and added, 'I mean it, Kathy. Walk away, for your own sake.'

~

Alun Hughes, a Cardiff boy, had a strong Welsh accent undiminished by thirty years working in London. At times of great stress it became almost unintelligible. He was stressed now.

'Two honour killings one murder/suicide mysterious deaths in an old folks' home a gang of thrill-killers on the loose and half my team down with flu and I'm expected to clear up your mess, Kathy! What's going on in your neck of the woods? Is it contagious?'

When he'd got that off his chest, he calmed down a little. 'I've always admired Brock, a bloody good detective, one of the best. What the hell's become of him, Kathy? No, don't tell me. I'll have to work that out for myself. Just fill me in on what's happened.'

So she did, the whole story—Pettigrew, Maggie Ferguson, Uzma Jamali, Elena Vasile and her friends.

When she'd finished, Hughes looked up from his notes. He gave a grim little chuckle. 'That cunning old bugger. He sniffed out the cleaning girl, trailed Vasile halfway across London, got himself mugged and identified your murder victim when none of you could do it.'

'Yes, well . . .'

'So did he murder Vasile, Kathy? Your honest opinion.'

'No, of course not. Not in a million years.' She smothered the unwanted thought that came into her head: *He's been framed, just like Pettigrew.*

'Hmm. Well, maybe this will be more interesting than the other rubbish piling up on my desk. Interesting but unrewarding. No one is going to thank the senior investigating officer on this one, Kathy, regardless of the outcome.'

~

Brock, dressed in a baggy tracksuit and slippers, shuffled into the interview room and took a seat at the table. After ten minutes a constable showed Maggie Ferguson in. She stared at him in horror. 'Brock! . . . I'm speechless.'

'That's not like you, Maggie. Come and sit down.'

She pulled out a chair, thumped her heavy document bag onto the table and extracted a recorder and notebook. 'Better tell me all about it.'

So he did.

She stared at her notes with a sigh. 'I can't get you out tonight. Tomorrow I'll apply for bail, but . . . a murder charge, you know. And the knuckleduster doesn't help.'

'I know. I just can't work out why they haven't realised their mistake by now.'

'Suzanne is outside. They'll let you have five minutes together, but an officer will have to be present.'

He nodded.

Maggie went on, 'I tried to talk to Kathy Kolla, but she's been forbidden from involvement in the case. Another team is taking over. I don't know who.'

'But is Kathy still running the Pettigrew case?'

'As far as I know. I made the point to her that there's an overlap.'

'More than that, Maggie. They are one and the same case.'

'Hmm. I'm not so sure about that. They certainly don't seem to see it that way.' She frowned at him. 'You're taking this remarkably calmly, Brock.'

'Truth will finally and powerfully prevail, Maggie.'

'What idiot said that?'

'Thomas Paine.'

'And what happened to him?'

Brock smiled grimly. 'He was ostracised in the end, because nobody wanted to hear the truth.'

After Maggie left, Suzanne was shown in. They talked about banal, practical things, but as their time came to an end Suzanne took hold of his hands and held them in a fierce grip, and the constable had to tell her firmly to leave.

After a while they brought him his supper, a carton of pie and chips from the high street and a plastic mug of tea. Afterwards he lay on the bunk and thought it all through again. And when the lights were turned out, and the sounds of the station faded away, and still no one had come to apologise and set him free, he seriously began to wonder if he was losing it. First getting beaten up, now this. It was absurd, impossible. It would never have happened to him when he'd been in the force, in the thick of it. Perhaps he'd gone soft, lost his touch, his wits.

13

They interviewed him at eleven the next morning. Alun Hughes bustled in with a young female officer in tow, establishing himself laboriously, dumping his bag, methodically setting out a fat file, a notebook and four coloured pens, a tube of Polo mints and a plastic cup of black coffee on his side of the table. On the opposite side Brock sat with the solicitor that Maggie had insisted be present, a young woman who had just arrived and was immersed in her notes.

'Brock,' Hughes said, 'David,' and reached across the table to shake Brock's hand. 'My God, I never thought I'd find myself in this situation. This here is Detective Sergeant Mercy Bulimore, but don't expect any mercy from her— she's a holy terror. Whereas I, I've always been such a great admirer of yours, almost a disciple you might say. And here I am, ordered to question you like a common criminal.'

Brock nodded, scratched at his white beard. 'These things happen, Alun.'

'Ach . . .' Hughes shook his head. 'Well, I'd better do my job, I suppose. So, a factual matter—have you ever seen this before?' And he reached into his bag and heaved out a transparent plastic pouch containing a large, horn-handled knife.

Brock carefully examined the knife, the blade, the grip, then slowly nodded. 'Yes, this is mine.'

'Uh-huh. Go on.'

Brock's solicitor interrupted. 'No, my client wishes to withdraw his remark. He can't possibly be sure.'

'It belonged to my father,' Brock said. 'See, there are his initials engraved on the blade—MB. In his youth, he was a keen boy scout. When I turned eleven, I joined the local troop and he gave it to me. In those days, scouts openly wore sheath knives as part of their uniform. I don't suppose they're allowed to do that now.'

The solicitor tried to intervene again, but Hughes chuckled. 'Ah, those were the days. And where did you keep this special knife?'

'In a drawer for odds and ends in the spare bedroom at my home in Warren Lane. You've been there?'

Hughes nodded apologetically.

Brock said, 'And you found the knife in that drawer?'

'No, no. We found it in the boot of the red Mercedes roadster—a lovely car, may I say—along with the body of Elena Vasile, covered in her blood and bearing traces of your DNA—the knife, that is.'

A pause, while Hughes took a sip of coffee and gazed glumly at his notebook. 'You see my difficulty, Brock?'

'Yes, Alun, I do see.'

Brock's solicitor cut in again. 'I need to suspend this interview to talk to my client.'

'It's all right, Amanda,' Brock said. 'I'd like to know what Alun's thinking.'

'Edmanda,' she corrected him. 'And if we could just have a few words in private . . .'

'Let's hear a bit more,' Brock said firmly, and nodded at Hughes. 'Have you any other difficulties, Alun?'

'Oh yes.' He reached into his bag for another pouch, containing the knuckleduster. 'This was in your pocket when you were arrested, right?'

'True enough.'

'Why?'

'A precaution. The last time I met Elena Vasile one of her friends turned up and gave me a beating. So I was cautious about meeting her again.' Brock nodded at the brass knuckles. 'That's an historic artefact, Alun; once belonged to Ronnie Kray.'

'*The* Ronnie Kray, of the Kray twins? You're joking!'

'It's true. It was souvenired by one of Nipper Read's team that arrested them, and when he died he left it to me as a thank you for something I'd done for him. So look after it.'

'Well, well.' Hughes picked the pouch up reverently and put it back in his bag. 'So where did you keep this historic artefact, Brock? I don't remember seeing a glass case of memorabilia.'

'No, no, just in the same drawer of oddments.'

'And when you wanted to take precautions for this meeting on the Heath, you went to the drawer and took out the brass knuckles and the knife ...'

'No, not the knife.'

'But you would have seen it in there?'

Brock frowned, trying to picture it. 'No, I don't remember seeing the knife, now you mention it. There's a lot of junk in that drawer. Someone must have taken it.'

'But you groped around in the junk and found the knuckles, but didn't notice that the much larger knife was missing?'

'I suppose so.'

Edmanda drew an audible breath and shook her head. 'Please ...'

'Let's cut to the chase,' Hughes said briskly. 'Why don't you just tell me exactly your version of events yesterday morning, Brock, from go to whoa.'

When Brock finished, there was a long moment of silence. Hughes hung his head as if at a loss where to begin, DS Bulimore had an odd expression like a barely suppressed wolfish grin, and Edmanda looked despairing.

Hughes took him through it again, step by step, getting him to elaborate on certain points. The usual thing, Brock thought, probing for contradictions, but Hughes's heart didn't seem to be in it, when faced by so many improbabilities.

Finally, Brock said, 'Tell me, Alun, how did the patrol car arrive so promptly?'

'You were seen, Brock, in the car park after you returned from the viaduct. A witness called 999 to report seeing a man matching your description trying to bundle a woman's body into the boot of a red sports car.'

'No, that's not possible. I only arrived in the car park a few seconds before I heard the siren. I got lost on the way back from the Viaduct Pond. There was no one in the car park. Have you interviewed the witness?'

'We will.'

'Male or female?'

'A woman.'

'And you have her name, her phone number?'

'Don't you worry about that.'

'Hmm.' Brock rubbed his hand over his chin. 'They'd have to do that of course, so that you could catch me red-handed. Literally. They almost got it wrong—if I'd been delayed a bit longer the patrol car would have got there before I did.'

'You're suggesting you've been set up?'

'Of course I was, Alun.'

Hughes shook his head. 'I'd have a few difficulties with that idea. You changed your car at the last minute. How would they know what car you were driving? How would they know, out of all the possible places around Hampstead Heath, that you'd park where you did? Of course, we can check whether someone tailed you all the way up to Hampstead from Battle. We can look at cameras along your route. But wouldn't you have noticed a tail?'

'Maybe they bugged both cars.'

'No, they didn't. We checked. And then there's the question of motive. Who would go to such lengths to frame you, Brock?'

Brock sensed the unspoken words: *a harmless, spent old man like you.*

'I don't know. So what do you think happened, Alun?'

Hughes eased back in his chair, folded his arms, sighed and considered Brock gravely. 'One theory is that you had a brain snap. You'd hyped yourself up for this meeting, traumatised by the terrible beating you got from Elena's friend, arming yourself with knuckleduster and knife. And when she started taunting you, pushing you around, you lost it. Understand-able, really.'

Brock began to object, but Hughes went on, 'And maybe he was there too, her bully boy? Is that what spooked you, made you lash out? Hell, you were acting in self-defence, right? Did she get in the way and take the blow you'd aimed at her boyfriend?'

'No.'

'No. Frankly I don't buy it either. She was stabbed three times, in the back. And you wouldn't have put her into your boot and made off without telling anyone.'

'But, using your own argument, how did Elena find my car?'

'Exactly! How did she do that? Well, the obvious way of, course. You told her where it was! When you were on the viaduct and she phoned you to say she was running late. We've tracked the phone call to the south side of the Heath, not far from the car park. You told her to meet you by the red sports car instead of at the viaduct because you didn't want your meeting to be observed by the waiting cops. And that puts a darker complexion on things, doesn't it? It smacks of devious intent. You wanted to get her alone to force the truth out of her, about this mystery manuscript and Uzma Jamali's game. And things got out of hand, she fought back, and something tragic happened, a momentary overreaction, the heat of the moment ...'

Silence. Brock was aware of three pairs of eyes on him. He'd underestimated Alun Hughes, he realised. In fact, he'd underestimated the whole situation.

Hughes leaned forward across the table, spoke softly. 'Think about it, Brock. It isn't just my fancy. The forensics all support it. Maggie Ferguson will make the best of it for you—your head injuries, your genuine perception of a threat. Talk it over with her. Let her do her job.'

The same as she's done for Charles Pettigrew, Brock thought. Exactly the same.

After the police left the room, the solicitor said quietly, 'I'm not optimistic about bail, Mr Brock. I'm sorry. I have the feeling that the police are bending over backwards to avoid any impression that they're going soft on one of their own.'

'Yes, I imagine they are. Don't worry, Edmanda, I'll cope.'

She fiddled with her pen, reluctant to go on. He waited and finally she said, 'I think Maggie will want you to see a psychiatrist to assess your mental condition as soon after the event as possible.'

'I see. Yes.'

'Good.' She seemed relieved. 'Is there anything I can do for you?'

'Just find out as much as you can about the facts of the case. This mystery witness, for example, who called 999.'

'Yes, yes, of course.'

'Edmanda, somebody killed Elena, and it wasn't me. Whatever you and Maggie might privately suspect, I want you to act as if what I'm saying is true. Someone else must have been in that car park and killed Elena immediately before I arrived. The timeframe was very tight. It was probably

Elena's Romanian friend Marku Constantin, who attacked me three weeks ago. Have the police interviewed him? Did he leave any traces? Did anyone—a dog-walker, a bird-spotter, a jogger—catch sight of him?'

Edmanda nodded, trying hard not to look sceptical. 'Right. Got that.'

~

Later that afternoon he was transferred to Highbury Corner Magistrates' Court, another old haunt, for his hearing. On Maggie's instructions, Suzanne had brought him two sets of clothes—his best suit and tie for the court appearance, and a set of casual clothes for later. After what seemed like an interminable wait he was taken up to the courtroom and told to sit down, while around him the court officers got on with their business, conferring in a familiar low murmur. He looked around, remembering previous visits, trying to recall the cases. His eyes turned to the visitors' seats, where Suzanne was sitting in the middle of a row of unhappy women. She gave him a brave encouraging smile, as if she already knew the verdict.

Finally the magistrate raised his head, the lawyers moved back to their places and his case was called. It didn't take long; an outline of the prosecution case, a rebuttal from Maggie, some to and fro, a couple of questions from the magistrate and then the ruling—in consideration of the seriousness of the crime and the weight of evidence, and notwithstanding his previous exemplary record as a police officer, the accused was refused bail. Although it wasn't unexpected, the decision still hit him like a blow. Ahead of him lay long months in prison, waiting while others, free to come and go, would work on bringing him to trial.

Downstairs, in the processing area, he changed into the casual clothes that Suzanne had brought—as a remand prisoner awaiting trial he would be allowed to wear his own clothes in prison. Suzanne had also brought a bag of other things, some of which (pens and pads of paper, books) were allowed, the rest (chocolates, apples, a bottle of Scotch) refused.

'Where am I going?' he asked, and a court officer consulted his clipboard and grunted, 'HMP Belmarsh, mate.'

There were three others in the van, young men, subdued. They all stared out the window at the dark streets, the rhythm of streetlights flashing past, shopfronts, houses, all now given a heightened significance by being out of reach.

Belmarsh, Brock thought. They used to refer to the place laughingly as Hellmarsh. Now the joke wasn't so funny. Less than a month ago he had come here to visit Pettigrew. How relaxed he'd been, how objective and uninvolved, totally unaware that he was beginning a journey that would bring him back here, humiliated, to the prison gates.

The van came to a stop and they stumbled out and were led through to the reception bay for processing. Their possessions were carefully examined, their bodies searched. Brock was allocated a two-man cell in house block four, reserved for vulnerable and remand prisoners, and given a stream of information and instructions, half of which he barely took in.

A prison officer led him through the communal areas, now full of prisoners in association time, some playing cards and table tennis, others watching sport on a big TV screen.

Brock scanned their faces, dreading the thought that he might see someone he had put here. They continued along a corridor to house block four. This was a modern prison, built in the 1970s, and the utilitarian design of the four cruci-form arms, double-storeyed, made Brock think of a grim and Spartan shopping mall with identical blank shopfronts. He was shown to a cell on the upper floor. Inside there was a bed on each side of a narrow central space, a stainless-steel toilet, a window at the far end. The belongings of the other occupant were scattered everywhere—radio, kettle and toaster, clothes, magazines, toiletries—and on a pinboard were photographs, one of a young girl and another of a group of men wearing blue Chelsea scarfs. There was a smell of baked beans, after-shave and male body odour.

Brock dropped his few belongings on the least-occupied bed and was led back down to the communal areas. He had missed the evening meal, and was taken to the dining room for a late sitting. A dozen others were there, huddled over plates of food, eating in silence.

When he'd cleaned his plate, Brock went out to the social area and found a seat on the edge of the TV crowd. They were all male, of course, for this was a men-only prison, and mostly young, but he spotted a few who must have been over fifty, one distinctly elderly, staring expressionless at the big screen. He didn't recognise any of them.

When the clock on the wall showed eight thirty, a bell rang for the end of association time, the TV was switched off and everyone got to their feet and headed for their wings. Brock found his way back to his cell, where a man of about thirty-five was stacking magazines on a shelf.

'Hello,' the man said, turning to Brock. 'Dave, is it?' He gestured at the label on Brock's bag. 'I'm Danny.' He offered his hand, which Brock shook. The hand was soft, plump and pale, like the rest of Danny's anatomy.

'I'm just moving all my stuff over here, Dave, out of your way. Had the place to meself last four days, so I spread out a bit.' He chuckled. 'Fancy a cup of tea?'

This was the preamble to a getting-to-know-you session. They sat on their beds facing each other, sipping their tea, as Danny explained a few useful things about the way things were done.

'Your first time inside, Dave?'

'Yes.'

'Bit of getting used to then. Same for me when I came in, four months ago, but you adjust. We all adjust. You're on remand?'

'Yes.'

'Me too. What they got you for, Dave? Fraud, is it? I'm just guessing. You look the bookish type.'

'Murder,' Brock said.

'Ah! Fancy that. Me too.'

'Really?'

'Yes. Killed my missus. You'll find quite a few of us in here did that. You?'

'No, another woman. At least, that's what they say.'

'Oh yes? What, you're going for manslaughter, like me, are you? Provocation, that's the thing, innit? I fell for a cute little bum and discovered I'd married a big vicious mouth. The bitch gave me a hard time for years. One evening we both had a bit to drink and she started on at me again and I couldn't stand it no more and I whacked her with the ketchup bottle. A bit too hard as it turned out. But it was provocation. Is that how it was for you, Dave?'

'Not exactly, Danny, no. I didn't do it.'

'Oh.' Danny looked disappointed, as if Brock had broken some unspoken rule of etiquette. 'There's no hidden microphones in here, mate,' he said, sounding offended. 'I'm not a bloody nark.'

'I'm sure you're not, Danny, but that's just the way it is. I was in the wrong place at the wrong time.'

From Danny's expression it was clear this wasn't good enough. He said, 'Suit yourself,' and took their mugs to the sink and rinsed them, turning his back on Brock.

14

A cold and blustery Sunday evening, with rain hammering in vicious gusts against the big windows. Kathy turned the heating up a notch and buried herself in a corner of her sofa. Sometimes she missed the stuffy, closeted atmosphere of her old flat, the walls of masonry instead of glass, the creaky old lifts, the muffled sounds of neighbours' music or arguments instead of the utter silence of this building, where most of the apartments were owned by absentee overseas investors.

Somehow, by default it seemed, she had become the senior investigating officer reporting to the ad hoc committee, codenamed the Falstaff Committee, advising the commissioner on the Walcott case. It was her task to review the investigation into Walcott's death as a matter of urgency, though not quite as much urgency, she sensed, as another team from the

Directorate of Professional Standards investigating how the hell the story had leaked to the papers. She had her own theory about that, centring on the recently retired DI O'Hare, now apparently impossible to locate. Kathy's team was busy reinterviewing everyone else involved in the original investigation and re-examining every scrap of evidence, but it was becoming clear that the hard nub of truth lay inside the judge's computers—the laptop found in the hotel room and the desktop unit in his home—in which all the incriminating links to paedophile rings and to Selwyn Jarvis were contained. For that sort of truth, she could only sit and wait for the experts to pronounce. While waiting, she'd got a team searching for every instance they could find of connections between the two judges. It was already an impressive list, from the Lord Mayor of London's annual banquet to a shared yachting holiday in the Caribbean, apart from hundreds of more mundane professional and social contacts. It didn't help that, among her team's paperwork spread out on the sofa and floor and coffee table around her, was Saturday's newspaper, naming Jarvis as the second paedophile judge.

The phone rang. Suzanne's voice, sounding breathless. 'Kathy, hello! Am I disturbing you?'

'Not at all, Suzanne. Where are you?'

'On my way to London Bridge to catch the train home.'

'You've been to see Brock?'

'Yes, it was such a crowd, the prison visitors. I was wondering . . .'

'Have you got time to call in?'

'That would be wonderful.' Kathy heard the relief in her voice.

She arrived half an hour later, wet and exhausted, and sank into a chair with relief.

'Kick your shoes off,' Kathy said. 'Tea, or something stronger?'

'Oh yes, please. Mother's ruin, if you've got it.'

Kathy poured a couple of stiff gin and tonics and Suzanne began to relax. 'You just get used to it, I suppose, the whole paraphernalia. I got into trouble because I had a five-pound note in my pocket and you're only allowed to take in coins. And then when I came out I couldn't find my locker key. I'll know better next time. But, Kathy, to think people are doing this for years and years. Some of those poor women, dragging their kids along . . .'

'And how was he?'

'Trying to give the impression he was perfectly happy and immensely interested in it all. But I could tell he was embarrassed and ashamed, even though he's done nothing wrong. You do believe that, don't you, Kathy?' And suddenly her eyes were sharp and focused.

'Yes, Suzanne, of course I do. It's all a terrible, absurd mistake.'

'And yet, knowing him, the kind of man he is, his long record of service, they still arrested him and charged him with murder. Can't you make them see sense?'

'I've been told to keep away, because we worked together for so long, but I am able to access information about the case as it develops. The detective they've put in charge is very competent and experienced, and I'm confident he'll get to the truth.'

Actually she wasn't, not after what she'd been reading recently. Alun Hughes's notes on his last interview with Brock and on the forensic reports were not encouraging at all.

'But is that enough, Kathy? Can't we do something? Something to help Maggie Ferguson get him out of there? Although I do wonder about her.'

'How do you mean?'

'Well, she got him into this mess in the first place. Maybe she knows more than she's letting on. Maybe she's covering something up.'

'Oh, I don't think—'

'I just wonder if Brock shouldn't have got a different lawyer to represent him. I mean, why did Maggie approach him in the first place? They weren't particular friends, were they? And he wasn't looking for work. Why pick on him?'

Kathy was about to say something reassuring when it occurred to her that it wasn't a bad question. There were plenty of younger ex-detectives who'd moved into private investigation that Maggie could have thought of more readily.

'Why don't we ask her?' Kathy said, and picked up her phone.

After a moment she heard Maggie's voice. 'Kathy? How are you? Got something for me?'

'I wish I did, Maggie, but you know I can't interfere. I'm sitting here with Suzanne, who's just returned from visiting Brock, and she's very worried about how things are looking.'

'Yes, this is a bad time, but I'm hopeful that we'll see some progress later in the month.'

'That sounds like lawyer-speak for the case is hopeless.'

'Now, now. Put me on to her.'

'Okay, but just one thing—what made you approach Brock in the first place?'

'Over the Pettigrew affair? It was Pettigrew himself. He suggested I get Brock to help—was quite insistent, in fact.

Apparently he'd seen Brock in action in court and was very impressed.'

'Okay, I'll put Suzanne on.'

She handed the phone to Suzanne and half listened as she topped up their drinks.

Later, after Suzanne had caught a cab to London Bridge for her train home to Battle, Kathy got on to the police intranet and checked on her team's recent reports. There were new entries in the list of known connections between Jarvis and Walcott, and one of them caught her eye, a trial at the Old Bailey in Jarvis's prosecutor days, where Walcott had been the presiding judge. Not a paedophile case, thank goodness, but a 1999 murder trial at the Old Bailey that Kathy remembered well, *R v J. Causley and D. Causley*. Jarrod and Dean Causley were brothers, aged sixteen and fourteen, charged with the drowning murder of an eight-year-old girl, Chloe Honnery, after a rapid police investigation.

Kathy sat back, remembering the shock and outrage the murder had stirred up, given the youth of the murderers and the brutal nature of the crime. She hadn't been involved in that one, being on sick leave following her experiences in the Silvermeadow case, and her memories of that period were shaded by her own dark state of mind. But she'd followed the daily reports of the trial, mainly because the senior detective in charge of the case was Brock.

Brock, Walcott and Jarvis, all brought together sixteen years ago for the trial of the Causley boys, just one of those random events that you would expect within the restricted criminal justice community. But still, it seemed an ominous coincidence.

No, she decided, the important thing, the only thing she should be concentrating on, was finding flaws in Alun Hughes's case against Brock.

~

There were no prison visits on Mondays, and Brock sensed a mood of weary resignation among the inmates. He'd only been there a couple of days, but already he was beginning to understand what long-term imprisonment might be like. The first shock of a new and potentially hostile environment, alert to every novelty and nuance, was wearing off as his life narrowed into a range of tedious routines. His relationship with his cellmate had settled into a chilly acceptance, although Danny hadn't abandoned his campaign to get Brock to admit that he really had murdered a woman. Confined together in this small room, Brock felt like someone stuck in a claustrophobic marriage with a partner determined to get him to confess guilt—a partner who spent most of the day on his bed watching TV, who snored and farted in his sleep and who wouldn't keep his stuff to his own side of the room.

On the positive side, he'd struck up the beginnings of a friendship with one of the prison chaplains, who had encouraged him to get involved in practical activities, and he'd enrolled in courses of bricklaying and fitness for over-fifties in the gym, and had volunteered for a job in the library.

He had also made contact with Charles Pettigrew, whose cell was on the lower floor of the same house block four. He had spotted him on Sunday in the visits hall, where he had met Suzanne for one of the three half-hour sessions they would be allowed together each week. Pettigrew was sitting at his table with a grey-haired woman of around sixty, he guessed, who was speaking intently to him. Watching them together, Brock was struck by the contrast between them—she gesturing vigorously as she spoke, while he slumped listlessly over a plastic cup. Brock wondered if that was how Suzanne and he appeared. Later Brock caught up with Pettigrew as he was about to disappear into his cell. He looked at Brock with a wondering frown.

'I heard you were in here, Mr Brock. I thought they were pulling my leg. Murder, they told me. Can that be true?'

'So it seems, Charlie. But I see you've got a girlfriend.'

'Oh, one of my authors, Donna Priest, kind enough to pay me a visit. Probably after material. She writes true crime, you see. I think she wants to make a case study out of me.'

Seeing him close up, Brock was shocked by his pasty complexion and the dead tone of his voice. In less than three months he seemed to have become a broken man. Brock suggested they find a quiet corner and have a chat, but Pettigrew excused himself, saying he was feeling tired and wanted to lie down. Brock was so disturbed by the change in him that he mentioned it to one of the house warders, who shrugged and said Pettigrew had been having regular checks at the medical centre, and that some people just withdrew like that. 'Get him down to the gym,' he urged Brock. 'Get him to go outside, get a bit of fresh air.'

That night, lying sleepless in the narrow bed, Brock was filled with an overwhelming sense of dread, of fear of gradually losing touch with Suzanne and the outside world, and of dying here alone.

15

'You seem to have a rapport with Jarvis,' Torrens had said. 'Go and have a chat to him. He's under a lot of pressure now with the press articles. Maybe he'll come clean to you.' So, reluctantly, that's what Kathy was trying to do. The phone was hopeless, continuously engaged, and she imagined the press siege outside his house, so she tried his sister-in-law's home phone, also jammed, and then her mobile. Finally she got through, hearing the desperation in Audrey Gowe's voice.

'He's not here,' she said in a rushed half-whisper, as if afraid of being overheard. 'He left Highgate on Friday, thank God, and was with us on Saturday night. But the reporters were on our doorstep on Sunday morning and we barely managed to get him out through the back lane before they closed in. Oliver is incensed; we all are. It's madness, cruel madness.

You've no idea the messages posted on the web. Hateful, obscene things. Of course, it's all untrue, what they're saying about him. And coming on top of Caroline's murder ... I'm frightened for him.'

'I understand,' Kathy said. 'So where is he now?'

There was silence.

'Mrs Gowe? If you could tell me how to contact him, I may be able to help.'

Finally she answered, a chill in her voice, 'I'm not sure we can believe that anymore. All I can tell you is that he's no longer in England. If you really want to help, you can put a stop to this witch-hunt.'

~

Frustrated, Kathy called Alun Hughes, who invited her to share a sandwich lunch. They sat in a weak patch of sunlight glimmering through the glass curtain wall of the Box, looking out over the Broadway shopping centre and the constant stream of traffic on the Hammersmith flyover. Hughes unwrapped his lunch, complaining about the air-conditioning in his corner of the office, about the coffee and about the latest round of HR memos, then said, 'So is there something I can help you with, Kathy?'

'You know me, Alun, I'm biased. I worked with Brock for far too long to believe he killed that woman, so bear with me if I'm being a pain. But it seems to me the only way they knew where Brock parked his car was because they were tracking him, and the obvious way was by his phone. So I have to ask: are you absolutely sure his phone wasn't being tracked?'

'Oh ...' Hughes gave a disappointed sigh. 'You're surely not going to call me stupid or incompetent, are you, Kathy?'

Kathy winced, embarrassed. 'No, but ...'

'Of course we checked and rechecked his phone. There were no rogue apps or hidden spyware but, yes, he was being tracked.' He looked with satisfaction at his roast beef sandwich and sank his teeth into it.

Kathy blinked at him. 'He was?' She hadn't seen this in the technical reports.

Hughes chewed. 'He was.'

'Who by?'

'By his partner, Suzanne. Very simple with a smart phone, very useful for keeping tabs on wayward children or elderly men who are losing their marbles.'

'She told you this?'

'When we asked her, yes. She did it after he got mugged that time and drove home from London in a semiconscious state. She was worried that he needed watching. Not quite compos mentis. Her words.'

'Oh.' Kathy was deflated.

Hughes went on, 'But tell me, Kathy, who is this "they" who might be tracking him? This mysterious "they" you've dreamed up to avoid facing the bleedin' obvious? Who the hell are "they"?'

Kathy took a breath and said, 'What about Elena Vasile's thug friend, the one who beat up Brock in Walworth? Have you checked on him?'

'Of course we've bloody checked on him!' Hughes sounded distinctly annoyed now. 'Marku Constantin flew out of Gatwick on an easyJet flight to Bucharest on Christmas Eve, two weeks before Elena was murdered, and has not returned since.' He puffed out his cheeks, then said more calmly, 'Anything else?'

'Motive, Alun. He had absolutely no reason to kill that woman.'

'He just lost it, Kathy. That's my belief. Elena was working a scam, and when Brock realised she was playing him for a mug he just lost it, lashed out.'

'No, not Brock. Never.'

'People change, Kathy. He wasn't his old self. Elena's boyfriend had beaten the shit out of him just three weeks before. It must have had a devastating impact on him, forced to face the fact that he wasn't the man he'd once been. When she taunted him, turned her back on him, he saw red and let her have it.'

Kathy bowed her head. It was the same argument that she'd used to Brock about Pettigrew.

'I'm sorry, Kathy. Believe me, this grieves me too.'

~

Later that day Kathy was trying to understand a preliminary technical report on the contents of Jarvis's home computer when her mobile rang.

'Kathy? Hi, it's John.'

She recognised the Canadian accent of Brock's son with a mixture of pleasure and guilt that she hadn't contacted him. 'John! Hello. You've heard about Brock?'

'Yes. I'm still in shock. Suzanne finally decided to call me yesterday, and I caught the first flight I could.'

'You're here, in London?'

'Heathrow, yes. Look, I'd really appreciate having a talk with you about this. Any chance I can buy you dinner tonight?'

He had booked a room at a small hotel in Pimlico, he explained, and they agreed to meet at the Orange pub nearby.

~

The bar on the ground floor was crowded, and he didn't see her as she stepped inside, although she spotted him immediately—as tall as Brock but leaner in build, a lock of dark hair fallen forward over his forehead. She hesitated for a moment, watching him, the eyes half closed with the preoccupied look she recognised so well from his father. There was something else too that reminded her of Brock, a sense of self-possessed calm. In the older man it had always been reassuring, but with John it had a different effect on her, a quickening of the pulse. And then he glanced up suddenly and saw her and gave a big grin. They pushed their way through the crowd towards each other and hugged.

'Kathy,' he said, 'it's so good to see you again.'

Over a drink she told him what she could about Brock's situation and how it had come about. When she reached the end, he shook his head in disbelief. They finished their drinks and went upstairs to a table in the dining room with a view out onto Orange Square, pedestrians hunched against the wind hurrying across the small triangular open space beneath the skeletal trees.

John said, 'Both Pettigrew and Brock were caught up in this because of *The Promised Land* manuscript, and in both cases the woman who was trying to sell it was murdered.

Why? In order to frame them? That sounds so crazy, Kathy. It's not surprising the police don't believe it. It's like the plot of some weird Jacobean tragedy.'

'Yes. And part of me doesn't want to believe it either. You have to remember that I'm leading the team that's bringing the case against Charles Pettigrew, so I'm not a disinterested observer, and I can't be as open with you as I'd like. But if you can tell me anything useful about that manuscript I'd be grateful, wherever it leads. Brock sent you a copy of that first page, didn't he?'

'And of the second page too, yes. In fact, I was planning to come over anyway to talk to him about it. I showed the pages to a colleague in the university who's a specialist in mid-twentieth-century literature, and she's very interested.'

'What, she thinks they could be genuine?'

'She doesn't go that far, but she certainly considers it's a possibility.'

A waiter came to the table and they gave their order, then Kathy said, 'Go on, convince me.'

'Well, I'm not sure I can do that, but it's intriguing. Orwell was fascinated with utopias gone wrong, as in his last two novels, *Animal Farm* and *Nineteen Eighty-Four*, and the idea of a third and last one, challenging the utopian uber-text, Thomas More's sixteenth-century book *Utopia*, head on is certainly appealing. And those first two pages are scattered with sly references to More's book. In that story the narrator meets a traveller called Raphael Hythloday, while in *The Promised Land* he meets Ralph Halliday. The visionary who founded the ideal state is called Utopas in More's book and Ulisses Topaz in this one, and the main settlement is called Amaurot in one and its exact opposite Toruama in the other. There are other cross-references—the Portuguese nationality, for instance, and the promised land utopia being on an island. So it's got the appeal of a puzzle text, and Kimberly, the professor who's been helping me out on this, was very taken with that idea. But would Orwell/Blair have done that? I thought his writing was more straightforward and blunt than that, but Kimberly could quote me examples where he made allusions to other books.

'There are also lots of references to Orwell's own early life in Burma: the Strand Hotel in Rangoon, which he certainly knew well; the teak timber business which also features in his first novel *Burmese Days*; and the floating island farms like those on Inle Lake in central Burma, which he would have been familiar with. So those also have an appeal, with Blair, knowing he was near the end of his life, returning to his literary roots in Burma to write the definitive dystopian novel, and under his real name.

'Well, that's Kimberly's area; mine is the more mundane things like sentence structure, word choice and frequency, that kind of thing. Orwell recorded his views on literary style, favouring a no-nonsense approach—avoid long words, elaborate figures of speech, jargon and the passive sense—and *The Promised Land* pretty much follows that line. It also has some slightly dated words—"piteous", for example—that would be right for Orwell's era. And the opening—"The Strand Hotel, Rangoon, six in the evening"—it's pure Orwell; compare the opening sentence of his *Down and Out in Paris and London*: "The Rue du Coq d'Or, Paris, seven in the morning."'

'So you really think it could be genuine?' Kathy asked.

'I haven't made up my mind yet. The problem for Kimberly is that she's never heard of "my dear friend Amar Dasgupta" to whom Blair dedicates the manuscript, and she can't find any reference to him anywhere. So what I was intending to do, before this bombshell with Brock, was to spend time in the Orwell Archive at University College London trying to find him. If Dasgupta isn't there, then I think we have to conclude that someone has been playing us all in the most elaborate and monstrous game imaginable. Two men in prison. Two women dead!'

Four, Kathy thought, thinking of the murders of Andrea Giannopoulos and Caroline Jarvis. 'Anyway,' she said, 'Brock'll be really glad to see you.'

A cloud seemed to pass over John's face. 'How's he doing? Suzanne said he was managing pretty well, but I had the feeling she was pretty worried.'

'I haven't been able to see him yet myself.'

John focused on straightening the fork on the table in front of him. 'The thing is, I'm not sure whether I should visit him.'

'Why not?'

He finally met her eyes. 'I don't think he's ever accepted me, Kathy, not really. Despite all we went through together on the Chelsea Mansions case, I always had the feeling I was an embarrassment, the unknown son who suddenly barged into his life uninvited. I think he would hate it, me seeing him like that, locked up in prison, humiliated.'

'But he asked you to get involved in this case, John. He wanted your help.'

'Yeah, technical advice, nothing personal.'

There was some truth in what John was saying, Kathy thought. She'd sensed Brock's reluctance to get involved, and had wondered if John was a reminder of a stage in Brock's life that he'd prefer to forget. And there was something else, something more personal to her. On his last visit, she and John had discovered a rapport between them, an easiness of manner, and perhaps something more than that. But Kathy had been aware that Brock had noticed this and perhaps resented it, and it had made for a strange awkwardness between the three of them.

'Well, you've come all this way, John. I think you should give it a try. It might be uncomfortable at first, but I do know him, and I think he'll appreciate the effort.'

'I'm not sure. Would you come with me?'

Kathy thought about that. Finally she said, 'Okay, we'll go together, but we'll play it my way, okay?'

~

The following morning Kathy sat alone at her table in the visit room at Belmarsh, waiting for Brock to appear. Around her prisoners were bent in conversation with wives, mothers, a few with children. Trying not to appear as if she was listening, she picked up the tone of these strange meetings, some stilted and awkward, one bursting with suppressed anger, most with an effort at cheerfulness. She noticed Charles Pettigrew and calculated that it was about six weeks since she'd last seen him. She saw the change in him, his posture slumped, complexion pale. He was sitting with a grey-haired woman who was gesticulating, talking urgently to him while he sat silent, unresponsive. As Kathy watched he turned suddenly and stared directly at her, and she looked quickly away and saw Brock coming through the door.

He strode in, head up, shoulders back, casting a look around him as if he owned the place, then made his way across to Kathy's table as she got to her feet, wondering how they should greet each other. He held out his hand with a wry smile and she took it, suddenly overcome with a sense of terrible pity, and of anger, seeing him here like this.

'Well,' he said, pulling out his chair. 'Good to see you, Kathy . . . at last.'

She began to frame an explanation, but he waved his hand. 'No, no, of course I understand. Honestly, I didn't think you'd be able to come at all. Are you sure you're not compromising yourself?'

She took a deep breath, steadied herself. 'Don't worry about that. How are you?'

'Fine, fine.' He sat back, folding his arms. 'This is an education. I think every young copper should be sent inside for a few weeks to get a perspective on things. And I'm learning bricklaying! How about that?'

'That's great. Food?'

'Not bad.' He shrugged dismissively and gazed around. 'There's old Pettigrew over there—not doing too well, I'm afraid. I see true crime has come to cheer him up. About the last thing he needs, I'd have thought.'

'Who's that?'

'One of his authors, Donna Priest. She writes about real murder cases apparently. Probably planning a blockbuster on poor old Charlie, I shouldn't wonder. She'll be wanting to interview you next.'

Or you, Kathy thought, but didn't say it.

'But tell me about yourself and the big wide world,' Brock went on. 'That's much more interesting. What's this I've been hearing about those bloody judges? What's the inside story, eh?'

'Oh.' She shrugged. 'A mess. They've put me in charge of the review of the circumstances of Walcott's suicide.'

'A poisoned chalice, I can imagine. He was the first one, right?'

'Yes, and now there's Selwyn Jarvis.'

'I remember him from way back, when he was a Crown prosecutor. Decent bloke, I always thought.'

'And his wife was Caroline Jarvis, who was Charles Pettigrew's second victim.'

That stopped Brock dead. 'Eh?'

'Yes.'

'I hadn't . . . God, I hadn't made the connection.'

'You've had too much else on your mind.'

'Yes, but that's . . . bizarre.'

'Yes. And Walcott, you must have come up against him, didn't you?'

'Oh yes, several times. Pompous, but he always got it right on my cases.'

'There was at least one trial where all three of you were involved—you, Jarvis and Walcott. September 1999, the trial of the Causley brothers, remember it?'

'Of course. You weren't with me on that one, were you? Chloe Honnery, eight years old, as sweet a little girl as you can imagine. The Causley brothers tortured and drowned her just for fun. The thing that particularly shocked people, apart from the brutality of the crime itself, was that they came from a decent middle-class family in an ordinary law-abiding London suburb. As far as we could discover they had never suffered abuse or deprivation of any kind, both intelligent and well nurtured. They were just plain evil. Different personalities— Jarrod articulate with excellent school results and a prize for debating, and Dean silent, introspective, with an interest in computers and art—and both psychopaths. The judge, Walcott, took the view that Jarrod was the instigator and more culpable, but they seemed to me to be two sides of the same coin. There was some kind of unhealthy bond between them.'

Kathy said, 'You were the senior investigating officer, Jarvis was the Crown prosecutor, and Walcott was the judge.'

'True.'

'We've been looking at all the links we can find between Jarvis and Walcott, and I noticed that one because I remembered you were involved.'

'So?'

'Well . . . three very senior law officers all publicly disgraced and under investigation within the space of a few weeks. It's a coincidence.'

'Yes, but we three have had many contacts over the years— committees, conferences, other trials. As a matter of fact, we all expressed misgivings about the appointment of the present police commissioner. Maybe he's framed us.' He chuckled, then added, 'Come to that, Pettigrew was at the Causley trial too.'

'Pettigrew?'

'Yes, he told me. He saw me in the witness box there, and that's why he suggested to Maggie Ferguson that I'd be good to advise on his case. But that's neither here nor there.' He leaned forward across the table. 'No, the Jarvis and Walcott cases are completely different from my problem. If you want to do us both a bit of good—you with your case against Pettigrew and me with my present incarceration—you should concentrate on that Orwell novel. That's the key to both investigations. You said before that only that first page of the manuscript existed and the rest was just a fantasy of Charlie Pettigrew's, but now we know that isn't so, because Elena Vasile sent me a second page two months after Pettigrew was locked up in here. Either Pettigrew and I were innocent bystanders who got caught up in a fight to possess that manuscript, or else it was used to trap us both. So where did it come from? Who's got it now? Did Uzma Jamali forge it, or did she steal it from the real Shari Mitra, wherever she is? Is it real or is it a fake?'

'Yes, I've got an expert working on that.'

'Really? I wish I could talk to them.'

'You can. I brought him with me. I'll get him in, shall I?'

'Certainly.'

Kathy went out to the lobby where John was waiting. She gave him an encouraging smile, nodded her head in the direction of the door and watched him go in. Next to the visit room entrance was a small room with a one-way window for guards to observe, and Kathy slipped in there and watched John approach his father. She saw the shock register on Brock's face, his air of confidence disappear as he got to his feet. For a moment, as they stood facing each other, she wondered if she'd made a terrible mistake, but then John stepped around the table that stood between them and put his arms out and wrapped his father in a hug. Kathy registered the surprise on Brock's face, and then a flash of something like relief as he embraced his son in return. They sat down and began to talk, and soon were deep in conversation, poring over the papers that John took from his jacket pocket.

She watched them for a while, then went out to the coffee machine and bought three cups. As she was waiting for them to fill she was aware of someone coming up behind her. She turned and recognised the woman who had been sitting with Charles Pettigrew. The woman smiled cautiously at her and said, 'Hello. You're Detective Chief Inspector Kolla, aren't you? I've been a long-time admirer of your work with DCI Brock. I should explain: I'm an author and write about true crime cases. Donna Priest.' She handed Kathy a card.

Kathy said, 'I noticed you sitting with Charles Pettigrew. I'm afraid I can't talk about his case.'

'Oh no, no, of course not. I'm here as a friend really—he's been my publisher for many years and I feel so sorry for him. He seems to have been abandoned by all his other former colleagues. But it is an intriguing case. Maybe when it's all over we could have a chat?'

'Maybe.'

'And we have another connection, actually. I know your aunt and uncle in Sheffield, Mary and Tom.'

'Seriously? How?'

'I was up there doing some research on Peter Sutcliffe, the Yorkshire Ripper, and one evening I went to see a show at the Playhouse, and in the interval I got into conversation with this lovely couple, Mary and Tom, and they told me about their wonderful niece who was a detective with the Met in London. Well, of course I'd heard of you, and we struck up a friendship. How are they?'

'I'm afraid they both died last year.'

'Oh, I'm so sorry. They thought the world of you. Such a lovely couple, real characters.'

'They were. But that's amazing that you met them,' Kathy said. 'Small world.'

'Yes, indeed. But I think the real world is full of coincidences like that, isn't it? Unlike the world of fiction, where it's not allowed.'

Kathy smiled. The woman, probably in her early sixties, had a bright, intelligent manner. Was this how authors worked, cultivating contacts with useful people in the real world? 'Have you always been an author?' she asked.

'Oh no. Once I worked in finance in the City, but although it was exciting in its way, I never felt satisfied. To me it didn't get close to the mysteries of the human condition. Does that sound pretentious?'

'No, I think I understand. That's what makes police work so compelling for me.'

'Exactly! Look, Kathy—may I call you that? I feel I know you so well already—might I send you a copy of one of my books? You may have a dull moment one day to glance at it.'

Kathy gave her a card with a smile and took the coffees over to Brock's table. The two men barely looked up, intent on examining some quirk in the handwriting on the first page of the manuscript. As she waited for them to finish she thought about Donna Priest's story and about the Yorkshire Ripper, who had also attacked his victims—thirteen who died and seven who survived—with a hammer. Could that have been an inspiration for Pettigrew?

~

On the way back Kathy said, 'So it went all right then?'

John nodded. 'Yes. A bit awkward at first, for both of us, but then it was okay. The worst bit was walking away and leaving him in that place. Has he got a decent lawyer? If it's a matter of money, I could help.'

'I'll give you her contact details. I'm sure she'll be happy to talk to you, John.'

'Right. And thanks, Kathy, for bringing me today.'

'He seemed very taken up in what you had to tell him.'

'He's kind of obsessed with that Orwell manuscript—he's been reading all the Orwell stuff he can get hold of, starting with *Burmese Days*. We were talking over the research I'm going to do at UCL.'

He explained that he'd phoned the Special Collections office of the university in Gower Street, not far from the British Museum, and they had arranged a pass for him to access the main part of the Orwell documents held in the National Archives, ten miles upriver on the Thames at Kew. She drove him there from the prison, then returned to her desk in the Box.

Later, when she'd cleared the backlog of requests and reports, she thought about her conversation with Brock about the Causley case and his remark that Pettigrew had also been there. It was an extraordinary coincidence, surely? Why was he there? She'd have to ask him or Maggie. She opened her file on the court documents again and searched them for the name Pettigrew. And when it came up she frowned and read it again. Pettigrew hadn't been just a casual onlooker; he'd been a member of the jury. In fact, he'd been their foreman, and had been the one who'd delivered their verdict to the court.

Kathy sat back, took a deep breath and tried not to get it out of perspective. But every way she thought of it brought her back to the same inescapable fact—that the four key people involved in locking up the Causley brothers were now, within the space of a few months, themselves in deep trouble with the law. What were the odds? A million to one?

She thought: What do I do?

The first thing was to find out more about the Causleys, sixteen years on. She began with their parole board reports. Dean, the younger boy, seemed to have suffered from a considerable amount of aggression and abuse while in jail, and was said to have become very withdrawn and uncommunicative. He was released under licence into the community after serving ten of his fifteen-year sentence and was given assistance to change his identity after receiving death threats. That was six years ago. He had kept out of trouble and after five years the licence period was completed and the monitoring stopped. His brother Jarrod, sentenced to twenty years, was described as having an exemplary prison record, completing an arts degree with the Open University and a postgraduate diploma in librarianship. He had been released two years ago, and was currently working as a trainee assistant librarian at a public library in North London. He was now thirty-two, his brother thirty, both having spent almost half their lives in prison.

Kathy was searching for the contact details for Jarrod's probation officer when her mobile rang. It was John.

'Kathy, are you still at work?'

'Yep. How did it go at the National Archives?'

'I made a start, but there's a lot of stuff to get through. But look, I think you need a break. How about taking some time off tomorrow?'

'I wish.'

'No, I'm serious. I thought you looked exhausted today. They're forecasting a break in the weather tomorrow, a sunny spring-like day they say, and I thought we could take a boat up the river to Kew and have lunch in a nice little pub to discuss developments in *The Promised Land* mystery, and then we could call in at the National Archives and I could show you their Orwell holdings. Consider it a work assignment—research.'

'Sounds good. Let me see . . .' She had the joint task-force meeting at nine, the HR briefing later in the afternoon, but the prospect of a few hours off and time to get reacquainted with John was tempting. 'Yes, okay. I'll work something out.'

'That would be wonderful, Kathy. Thanks.'

When she rang off, Kathy thought how keen he'd sounded, and wondered how she really felt about that. She set about rearranging her commitments, then remembered Jarrod Causley's probation officer. She found the number and explained that she wanted information on Jarrod's current situation.

The woman sounded worried. 'He's not in trouble, is he?'

'No. His name came up as a possible witness in another case, but I think it's unlikely he can help us.'

'Oh, something to do with the library, do you mean?'

'He works there full-time, does he?'

'Yes. From what I hear they're very happy with him.'

'Do they know his background?'

'Oh yes, but he came out of prison with full marks for motivation and the head librarian was keen to give him a chance to rehabilitate himself. She interviewed him and was impressed. He can be pretty plausible when he wants to be.'

'You sound sceptical.'

'Just between us? I've met his type before, manipulative and totally self-centred. And he's never expressed guilt or remorse for what they did to Chloe Honnery. But I can't complain about his behaviour on probation. He's done it all by the book. Never tried to cut corners.'

'Friends? Girlfriend?'

'Not that I know of. He seems to get on all right with the other library staff.'

'What's his brother up to, do you know?'

'No idea. I hear he got beaten up when he came out of prison and changed his name and moved away. I did meet him the once, at Belmarsh, when he was visiting Jarrod towards the end of his brother's sentence. He didn't say a word to me, and Jarrod didn't tell me anything about him except that it was unlikely they'd have much to do with each other when he got out. Their parents both died during the period they were inside, and they were left the house and a bit of capital, so they're neither of them on the breadline. Was there anything specific you wanted?'

'There's a time I'd like to check whether Jarrod was at work at the library. I'd prefer not to approach the staff myself, in case they get the wrong idea and think he's in trouble.'

'Good point. I could ask them if you like.'

'That would be a great help. The time I'm interested in is the morning of Friday, January the eighth, between nine and eleven.'

'I'll get back to you.'

Jarrod was in Belmarsh too, Kathy thought as she rang off. So many coincidences. She put a call through to the prison and spoke to the office manager. She explained that she wanted to identify a twenty-eight-year-old male who'd visited Jarrod Causley in the period immediately before his release in 2013. Within half an hour she got an email attaching the visit application form for someone called Ethan Hawke. There was also an image of Hawke's ID, a driver's licence with a photograph of a pinched, surly-faced man with a shaved head who didn't look a bit like the American film star of that name, but was recognisable from earlier pictures of Dean Causley. The address given was the Causley family's home that, on checking, Kathy found had been sold by the two boys soon after Jarrod was released. She wasn't able to trace an address for Dean Causley or Ethan Hawke since then.

Something about the face on the driver's licence bothered her. She thought she'd seen it before somewhere, but couldn't place it.

She made a check of social media sites, and found a number of photographs and postings of the older brother, Jarrod, seemingly not the least subdued by his prison experience but, on the contrary, quite jaunty and full of himself. On the website for the library where he worked there was an image of him running a workshop for a group of schoolchildren.

16

The weather was exactly as John had predicted, a crystal blue sky, sunlight glittering on the water. Kathy stood on the Embankment by Cleopatra's Needle across the Thames from the Festival Hall. She turned towards Hungerford Bridge and spotted him emerging from the tube station, tall, purposeful, looking around for her. Kathy smiled and waved.

'Hi.' John put out his arms and kissed her cheek. 'Wasn't I right? It's a beautiful day. Let's get a ticket.'

They walked to Embankment Pier, where they went down the ramp to the ticket office and took their seats on the open upper deck of the waiting boat. Kathy pointed out the tall spike of the Shard and described Brock's night spent tracking down Elena Vasile a month earlier, back and forward across the river.

John laughed and shook his head. 'You've got to hand it to the old man. Once a cop always a cop. Does that apply to you, Kathy? You wouldn't want to do anything else?'

'Once or twice I've thought of doing something different, but not for long. How about you?'

'Oh, when I was younger I did, but I do like academic work, my research and teaching. I have to admit, though, that my occasional forays with the SPVM—the Montreal police—and that time over here with you and Brock have been a lot more exciting.'

'Hair-raising, I should think.' Kathy laughed. 'You nearly got yourself killed at Chelsea Mansions.'

'True enough.'

She'd worked out that he was eight years younger than her, and the difference was crucial, she thought. In his thirties, he had his future open in front of him, full of choices, whereas she, in her mid-forties, was feeling very set in her path.

They moved off upriver, past the London Eye and the Houses of Parliament and under Westminster and Lambeth bridges. Beyond Vauxhall Bridge, John pointed to the apartment towers along the curve of the south bank. 'Wouldn't mind living somewhere like that, eh?'

'Actually,' Kathy said, 'that's where I do live. That one over there, twelfth floor.'

'Wow, seriously? I thought you lived in Finchley.'

'I used to. I moved here last August.' She told him the story of her aunt and uncle's legacy. 'We could call in on our way back, if you like. There's a great view.'

'That would be wonderful. I should get you a house-warming present.'

'A definite opinion about *The Promised Land* would be great.'

'Well, I've made a start, and I have come across something interesting. You have to register and apply in advance for what you want to access in the Orwell Archive,' he said. 'And because I'd turned up at short notice, they said it might take a while to retrieve the stuff I was after. They were very helpful, and told me I was in luck—another researcher was investigating the material for 1949, so it hadn't been returned to storage. They said that this other researcher had booked to return this afternoon at two, and they mentioned his name—Sir Mortimer Hartley. Well, Kimberly, my Orwell expert at McGill, had told me about Hartley. He's reckoned to be the foremost Orwell specialist in the world—he's written the definitive biography—and she told me it would be brilliant if we could get him to look at *The Promised Land* document. So, I've brought a photocopy of page one and thought I might try to catch him today and ask him to look at it. What do you reckon?'

Kathy thought about it. The document would become public knowledge soon anyway when Pettigrew was brought to trial. 'Yes, okay. It would be interesting to know why he was looking at 1949, specifically.'

'Yes, that's true. It'd be good if we could ask him that.'

They disembarked at Kew Pier, walked to the Greyhound pub and found a table by a window looking out over Kew Green. John went off to the bar, returning with their drinks and a lunch menu. 'Here we are. One glass of semillon, one pint of best. Cheers.'

After they'd ordered their lunch, Kathy watched John toying with a beer mat, a frown on his face, and sensed that he had something on his mind. She waited, and finally he said, 'It's been hard coming back to London. Harder than I expected.'

'Of course, seeing your dad locked up in jail.'

'Yes, that, certainly. But also . . . I've missed you both, you and Brock. You especially, Kathy. It really hit me, seeing you again. In a way, it felt like coming home.' He hesitated, then said, 'Tell me to shut up.'

'No,' she said, a little surprised by this. She reached across the table and took his hand. 'Don't shut up.'

And at that moment she felt her phone vibrate in her pocket. 'Damn.' She looked at the screen—Commander Torrens's secretary. 'Damn, damn. I'll have to take this.' She pressed buttons. 'Hello?'

'Kathy, sorry to disturb you, but Commander Torrens asks if you could attend an emergency meeting of the Falstaff Committee in an hour. He says it is very important.'

'I see. All right.'

'Shall I send a car for you?'

'Please.' She gave the address and rang off, turned back to John who was watching her. 'I'm sorry, John. I'm going to have to go. Work emergency. What were you going to say?'

'Oh . . . it can wait. Maybe we could catch up later? Dinner?'

'Yes, let's hope so. I've no idea how long this will take.'

'They're coming to pick you up, are they? What about your lunch?'

'I'd better cancel it.'

'I'll do it.'

He got to his feet and returned from the bar with a sandwich and a bottle of water for her. 'You've got to eat.'

A police patrol car drew to a halt in front of the pub, light flashing, and they went outside. She kissed him on the cheek and said, 'I'll call you.'

She got in quickly and the car sped away. As they drove towards headquarters she stared out the window and wondered where their conversation might have led if it hadn't been brought so abruptly to an end. She liked John very much, but wasn't sure she wanted a closer relationship. In many respects, he was exactly what she might look for in a man, but her feelings were unsettled by the fact that he was Brock's son and resembled him in so many subtle ways.

When she reached headquarters, she learned the cause of the panic. The body of Selwyn Jarvis had been found lying in the heather in the grounds of a friend's house in the Scottish Highlands where he had taken refuge. He had left a suicide note, denying all of the 'vile and malicious rumours' against Roger Walcott and himself.

Feeling troubled, Kathy waited while the Falstaff Committee met with the Home Secretary and Cabinet Secretary. While she was waiting, she got a text message from Jarrod Causley's probation officer to tell her that Jarrod had taken a day's leave on January the eighth. So he hadn't been at work at the library at the time that Elena Vasile was murdered and Brock arrested. The more she thought about it, the more unsettled Kathy felt. What if they'd been following the wrong trail all along?

When the committee returned from Whitehall, Commander Torrens buzzed for her to come to his office. It had been decided that in the following week the Home Secretary would announce a parliamentary inquiry into the

Walcott/Jarvis affair. Kathy's priority would be to bring her team's work to a rapid conclusion and to compile the results in a report for the inquiry.

'So,' Torrens said, 'you've got forty-eight hours. They're in a hurry.'

Kathy tried to explain that the computer experts were still divided over whether the incriminating items on the two judges' computers were genuine, or whether it was possible that a third party had planted them there, either at the times recorded or perhaps later, using a backdate utility.

Torrens shook his head impatiently. 'Nonsense. What third party?'

'It is possible, sir. Someone might have an interest in having their judgments overturned. Perhaps a paedophile ring, or . . . someone else.'

'Well, put that in your report if you think it's a remote possibility. Let them sort it out. The crucial thing is that you haven't discovered anything to suggest that the original police investigation into Walcott's suicide was in any way at fault.'

'That's correct.'

'Okay, well, get on with it then.'

'There's something that's come up that I'd like to discuss with you, sir. It concerns both the Walcott and Jarvis cases, and Pettigrew and Brock as well. I think I've found a connection.'

'A connection?' Torrens checked his watch. 'I have to go. If it's urgent, talk to Jean and make a time to see me later. If it concerns the Brock case, you'd better get Alun Hughes too.' He turned and paced away.

Kathy spoke to Torrens's secretary and found a time slot later in the afternoon, then returned to her office and set about planning her report to the committee. There were several loose ends that would have to be brought to some sort of conclusion and she would have to coordinate half a dozen specialists to write up technical sections. First she rang John to apologise again for leaving so suddenly at Kew, and for the fact that she'd be tied up all weekend.

'Can't be helped,' he said.

'Did you manage to find your Orwell expert in the archives?'

'Mortimer Hartley, yes, I did track him down eventually. It was the strangest thing.'

'How do you mean?'

'Well, I showed him the photocopy of that first page of the manuscript, and I could have sworn he'd seen it before.'

'Really?'

'Yes. His reaction was odd. There was an initial shock of recognition when he first looked at it, but then he said he'd never heard of *The Promised Land* or Amar Dasgupta and dismissed it as a crude forgery. But he was very interested to know how I'd got hold of it, and what my involvement with the police investigation was all about, and he asked to keep the photocopy.'

Kathy's desk phone began ringing and she said, 'I'll have to go, John. But we'll catch up, I promise.'

The call was from the IT expert in charge of the group investigating the two judges' computers, wanting to see her to discuss their report. When he arrived, he showed her the draft summary. He explained that the two judges, Jarvis and Walcott, had regularly exchanged interesting or humorous items— jokes, YouTube clips, photographs—with each other as email attachments, which they in turn had received from a variety of online acquaintances. The offensive material—mostly stills and videos of naked children—had been planted as a hidden backdoor element within these innocent attachments and ended up on the download files of the host computer.

'The thing is,' the man explained, 'Jarvis and Walcott passed their email clips on to other friends, who also received the hidden material, unknown to them, and who in turn passed it on to others. We've traced dozens of these innocent recipients.'

'So, could Jarvis and Walcott be innocent too?'

'Well, maybe not. It turns out that email clips they received from third parties were clean, and only became contaminated after they'd passed through the two judges' computers, and from one to the other.'

'And is there any evidence that the judges ever opened those hidden files?'

'Apart from the ones that were open on Walcott's file when he was found, no, we can't say.'

Kathy frowned, trying to get her head around this. 'But if the stuff they received from third parties was clean, where did the illicit files come from? What was their source?'

'We don't know. Both of their computers contained a computer worm, a relatively recent one called Miwar which installed a back door in their computers through which we think the material arrived. But we can't trace its source. It might be a paedophile ring, or it might just be a malicious hacker with a thing against judges. Miwar is receiving a lot of attention at present, and we may eventually learn more, but at the moment that's all we can say.

'Oh,' he added, 'one other thing: Miwar originated in Eastern Europe—Romania.'

'Like Marku Constantin,' Kathy said.

'Yes, but we haven't been able to find any evidence that he was computer-savvy. Nothing at all. Sorry, boss, it's all pretty inconclusive.'

Kathy considered this, then said, 'Well, if that's the case, that's all we can report.'

'Yep.' The man began gathering up his papers.

Kathy said, 'This business of passing hidden stuff between the two judges—was it known to the people who looked into Walcott's computer immediately after he died?'

'Yes, they discovered that all right. That's what first cast doubt on Jarvis.'

'So it would have been known to the detectives working that case?'

'Sure. Well, DI O'Hare, certainly. I hear we haven't been able to contact him. You're wondering if he leaked it to the press?'

'They wouldn't have published without some kind of convincing evidence, and he would have had access to it.'

'Yes, that occurred to me too.'

'Well, you might like to include a paragraph about who did have access to that material back in December. Just to protect yourself and your team.'

~

Out in the exercise yard, enjoying the unseasonable sunshine, Brock spotted Pettigrew sitting on a bench, staring glumly at a group of older inmates doing Pilates. Since Kathy's visit and her comments about the Causley trial he'd been wanting to speak to Pettigrew. Not that he really thought there could be anything in what Kathy had said, but still.

He wiped the seat beside Pettigrew and sat down. 'How are you doing, Charlie?'

'Oh, hello, Brock. All right, I suppose.'

'I've been wanting to ask you something. When we first met, you mentioned you'd seen me at the Old Bailey, the Causley brothers' trial.'

'That's right. I was most impressed.'

'You were there just out of interest?'

'Oh, a bit more than that. I was on the jury. In fact, I was foreman of the jury.'

'Really?'

'Oh yes. In point of fact—' Pettigrew leaned over to Brock, lowering his voice '—you could say that I was responsible for having those two locked up.'

'How come?'

'You remember the fuss the defence made about that witness sighting, the possibility of mistaken identity? How the witness may have confused the Causley brothers with two other boys?'

'Yes, I remember. It was their main line of defence.'

'Exactly, and several members of the jury were taken in by it, thought there was a sufficient element of doubt. It took me a while to make them see sense.'

'I remember, the jury was out for days.'

'Three days—three long days. It was a gruelling experience, one I wouldn't like to repeat, but I felt I had to put my foot down. Those two boys were guilty, no doubt about it. You made that perfectly plain, and it was your detective work on that case that made me suggest your name to Maggie Ferguson. Well, actually, it was Donna Priest who first suggested it to me, and I thought it was a brilliant idea and spoke to Maggie.'

'Your author Donna Priest suggested it?'

'That's right, she's a big fan of yours. She was there too, at the Causley trial, doing research. Up till then she'd been writing crime fiction, but she'd fallen into a mid-list trough with poor sales and was thinking of turning her hand to non-fiction crime. She recognised me at the trial and afterwards she approached me with her idea for a true-crime book called *Psychopaths*.' Pettigrew smiled. 'Donna doesn't believe in subtle book titles. I checked the sales of her previous crime novels and they were not encouraging, but I was flushed with my experience of the Causley trial and decided to give it a go. And it did reasonably well. She's not a bad writer and she's meticulous in her research. But look, you should talk to her yourself—I know she'd love to meet you.'

'Oh, I don't think so, Charlie.'

'After the trial she dug up a lot of fresh stuff about the Causley story, much of which we couldn't publish for legal reasons. For example, she believes that Chloe Honnery wasn't their first victim.'

'You're kidding.'

'No. She discovered that the previous year a girl was drowned one night in a hotel swimming pool in Majorca. The Causley family were on holiday there at the same time, and Donna spoke to some of the staff who said they'd seen Jarrod Causley hassling her. The Spanish police never followed it up.'

'That is interesting.'

'Yes. And now, of course, she's fascinated with our two cases. She's convinced the same people have set us both up, and she's trying to gather evidence to help us. It would really be worth your while talking to her, Brock.'

He squinted up at the sky, a cloud had passed over the sun and Brock felt the first spots of rain. 'I'll think about it,' he said. 'Now we'd better get back inside.'

Brock strolled back to his cell to get changed for his next gym session. The door was unlocked but closed, and there were none of the usual sounds of daytime TV from inside the cell. Brock peered through the spy hole and saw Danny sitting on Brock's bed, holding Brock's notebook, a pencil in his hand. Brock stepped back, then slammed the door open hard and walked in. Danny leaped to his feet, dropping the notebook on the floor between them. They stared at one another, and for a moment it seemed that Danny would be defiant, but then he looked at the pencil in his hand and sagged, bowed his head and muttered, 'Fuck.'

Brock picked up the notebook and flicked through the pages until he came to a passage written in a script that vaguely resembled his own. It read, *I'm still denying I killed the Vasile bitch, but Danny can see through my lies.*

'Well,' Brock said, 'I can see you're not in here for forgery, Danny. Do I detect an element of desperation?'

Danny said nothing, standing there, staring at the floor, fists clenched tight.

Brock said finally, 'Sit down, old son. Tell me all about it.' He sat and waited until Danny finally slumped onto the edge of his bunk.

Brock checked through the rest of the notebook, frowning like a disapproving schoolmaster. 'They're putting the hard word on you, are they?'

Danny's bowed head gave a little nod.

'Come on then, you might as well tell me.'

He sighed and finally spoke. 'I've got a little girl, Isabella.' He nodded at the photograph on the pinboard. 'She's eight. They've taken her into care. They say she's at risk and they've told her her dad's a murderer. She won't come to see me.'

He sniffed. 'The cop told me they'll fix it for me to get manslaughter with mitigating factors and be out of here in three years, if I do what they want. That way there's a chance I can make things good with Isabella. But if I don't, they'll make sure I get eighteen years minimum, and she'll be grown up by the time I get out, and it'll be too late.'

'And what do they want you to do?'

'To get you to tell me why you killed that woman.'

'And if I don't tell you?'

'Then I'll probably never see my little girl again.'

'That's rough,' Brock said. He went over and studied Isabella's photograph. He'd sometimes wondered what it would have been like to have had a daughter, if things had worked out differently. 'She's very pretty.'

'Yeah, and bright. My little angel.'

'This detective have a name?'

'Flint.' Danny shuddered. 'Hard as.'

'Well, the only comfort I can offer you is that things could be a lot worse.'

Danny snorted. 'Oh really? How?'

'I'm not going to confess to you, and I'm not going to

tell you why I killed that woman, because I didn't. And if you go ahead and tell them I did, and invent a lot of bullshit like this—' Brock shook the notebook at him '—then on top of everything else you're going to find yourself up on charges of perjury and trying to pervert the course of justice, and you'll have another three years minimum added to your sentence.'

'Jesus.' Danny buried his face in his hands and his shoulders shook. 'What can I do?'

Brock sat silent for a while, then said softly, 'Leave it with me, old son.'

~

It was after eight that evening when Kathy finally met with Torrens and Hughes. Torrens was in his shirtsleeves, tie loosened and looking weary. He took a bottle of Scotch from a cupboard and poured three glasses. 'It's been a bugger of a day,' he said. 'So I hope you're not going to make it any worse, Kathy. What's the problem? A connection, you said?'

'Yes. As you know, we've been trying to track down connections between Walcott and Jarvis, and we came up with something odd. Seventeen years ago they were both involved with a criminal trial which was highly publicised at the time—the Causley brothers.'

Torrens nodded. 'Yes, I remember.'

'Walcott was the judge and Jarvis the Crown prosecutor. But it turns out that both Brock and Pettigrew were central figures in that trial as well, Brock as SIO and Pettigrew as jury foreman.'

'Really? Quite a coincidence, but so what?'

'I wonder if it's too much of a coincidence, given what's happened to those four men since the Causley brothers got out of jail.' And Kathy told them what she'd learned about the Causleys since their release. As she spoke she saw the frowns deepen on their faces. 'I think it's a possibility that the Causley brothers might be involved in our four current cases, and I believe it's a possibility that we can't afford to ignore.'

'Hm.' Torrens glanced at Hughes. 'Alun?'

'Well ... this is the first I've heard of this notion, but frankly, sir, I think it's extremely fanciful. The Walcott and Jarvis cases are entirely different from the other two. It may be that there is some link between the Pettigrew and Brock cases that we haven't completely clarified as yet, concerning the Orwell manuscript, but that's got nothing to do with the Causley brothers, surely. No, no, I'm sorry, Kathy. I don't buy it. Coincidences happen all the time. That's all this is.'

'I agree,' Torrens said shortly.

'Sir,' Kathy said, 'I've established that neither brother appears to have an alibi for the morning of the eighth of January, when Elena Vasile was murdered. I'd like your approval to test this in the least intrusive way, by tapping Jarrod Causley's phones, accessing his bank accounts and monitoring his movements, and to mount a search for Dean Causley's present identity and whereabouts. Neither of them need be aware of our investigation.'

Torrens yawned, shook his head. 'No. Not on the basis of what you've told us. I can't see any judge approving it. And apart from that, it's a distraction from the Falstaff investigation that we just don't need.'

Outside, in the corridor, Hughes said, 'Didn't see that one

coming, Kathy. You'll do anything to get your pal Brock off the hook, won't you? Bloody brilliant, but it doesn't fly. And hell, woman, you'd be undermining your own case against Pettigrew.'

'Brock taught me that sometimes we pursue a wrong idea because we simply can't bear to dump all we've invested in it. He said a good detective knows when it has to be done.'

'And sometimes we get distracted from the truth because we just don't want to acknowledge what's staring us in the face. Pettigrew and Brock are both guilty, Kathy. The forensic evidence is unequivocal. If you want to cooperate on finding out where that manuscript fits in, I'll be very willing to help. But not with this fanciful nonsense.'

He was right of course. But as she drove back to the office she remembered Brock's argument that the forensics could have been forged—Pettigrew's DNA planted at Caroline Jarvis's murder scene, her necklace placed in Pettigrew's house. It seemed hardly credible, but was it possible?

There was a voice message waiting for her from Brock. *God, Kathy, I had to queue for an hour to get a turn on this bloody phone and you're not there! I need to talk to you!*

She sighed. She couldn't ring him back at the prison. He'd just have to wait.

~

The following day, halfway through the rush to finish her unit's report on the Walcott/Jarvis cases, Kathy went through her checklist of tasks. There were several lines of inquiry left unfinished, and one that particularly bothered her was a follow-up on the report from the coroner's office on Walcott's death. The coroner had never referred the case to Homicide and Serious Crime as a possible murder, rather than a suicide, and she wasn't sure whether the possibility of murder had ever been seriously tested. So, hyped up on strong coffee after an almost sleepless night, she phoned the coroner's office and was eventually put through to the police officer there who'd worked on the case.

'Yes, ma'am. I advised the coroner on the Walcott death.' He sounded cautious. 'I authored the report that was sent through to you for the Falstaff Committee.'

'Yes, thanks, I've read it. I just wanted to clear up one point. I know that hangings are usually assumed to be suicides, but surely in the case of a High Court judge the coroner would have referred the case to Homicide for investigation?'

'Oh no. Hanging is such a common form of suicide that they're only referred in cases of exceptional anomalies. I've seen hangings where the hands of the deceased were bound with tape and they still weren't referred. Suicides sometimes do that, you see, to try to prevent themselves changing their minds at the last minute. There were no exceptional circumstances in the Walcott case to indicate homicide. On the contrary, the location, the open computer, the nature of the bruises, all suggested an accidental autoerotic suicide. We've seen a few of those, believe me.'

'And the teddy bear,' Kathy added.

'Yes, ma'am, the teddy bear. But most of all the computer. It was full of child abuse videos. The screen was unlocked, and he'd obviously been looking at it just before he died.'

'How can you be sure of that?'

'Well, someone had, and there were no signs of anyone else having been there.'

'No obvious signs,' Kathy said. 'So would it be true to say that it was never investigated seriously as a homicide?'

'You'd need to talk to forensic services, but that is my understanding.'

Kathy had already done that. Volume crime cases in the Metropolitan Police area were handled by crime scene *examiners*, who together had to deal with over eleven thousand cases in an average month. More serious crime scenes were referred to crime scene *managers*, who could spend much longer on each scene. The Walcott case had been handled by a crime scene examiner. Kathy wished she could have talked to the senior investigating officer again, Detective Inspector O'Hare, to find out who'd made that decision, but of course he was presently lying on some distant beach, unable or unwilling to take messages.

~

The following night, short of sleep and headache throbbing, Kathy finally delivered her report to Torrens's office and headed home. After Thursday's brief spell of spring-like weather, winter had returned in earnest, with a freezing wind and hard rain lashing the city, and by the time she reached home she was sure she had a cold coming on. She hung up her coat, kicked off her shoes and made herself a hot toddy to her Uncle Tom's recipe—whisky, hot water, honey and a squeeze of lemon juice. She slumped down into the armchair with a sigh.

The phone at her elbow rang. It was John, and for a moment she had the thought that he must have been watching the tower to see her light come on.

'Hi, Kathy. How did it go?'

'Oh, okay, I hope. I've just got in. Where are you?'

'In Battle. Suzanne invited me down here for a day or two.'

'That's nice.'

'You sound exhausted. Any chance you can join us? Suzanne told me to ask.'

'That's good of her. Please thank her, but I'm going to have to stay around here in case I'm needed.'

'Sure.'

There was a moment's silence. She tried to think of something to say. 'Any more luck with *The Promised Land*?'

'Maybe. I found ...' He hesitated, then said, 'It's a bit complicated. I really need to show you. Not to worry. You sound bushed. You need to get a good night's sleep.'

'Yes, you too.'

She rang off, thinking she should have found something more to say, something encouraging, but she was just too tired to think.

~

John hung up. He returned to the living room where Suzanne was drinking a mug of hot chocolate and sat down.

'How's Kathy?'

'Very tired. I did pass on your invitation, but she's too tied up to leave town.'

'That's a shame.'

He was aware of her observing him over the rim of the mug.

'You all right, John? Worried about your dad?'

'He seemed to be coping better than I expected. I had these visions of an ex-cop being bashed by the other convicts, but it was nothing like that.'

'I know what you mean—I think boredom must be the worst thing.'

'Yes. Imagine spending the rest of your life in such a place.'

'I'm hoping it won't come to that. But maybe you're bored, down here.'

'No, no.'

'Something's bothering you though.'

John smiled, remembering what Brock had once said about Suzanne's interrogation technique. 'Well . . . I feel kind of useless and in the way.'

'Of course you're not. Why do you say that?'

'Well . . . I tried to have a chat with Stewart, but he made it pretty plain he wasn't interested in having me around.'

'Oh, I'm so sorry. He's impossible. He drives—drove—Brock mad. He's rude, has almost no real friends and his school results are going downhill. These last weeks he's been worse than ever. I don't know what to do. The trouble is, I can see his mother in him. She was just the same at that age.'

'I was wondering . . .'

'Go on.'

'Something Brock said when I saw him, about how he would have liked to take up gliding again, and how he now knew how a caged bird must feel. He mentioned a gliding club over by Lewes.'

'Yes, we did talk about that. I stopped him going, but now I wish I hadn't, then he might never have got mixed up with Maggie Ferguson and got into this mess.'

John said, 'I checked the club out on the web, and they have trial lessons on Sundays, taking people up for a first flight to get them interested. I wondered if I could persuade Stewart to come with me tomorrow, just the two of us.'

'John, it would be a miracle if you could get him off that computer and out of his room for a few hours.'

~

Kathy stared at her dining table, which was looking much like her desk at work, covered with notes, photocopies and computer printouts. Among them lay the enlarged image of Dean Causley's face taken from his driver's licence in the name of Ethan Hawke. She felt weary and defeated just looking at the mess.

She forced herself to her feet, went into her bedroom and fell immediately to sleep.

Three hours later she opened her eyes wide and said, 'The Spaniards Inn.'

She got up and washed her face with cold water, then went through to her computer, logged on to the MPS intranet and into the files of the Heath murder investigations. At the time they were investigating the plumber's van in the car park of the Spaniards Inn they had accessed the pub's external security camera for the periods around both the Giannopoulos and Jarvis murders, and from these they had enlarged and enhanced images for every person recorded passing by. Kathy now began scrolling through those images until she came to the one she wanted—an unidentified male carrying a shoulder bag, walking along Spaniards Road opposite the pub at seven sixteen on the morning of Andrea Giannopoulos's murder. She zoomed in on the face, then copied and pasted it alongside the face from Ethan Hawke's driver's licence.

'It's possible,' she murmured. 'Very possible.'

17

The following morning at the breakfast table, despite Suzanne's prediction, a small miracle did happen. Stewart sat as usual, head down, saying nothing, when John took the seat next to him and slapped a sheet of paper down in front of him.

'What do you reckon, mate?' He tapped the sheet.

'What?' Stewart mumbled, stared at the paper, shrugged and continued eating his porridge.

'You and me. We've got flying lessons today.'

'What!' Miranda cried. 'You're going flying?'

'Yep. Stewart and I are booked to go up at midday.'

'That's fantastic!' She punched her brother on the arm. 'You lucky thing.'

'No.' Stewart shook his head. 'No way.'

'Come on,' John said. 'I've paid. Don't let me down, mate.'

'You're not scared, are you?' Miranda goaded.

Stewart looked in alarm at the two of them, then at his grandmother.

Suzanne said, 'You'll have to go, Stewart. Now John's paid.'

They didn't think he would, not until the last minute, when John appeared at the foot of the stairs with Stewart in tow, both with their coats on.

~

This time Edmanda was determined to put her foot down. 'I know you've been in a lot more police interviews than I have, Brock, but you've never been on this side of the table before, have you?'

Brock nodded humbly. 'True enough, Edmanda. True enough.'

'And I think, despite your long experience, that I may know the law a little bit better than you. So please, let me do my job.'

'Point taken.'

'Maggie told me that your most effective technique when interviewing suspects was your silences. Let's try that now.'

Alun Hughes came bustling in, the merciless DS Bulimore at his heels. 'Morning, morning. How are we this wet and dreary morning?'

Silence from Brock.

Hughes looked a little disconcerted. 'Well, let's get down to it, shall we?' He unpacked his bag and took up his notebook. 'Nothing major, Brock. Just a few little odds and ends, points of detail I'd like to clear up, that's all. Hmm . . .' He consulted his notes. 'Did you recognise anyone else on Hampstead Heath that Friday morning, the eighth of January?'

Silence.

Hughes tried again. 'Was Elena Vasile wearing the same clothes that day as on the previous time you met her, in Walworth on the nineteenth of December?'

Silence.

'On either occasion, did she have any visible bruises? Any signs of having been assaulted?'

It went on like this for some time, Brock saying not a word, until finally Hughes, exasperated, threw down his notebook. 'This won't do, Brock! It's all very well saying nothing at the beginning of an inquiry when the police are just fishing, but not now, not when we know everything. All it does is antagonise us, and strengthen the prosecution case.'

Brock made no response, and Hughes began again, going through his long list of questions and getting silence in return. Finally he closed his notebook with a snap. 'Very well. If you're not going to talk to me, there's nothing I can do for you. I'm disappointed, Brock. Very disappointed. I can see you spending the rest of your life in jail. Think of that. I am now suspending this interview.'

As he got to his feet, Brock said quietly, 'I'd like a word alone with you, Alun.'

Edmanda began to protest, but Brock interrupted, 'Nothing incriminating, I promise you.'

Hughes looked doubtful for a moment, then waved Mercy Bulimore out of the room. Edmanda followed with a reluctant frown.

Hughes waited till the door closed behind them, then nodded, 'Yes, Brock, man to man.'

Brock said, 'Switch off the tape, or whatever they have now. This is not to be recorded.'

Hughes shrugged, pressed a switch on the machine over on the side table. 'Okay.'

Brock said, 'I always thought you were an honest cop, Alun.'

'What are you talking about? Of course I am.'

'But you have a problem, don't you?'

'Oh, do I? What's that?'

'You really don't know what motive I had for killing Elena Vasile.'

Hughes smiled, leaned forward confidentially. 'Tell me then, Brock, just between us, and I'll see what I can do for you.'

Brock reached into the pocket of his baggy old trainer pants, took out his notebook and opened it to the page. He handed it to Hughes, pointing to the line, *I'm still denying I killed the Vasile bitch, but Danny can see through my lies.*

'Danny is my cellmate, Alun. A sad bugger who killed his wife and is desperately hoping for a manslaughter plea. From the moment I arrived he's been trying to get me to admit that I killed Elena Vasile. Then I discovered him with my notebook and found that crude attempt of his to forge my handwritten confession. We had a chat. Turns out he was visited by your DS Gavin Flint the day I arrived at Belmarsh. Flint put pressure on him—get me to confess why I killed Vasile and he'd make sure the prosecutors went easy on Danny. That's an attempt to corrupt a witness and pervert the course of justice.'

Hughes stared at him. 'Fuck.'

'What, fuck I found out, or fuck you didn't know?'

Hughes shook his head. 'Flint's a good detective. Keen, like. Maybe too keen.'

Brock said, 'There are two ways we can handle this. One, we resume the interview and I put this on the record . . .'

'Or?'

'Or you pull Flint into line, make your peace with Danny, and get it into your thick Welsh head that I didn't kill Elena Vasile.'

Hughes frowned. 'I can't compromise my investigation, Brock.'

'It's already compromised, Alun. All I'm saying is, do your job and find the *bloody truth*.'

Hughes stared at Brock's notebook, then said quietly, 'It's that damn manuscript, isn't it?' He sighed. 'I'm making in-quiries to see if Vasile's friend, Constantin, could have slipped back into the country undetected. One way or another, the poor girl was set up, wasn't she? Either by them or by you.'

'You haven't found the woman who phoned 999, have you?'

'No.'

'Thought not.'

~

Kathy arrived at Belmarsh soon afterwards. Brock was already seated at a table when she reached the visit room.

'Ah, Kathy.' He got to his feet, hand outstretched. 'Sit down, sit down. Good of you to come.' He scrutinised her face. 'You all right? You look worn out.'

'Oh, lot of things going on.'

'Of course. Well, good of you to make time to come out here.'

'You said you had something to tell me.'

He leaned closer. 'I was talking to Pettigrew about that Old Bailey trial where he saw me give evidence.'

'The Causley trial, yes.'

'And it made me wonder if there might be something in your suspicion about the coincidence—Walcott, Jarvis, Pettigrew and me all linked by that trial. Because it turns out that Pettigrew wasn't just a spectator there. No, he was the foreman of the bloody jury!'

'Yes, I know. I did a bit more digging and found that out.'

'Oh . . .' Brock looked disappointed. 'And did you find out that it was almost a hung jury until Pettigrew got them all to fall in behind a guilty verdict? They deliberated for three days.'

'No, I didn't know that.'

'And there was another person who attended that trial— Pettigrew's author, Donna Priest. She was researching her first true-crime book. Pettigrew told me that she did a lot of background research on the Causleys, and discovered another suspicious death they may have been involved in, the previous year.'

Kathy felt a chill go through her as Brock told her about the girl drowned in the hotel pool in Majorca. 'Alex Nicholson did a preliminary forensic psych report on the first two Heath murders,' she said, 'in which she drew attention to their location next to pools of water. She thought that might be significant.'

Brock nodded. 'Chloe Honnery and the girl in the Majorca pool. And now Andrea Giannopoulos and Caroline Jarvis.'

'And you were supposed to meet Elena Vasile by Viaduct Pond.'

'Right. I think we should talk to Donna Priest.'

We, Kathy noticed, like we're a team again. 'Maybe.'

'She's in here quite often. That's her over there, as a matter of fact, talking to that weird bloke. Don't know his name, but I've seen him around.' He pointed to another table where Priest and a prisoner were caught up in what looked like an intense discussion, he gesticulating and she trying to calm him down. As they watched, the man got abruptly to his feet and marched away. Donna Priest shook her head and began to gather up her belongings. As she stood up she glanced around the room and Brock raised his hand. Priest smiled and waved back then came over.

'Chief Inspector,' she said, taking his hand. 'I'm so glad to meet you at last.' Then, to Kathy, 'And to see you again, Chief Inspector. It's a great honour to meet you both. I've followed your cases with great interest over the years.'

She had a rather pedantic manner of speaking and fixing the other person with a questioning half-smile, Kathy noticed, as if she wasn't quite sure whether to believe them.

'I did actually speak to you once, Mr Brock, outside the Old Bailey following the conclusion of the Causley trial. I wanted to ask if I might interview you, but you were in a great hurry.'

'I'm afraid I didn't give interviews then, Donna. But I find myself in very different circumstances now.'

'Indeed, a monstrous miscarriage of justice. As also—' she turned to Kathy with a frown '—in the case of Charlie Pettigrew. I hope you don't mind me being blunt.'

'I'm always willing to listen to potential evidence,' Kathy said.

'Well, I don't have that, I'm afraid, but I've known Charlie a long time and I find the murder charge quite inconceivable.'

Brock waved to the free chair. 'Sit down if you've got a moment, Donna. Would you like a cup of coffee?'

'Thank you, no. But I'd love to have the chance to talk to you both. You know, you should be writing your memoirs, Mr Brock. They would be wonderful. I could help you if you liked.'

Brock smiled. 'Not sure about that.' But Kathy could see he was flattered by the idea.

'Call me Brock, by the way, Donna, and this is Kathy. We were just talking about the Causley trial. You wrote a book about it, I understand?'

'*Psychopaths*, yes. That trial was my first case study.'

'And you considered the Causley boys to be psychopaths?'

'The psychiatrist's evidence at the trial pretty well confirmed it, didn't it? The compulsive lying, the bullying, the torture of animals. I turned up a lot more evidence along those lines in the course of my research.'

Kathy said, 'But now Jarrod Causley appears to be a reformed character.'

'Psychopaths don't reform, Kathy. It's innate. All we can do is try to teach them about consequences. I've no doubt Jarrod had learned something about consequences by the time he reached sixteen, but it wasn't enough to stop him murdering Chloe Honnery. We can only hope that prison has taught him more.'

'And Dean?'

'I doubt if anything could get through to Dean. He was a dark and angry boy, and from what I hear his prison experience was traumatic. I think that will only have made him darker and angrier. I'd hate to meet him in a lonely alleyway.'

'Yes.' Brock nodded. 'They were very different: Jarrod hiding behind a brazen front; Dean trying to project no front at all.'

'Oh, I wish you'd let me speak to you before, Brock. I'd have loved to use that quote.'

Kathy asked, 'Have you had any contact with them since the trial?'

'With Jarrod, yes. When *Psychopaths* came out, he heard about it and wrote to me, care of Golden Press. He told me he thought it was a brilliant book, but I'd made one or two errors he'd like to discuss. For a while, when he was held up north at Wakefield, we corresponded by letter, but eventually, when they brought him down here to Belmarsh, I came to visit him. He was very smooth, tried to use flattery, but once or twice, when that didn't work, he flared up. It was interesting and rather frightening to watch, him struggling to control himself so the guards wouldn't see. He never pretended to me that he was innocent, and never expressed any sympathy for Chloe's poor parents, whose lives were devastated by his little experiment in sadistic violence.'

'Have you seen him since he came out?'

'I've spoken to him a couple of times. He's keen for me to write something—an article or blog—about his exemplary reform. I've resisted the idea.'

'What about Dean?'

'No, I've had no contact with him. I understand he

changed his name and moved away somewhere. Let's hope we don't hear of him again.'

Kathy bit her lip, thinking of the face captured by the Spaniards Inn camera.

'Was that one of your case studies you were talking to just now?' Brock asked.

'It was indeed—Arnold. Have you bumped into him? Actually, you'd be better not to—he was one of my psychopaths, been in prison for twenty years now, and, I would say, totally unreformed.'

'I must get hold of a copy of your book,' Brock said.

She gave a coy smile. 'Well now . . .' She reached into her bag and drew out a paperback. 'I do just happen to have a copy with me. I'd be honoured if you'd accept it.'

'Oh, that's very kind of you.' Brock examined the cover image, a pair of manic eyes staring through a red mist.

'Can I sign it for you?'

'Please.' He handed it back and she wrote inside with a flourish.

'I'm afraid I only have one copy with me,' Priest went on, 'but please let me send you a copy too, Kathy. You may find something of interest in there about the Causley boys. But tell me, do you have any particular reason for being interested in them? I ask because Charlie mentioned them to me. He reminded me that both you, Brock, and he were key figures in their conviction, and here you are now, both accused of murder under strangely similar circumstances. He asked me if I thought they could be behind it.'

'And do you?' Brock asked.

'Well, it's a big leap, but . . .'

'But?'

'Well, frankly, I think those boys would be capable of anything. Jarrod is very intelligent and he's had a long time to plan his revenge, if that's what it is. And as for Dean ...'

'Yes,' Kathy said, 'but why so elaborate? If they wanted to punish Brock and Pettigrew, why wouldn't they just kill them?'

'Good point,' Donna said. 'Perhaps they wanted you to suffer incarceration first, as they had to? You don't look convinced, Kathy. No, of course not—Charlie's is your case, isn't it?'

'It's not just that. Are you suggesting they killed Andrea Giannopoulos too? Why?'

'A trial run perhaps,' Brock said, 'to establish the pattern. They wanted Pettigrew to be known as a serial killer.'

'Just as they are,' Donna added. 'I'm sure Chloe Honnery wasn't their first victim, although Charlie's lawyers wouldn't let me put it in the book. I'd be very happy to expand on anything that interests you. I still have all my notes.'

'What about *The Promised Land*? Did Charlie tell you about that?'

'Oh yes. That is intriguing, isn't it? It's what we're all looking for, one way or another, isn't it—the promised land?'

'Was Jarrod capable of writing it?'

'I haven't seen it, so I couldn't say. But I believe he did study English literature with the Open University while he was in prison, didn't he? I suppose anything's possible with those two. Anyway, I'd better be going. It's been wonderful to meet you both. Do get in touch if I can be of any help.' She gave them each a card.

After she'd gone Kathy read the dedication she'd written at the front of the book she'd given Brock: *To a great detective, David Brock. With all best wishes from a long-time admirer, Donna Priest.*

'Well,' Kathy said, 'you've got a fan there.'

Brock waved a hand dismissively. 'Why don't you take the book, Kathy, see if it sparks any ideas.'

When Kathy got home, she opened Donna Priest's book. The style was much more lively than the crime reports she was used to reading, and in one or two places she was annoyed when Donna passed over some point that Kathy thought needed more explanation. But she couldn't deny that it was entertaining, and the description of Chloe's murder was gripping. But the most interesting thing for Kathy was a passage near the beginning, in which Donna described the boys' normal, relatively untroubled middle-class family life. On a school trip to France, Jarrod's class had visited the D-Day Normandy beaches, and at one point he had slipped and fallen into a rock pool, hitting his head. For a time he had lain unnoticed face down in the water, before he was hauled out and CPR applied. He recovered completely from the incident, but he described it to Donna as 'a near-death experience', and the start of a fascination with death.

~

By the time they reached the flying club, John was having doubts. The clouds overhead looked dark and forbidding, and when they stepped out of the car they were buffeted by gusts of cold wind. They made their way to the clubhouse at one end of the long grass field. A dozen gliders were parked nearby along with one small powered plane. They stepped inside to the sound of a radio crackling, and a man behind the counter gave them a beaming welcome.

'I wondered if you'd still be flying this morning,' John said, 'in this weather.'

'Oh, absolutely. You've got a booking?'

John showed him his receipt for two winch-launched flights.

'Right. I'll be taking you up first, Stewart, and Libby'll pilot you, John. Follow me.'

He led them outside and John watched as he took Stewart to the plane waiting at the end of the strip, explaining the drill and then helping him up into the two-man cockpit. To John's eyes, the machine looked incredibly fragile. His pilot, Libby, joined him and together they watched the first glider being hitched to the winch cable. Suddenly it lurched forward and set off across the field, faster and faster until it arced steeply upwards into the sky. 'Okay, John,' Libby said, 'our turn now.'

When he was strapped inside the little bubble and felt himself being flung up towards the clouds, John gave a whoop, wondering how Stewart was taking it. He could see the other glider high up ahead, banking and beginning to circle over the dark green forest of the South Downs National Park. Soon they were alongside, and John saw Stewart's pale face staring across at them. He gave a wave, and after a moment he got a wave back and what might have been a smile.

Together the two planes circled down and around, Libby giving a commentary on the features below. All too soon John saw the nose of the other glider dip and begin its descent towards the strip. Libby circled one more time then began to take them down, talking about airbrakes and crosswinds and calling their speed. They touched the ground at fifty knots and rolled to a halt where Stewart was standing watching them, eyes wide, long hair blowing in the breeze.

John clambered out and said, 'How was that?' and the boy grinned and said, 'Magic.'

John said, 'Don't know about you, but I could do with a drink.'

A club member directed them to a local pub where the grub was good, and gave Stewart a pamphlet about learning to become a pilot. The lad took it and shook his hand. John felt relieved at the way it had turned out.

It didn't last long. By the time they reached the pub and John had brought them a couple of beers to a table by the window, Stewart seemed to have regressed into some kind of introspective mood. After an unsuccessful attempt to make conversation he finally said, exasperated, 'What's the matter, Stewart? You in love or something?' and saw from the startled look on Stewart's face that he'd hit the bullseye. 'Me too, I think,' John went on. 'Don't fancy my chances though. How about you?'

Stewart looked away, that droop of the head again, and John thought he'd lost him. But then, so softly that John could barely hear, he said, 'She's dead. And that bastard killed her.'

'What?' John stared at him in astonishment. The boy looked over at the door as if he might bolt for it, but John put out his arm. 'No, wait. What are you talking about? Stewart, for God's sake talk to me. Who's dead? What's her name?'

Again John thought he'd lost him, but it was as if the boy had been bottling it up for so long that he could no longer hold it back, and gradually it came out, a strangled sentence at a time.

'Inga.'

It seemed that Inga lived in Riga in Latvia, and was studying computer technology. They had met on the web last November and had been skyping ever since, until about ten days ago when her messages abruptly stopped. She had spoken about her plan to come to England to see Stewart, and for a few days he had hoped to hear that she had arrived. But then he'd seen a report on the web.

He reached into his coat pocket and pulled out his phone, played with the buttons, then showed John a picture of a young, dark-haired woman, and beneath it the message, *Police are asking the public for information about the above woman, aged in her twenties and thought to be originally from Romania, who was found murdered recently in a car park on the edge of Hampstead Heath in London.*

'That's her,' Stewart said, and his eyes welled with tears.

'Are you quite sure?'

'Yes. Brock killed her. That bastard Brock. She warned me about him.'

'Wait, wait,' John said. 'That can't be right.'

'It is.' His teenage vocal cords cracked and he began sobbing. 'Brock was arrested on the same day I stopped hearing from Inga. It's her picture. They got the bit about Romania wrong.'

'Have you got any pictures of Inga?'

Stewart had several on his phone. They did look remarkably like the police image. John noticed that on some of Stewart's pictures a tattoo was visible on the left side of Inga's neck, which wasn't apparent on the police photo. He pulled out his own phone and rang Kathy's number.

'Kathy, hi, it's John. I'm here with Stewart. Something very strange has come up. The girl that Brock's accused of killing, Elena Vasile, did she have a small tattoo on her throat, the left side? Yes?' He hesitated, looking at Stewart's tortured face. 'Kathy, I think you'd better get down here right away. It seems she's been in touch with Stewart for months.'

He listened to the doubt in Kathy's voice and said, 'Hold on a moment.' He turned to Stewart. 'We need to send your pictures of Inga to Kathy. Okay?' The boy hesitated, seeming as if he might refuse, then he began tapping on his phone.

18

John opened the front door and ran out as Kathy drew up outside. He explained about the glider flight and his breakthrough with Stewart, and the boy's sudden confession. Suzanne and Miranda were at an equestrian event in Hastings, and knew nothing of this. He took Kathy inside and upstairs to Stewart's room, where the boy was waiting, an image of Inga on his computer screen. Kathy had never seen Elena alive herself, of course—only Brock had done that—but John was right about the tattoo, and the earrings were the same. She sat down beside him and he showed her a clip that he'd recorded from one of their conversations. The girl was lively and seductive, talking about her troubles at home and her dream of making a new life in England with Stewart.

'I can see what you saw in her,' Kathy said. 'Why don't you tell me all about it. When did it begin?'

'Early October last year,' Stewart mumbled. 'The third.'

So long ago, Kathy thought. Seventeen days before the first Heath murder.

'At first she didn't seem that interested,' Stewart explained. They had a mutual friend on Facebook, and she just wanted to chat to people in England about how things were and whether she'd be able to get a job if she came over. Gradually she told him about her life. Her parents had divorced when she was young and another man moved in with her mother. He was a brute, didn't have a job, and Inga had to put up with him abusing her. In turn, Stewart told her about himself, living with his grandmother, and Brock moving in. She told him that Brock was bad news, just like her stepfather, and how Brock would want to take over. And Stewart could see that what she said was true, that Brock was always hanging around with nothing to do, criticising, like he owned the place. It wasn't just Miranda and Gran and him anymore. Inga told him he had to be smart, and keep a close eye on Brock. He might have another woman somewhere; he might be stealing money from Gran's business.

Stewart paused. 'She was the only person I could really talk to. The only person who really understood where I was coming from, you know?'

'Yes, I can understand that. I really can. So, how did you keep an eye on Brock?'

'Oh, nothing, really.'

'Come on.' Kathy laughed. 'For an ex-cop, Brock's pretty useless with his own security, isn't he? I don't think he's even got a password to get into his laptop.'

Stewart gave a little smirk and avoided her eyes.

Kathy looked around the room, taking it in—the screen-shots for gaming sites, a movie poster image of Jonny Lee Miller in the 1995 crime film *Hackers*, and a copy of *AdvanceED ActionCoding 4.0* lying on the desk beside the computer.

'So . . .' Kathy said, 'you hacked his computer? His phone? His bank accounts?'

Stewart had gone very still, arms folded, head down.

Kathy leaned closer to him and spoke softly. 'I'm going to try to keep you out of trouble, Stewart, but to do that I need to know everything before the heavy mob move in. Let me explain to you how it is. Her real name is Elena Vasile and she came from Bucharest in Romania, not Riga. All the time she told you she was talking to you from Riga she was actually living in a flat in Walworth, South London, with a Romanian gangster, and with him she was involved in a scam to extort money and entrap Brock, which they did very successfully. Brock is now in jail accused of Elena's murder. They used you as a screen, to keep tabs on Brock without implicating themselves.'

She sat back, let that sink in, then went on, 'You were tracking his phone location through the app you set up for your gran, yes?'

Stewart had turned very pale. Finally he whispered, 'When Brock got beaten up that day, she was worried that she hadn't known where he was, and I said I could set it up so she could see where his phone was.'

Kathy detected something false in his tone. 'But Inga had already got you to do it before that, hadn't she?'

He nodded.

So they probably knew that Brock was trailing Elena from

the Shard that night, Kathy was thinking, and were waiting for him when he finally approached her in Walworth.

'Is there anything else I should know, Stewart?'

He shook his head.

'Okay. You and I are going to go to the local police station and you'll make a formal statement—I'll help you. At a later date, you may be called as a witness in court. I'll try to prevent that, but you should be prepared, and if you think of anything else relevant you must tell me.'

He didn't respond.

Kathy said, 'Understand one thing, Stewart: Brock did not murder Inga. She was a fiction invented to fool you, and one day you'll be able to look back on all this and tell great stories about it. But for now, the most important thing is that you tell us everything, okay?'

As she drove him over to Sussex Police headquarters at Lewes to record his statement, she wondered what else she didn't know. This was sounding more and more like a violent scam by the Romanians to extort money, first from Pettigrew and then from Brock, for a fake manuscript. Hughes was right: there was nothing to connect this with the Causley brothers. But there had to be a connection, she was almost sure of it.

Suzanne and Miranda were home when they returned from Lewes, and John explained to them what had happened. Kathy said she'd have to get back to London, but John said he had a couple of things he needed to tell her, and they sat together in the sunroom at the back of the house, at a table on which he had been working.

'I didn't thank you for getting that out of Stewart,' she said to him. 'That was brilliant. You'd make a great detective.'

He smiled. 'Hardly. But I did find something else that I need to show you.'

He picked up a thick book, *The Diaries of George Orwell*, and handed it to her. 'Just about every word that Orwell wrote—essays, letters, diaries—has been published.' He turned to a marked page. 'This is a typical diary entry, for the twenty-first of May 1949, transcribed for print.'

Kathy ran her eye down the page:

7am   Pulse and temperature taken. Try to get back to sleep.
7.30   Sputum cups changed.
8.00   Breakfast then request a bath, but not allowed as
I have already had two this week and they are considered to
be 'weakening'.
10.00 Rest.

The list of banal housekeeping events continued for page after page.

John said, 'Kimberly and I have searched through all the books like this that we could lay our hands on, trying to find a mention of Amar Dasgupta, and we came up with nothing. So, just to be absolutely sure, I thought I'd check some of the original documents, including the diary for his stay in the Cranham tuberculosis sanatorium.'

He picked up a sheet of paper from the table. 'This is a photocopy of the diary page for that day.'

He passed it to Kathy, who recognised the same handwriting she'd seen on the first page of *The Promised Land*.

'Look at the entry for ten that morning,' John said.

Kathy read: *10.00 Rest.* She said, 'It's the same in the printed version.'

'Yes, but look over there, on the right-hand margin.'

He pointed to a smudged scribble on the original page.

'I took a photograph,' John said, and showed her on his phone an enlargement of the scribble. She could make out two faint pencil letters, AD, and an exclamation mark.

'AD,' Kathy said, and looked at John. 'Amar Dasgupta?'

'I think so. I believe that's the day Amar arrived. And because Orwell believed the clinic staff were reading his diary he disguised the entry, and the editor who later transcribed the diaries for publication missed it too.'

Kathy reached across to grip his hand. 'So it's true! The manuscript is genuine.'

'Maybe.' He was looking down at her hand on his.

'What was the other thing you wanted to tell me?' she asked.

'I need to get back to Canada. Term started a week ago and I can't stay any longer. I've got a flight booked first thing on Tuesday.'

'Oh. But I've seen so little of you.'

'You've had a lot on your plate. I guess it's always like that. You have a very demanding job.' He looked sad. 'Anyway, it was good to catch up with you again, Kathy.'

He got to his feet and said, 'I won't hold you back any longer. Good luck.'

~

It was for the best, she told herself, as she drove back to London. But it didn't make her feel any better. She had an uneasy sense of having lost something important.

She shook off the feeling and headed to Walworth. The East Street market was busy as she made her way through the crowd to Rosie's store. Rosie was in the back office, making up an order, and she heaved herself to her feet when she saw Kathy.

'I seen that Roma girl's picture in the paper. Murdered, yeah? But you got the man okay?'

'We're still investigating, Rosie. Maybe you can help me.' She took her iPad from her bag and opened the file of photographs. 'We're looking for people who may have had contact with Elena recently. See if you can recognise any of these men.'

Rosie considered the faces, one by one. Among them were images for Jarrod and Dean Causley, but she didn't react to them. She shook her head.

'Sorry, luv. Don't recognise any of these. Have you tried Old Bert?'

'Who's he?'

'He's got a flat in the same block as the Romas, same floor, next to the stairs. Nosy old bugger, keeps an eye on everyone. Ask him.'

Kathy walked around to the block of flats and made her way up the stairs. When she reached the right floor, she saw the net curtain twitch in the window of the adjoining flat. She knocked on the door, but there was no reaction. She bent down to the letter flap and called out, 'Open up, Bert. I'm the police.'

Finally there was a shuffling sound and the door opened on a chain. 'Whaddya want?'

'I want to show you something.'

Reluctantly he let her in and she showed him the images. When he came to Dean Causley's picture, he pointed. 'Mean bugger. Threatened me he did.'

'Why?'

'Saw me watching him. Told me to fuck off or he'd bash me, him and the other one.'

'There was someone else with him?' She flicked through the images and he stopped her at Jarrod's.

'That's him. The two of them came to see the Romas, down there.'

'How often?'

'I seen them three or four times, maybe more.'

Kathy showed him Elena's picture.

'Oh yes, she was there, and that Paki girl, Uzma. Brasses, the pair of them.'

'Prostitutes?'

'Yeah, brasses, toms. 'Course they were.'

She couldn't get him to be more specific about when the Causleys had visited, or how often. She thanked him and returned to her car. She'd seen the empty bottles in the hallway and smelled it on his breath. It was a start, but she'd need more to convince Torrens. She wondered what other loose end she could probe and thought of John's impression that the Orwell expert, Mortimer Hartley, had already seen *The Promised Land* page. Was that possible? Was he involved? She checked with her office and got a number for Hartley's address. An answering service replied. Sir Mortimer was currently overseas. Did she want to record a message? Kathy said no.

Who else? She tried the number for Golden Press, and when Angela answered she asked her if she'd heard anything in publishing circles about Charlie's case or the manuscript that he'd claimed to have seen, *The Promised Land*.

'Nothing concrete,' Angela replied.

Kathy heard the caution in her voice, and said, 'Anything, Angela. Anything at all.'

There was silence for moment, then Angela said, 'I shouldn't really be talking to you, should I? You're the one who's trying to get him locked up for life. I went to see him the other day, at Belmarsh, and I was shocked at how he was. He broke down while we were talking. He burst into tears. It was so awful. He begged me not to believe he was guilty.'

'Angela, my job isn't to lock Charlie up, it's to discover the truth. It's just possible that he was the victim of a plan to extort money over that manuscript, and I need to know anything that might help me get to the truth.'

Another long silence, then, 'I did hear something . . . I'm not sure.'

'Go on.'

'When I first started here, I was pretty inexperienced, and the senior editor at the time took me under her wing, and we became good friends. After a couple of years she moved on to one of the big publishers, and later they sent her to New York, but we've stayed in touch. She rang me last night. I'd already told her all about Charlie's problems, of course, and she wanted to know if there were any developments. Then she told me the latest publishing gossip in New York. There was a rumour going round of a bidding war between three of the major publishers for a manuscript of an undiscovered novel by a famous writer, she didn't know who. What made her think of Charlie was that she'd seen the top Orwell authority, Sir Mortimer Hartley, in New York, having lunch with one of the publishers who was supposed to be bidding.'

'Did she have any idea who was selling this manuscript?'

'No, it's all very hush-hush. Big money, apparently. That's all I know.'

'Okay. Thank you, Angela. I promise I'll keep an open mind about Charlie until I'm sure I've learned everything. Let me know if you hear anything else, will you?'

Kathy rang off and said to herself, *Steve Weiner*. She turned the car and headed for Putney.

She found a space on the high street not far from the Sweet Pepper Café, parked and went inside. The corner table that served as Weiner's office was empty, and she asked the girl behind the counter where he was.

'Oh, he went to New York about a week ago . . . no, maybe it was longer than that. Full of it, he was, how he was going to take a big bite out of the Big Apple.'

An older woman came out of the kitchen with a tray of pastries and said, 'Talking about Steve?'

'Yes, I was just saying he's in New York.'

'No, he's back. Got back last night. He's . . . Steve!'

Kathy turned and saw the literary agent in the doorway. He looked different—hair groomed, a smart suit and gleaming white shirt, dark tie, and carrying a smart new travel bag. He frowned, recognising Kathy, and looked as if he might make a run for it.

'Mr Weiner,' Kathy said, and quickly went over to him. 'We need to talk.'

'No time, I'm afraid. On my way to the airport.' He waved to the women behind the counter and turned on his heel.

Kathy followed him outside, where a cab was waiting at the kerb. She pushed in front of Weiner, showing her police ID to the cabbie. 'The ride's cancelled,' she said. 'Get going.' The driver muttered something and took off.

'Hey!' Weiner yelled. 'I've got a plane to catch!'

'I'll give you a lift,' Kathy said. 'My car's over there.'

Weiner looked around, furious, then checked his watch and reluctantly followed her.

'Where to?' Kathy said as they set off.

'City Airport,' he snarled.

'And where are you flying to?'

'Mind your own fucking business.'

Kathy swerved into the kerb and pulled to a stop, snapping the door locks. 'This is going to be a slow journey if you don't cooperate.'

He swore softly.

'What was that?'

'Okay, okay. I'm going to Frankfurt. Get a fucking move on, I'm late.'

Kathy set off again. 'And who's in Frankfurt?'

Weiner said nothing, face turned away, and Kathy put her foot on the brake.

'Oh, Jesus,' he groaned. 'Welthammer.'

'Who's he?'

'The Welthammer Publishing Group.'

'Who are . . . ?'

'One of the big five global publishing houses, that's who.'

'And they're bidding for *The Promised Land*, are they?'

His head jerked around to face her. 'How . . . ?'

'I know a lot of things, Steve. And I'm sure Welthammer and the others would be interested to hear that you're involved in a criminal conspiracy to sell a forged manuscript.' She caught the expression on his face, shocked, appalled.

'No . . . no, that's not true.'

'You're going to have a big job convincing me of that. Everything you told me the last time was a lie. I think I may just drive you straight to the nearest cop shop and have you charged with fraud and conspiracy to murder.'

'No!' His voice was an agonised whine now. 'I know nothing about any murders. I bought exclusive rights to the *Promised Land* manuscript from Shari Mitra in good faith.'

'But you and I both know that Shari Mitra was not who she said she was. She was a fraud.'

'No, she wasn't. It was the name she used to stop her abusive husband finding her, that's all. But she—Uzma Jamali—was the great-granddaughter of Amar Dasgupta, who was George Orwell's close friend and the rightful owner of his last novel. I have proof of that.'

'You'll have to convince me.'

'Okay, okay . . . Hey, this isn't the way to the airport!'

'You're going to make a formal statement under caution, Steve. I don't care about the manuscript. I'm running a police investigation into the murder of Uzma Jamali, and you're a material witness.'

'Oh shit.' Weiner snatched out his phone and started frantically typing.

'What are you doing?'

'Finding out when the next flights to Frankfurt are. I'll tell you everything, but you've got to get me to Frankfurt today, otherwise I'm getting my lawyer and I won't say a word. There's a flight from Gatwick in three hours. Deal?'

'Deal,' Kathy said.

When she had him seated in an interview room in Gatwick security, Kathy cautioned him and he began his story.

'When Uzma ran from her pig of a husband, she had nowhere to go. She had no money and slept rough for a few nights until she met a Romanian girl, Elena Vasile, who was sorry for her and took her back to her place in Walworth. She got her a job in a kebab place, where she washed dishes. What she wanted was to go home to Pakistan, and eventually, with what she earned at her job and with a loan from Elena, she bought a cheap airline ticket back. But when she got home her family were furious. They disowned her and told her to go back to her husband. The only one who sided with her was her grandmother, who was the favourite daughter of Amar Dasgupta, who had left her an heirloom, the unpublished manuscript of the great English writer, George Orwell. She gave Uzma the manuscript and told her to go back to London and sell it to a publisher for lots of money. Uzma agreed and came to me—and also, although I didn't know it at the time, to Golden Press.'

'Why you?'

'When she returned, she told the story to Elena, who said she'd be better to get an agent. Elena looked on Google and reckoned I had the best website.'

'Can you prove any of this?'

'Uzma's story? Of course I can—people like Welthammer wouldn't give me the time of day if I couldn't. I've got copies of birth, marriage and death certificates of Amar and the others. I've got Orwell's letter to Amar at the Savoy Hotel and a photograph of them together at Cranham, and a copy of Amar's will leaving the manuscript to his daughter. I've also had a team of experts authenticate the manuscript—a forensic linguist, an Indian historian and the world's top authority on Orwell. They all agree that it's genuine.'

'What about a document scientist, to check the age of the paper and ink?'

'We confirmed that the typeface was that of a 1930s Smith Premier Home Portable typewriter, but we couldn't do the other tests because Uzma wouldn't release the original, only a photocopy. She was scared if she did people would steal it. She agreed to release it only when a contract had been signed, but then she was murdered and the original has never been found. That's why we're in a hurry. I have a binding agreement with Uzma to sell the book on her behalf, but I don't want whoever has the original to beat me to it.'

'All this must have cost you quite a bit.'

'Believe me, I've got everything riding on this.'

'Yes, I can see that. And when you heard that Uzma had also approached Charles Pettigrew you must have been very worried.'

'I didn't know anything about that, not until I read that she'd been murdered in Pettigrew's house. That scared the shit out of me—he might have killed me.'

'So you say, but to me it sounds like you have a big motive to get rid of competitors. I want to know where you were on the evening of Monday the twenty-sixth of October, the night Uzma died.'

Weiner checked his phone and came up with an evening with friends in a pub.

'Also the morning of Friday, January the eighth.'

'Why then?'

'Just check.'

He did. 'Oh yeah, I was in Oxford, with our Orwell expert, Sir Mortimer Hartley. But . . . I don't want you telling him I'm suspected of being involved in a murder case. He'd have a heart attack.'

'How did you travel to Oxford?'

'I caught an early train . . . yeah, here we are, the 7.23, and I came back in the afternoon, the 3.15, got into Paddington at 4.18.'

Kathy took him through it again, pressing for details and the names of people who could confirm aspects of his story. Finally she released him, just in time to catch the Frankfurt flight.

~

Kathy was able to arrange a telephone conference with Commander Torrens and Alun Hughes. She told them the new information she'd uncovered, and when she finished Torrens, as before, asked Hughes for his reaction.

'It's still pretty thin,' he said reluctantly. 'Kathy's provided a possible way in which an outsider could have tracked Brock's movements that morning, but she hasn't established that it did in fact happen. She's also got a blurry photograph of someone who might resemble Dean Causley near the scene of the first murder, and the opinion of "Old Bert"—' he said it with a derisive snort '—that he may have seen two men resembling the Causleys at some unspecified time and place, no doubt between bottles of cheap vodka.' Perhaps he realised that was probably overdoing it a bit, for he added, 'But full marks anyway, Kathy, for effort.'

'We have to follow it up,' Torrens said. 'For insurance, if nothing else. After our last meeting, I mentioned your Causley boys theory to the assistant commissioner, Kathy, and she was interested. If true, it would put an end to the Jarvis–Walcott debacle and to the embarrassment of having a former senior homicide detective up on a murder charge. All the more reason therefore why we—you—have to make it absolutely watertight, one way or the other, before the press get wind of it and accuse us of a whitewash. For that reason, we will keep it covert for the time being—electronic and physical surveillance only. See where that gets us. Any word on the other one—Dean?'

'No. He doesn't appear to be using his Ethan Hawke identity.'

'Could one of the brothers have done this on his own?'

'It's possible, sir, but I think unlikely.'

Kathy immediately organised a team of officers for the surveillance of Jarrod Causley, and the telecommunications intercept branch for the monitoring of his calls. 'At this stage,' she said, 'it's important that he doesn't know we're watching him. We want information on his movements on these dates in particular, and on any contacts with his younger brother Dean, whom we believe is living under an assumed name unknown to us.'

By the end of the afternoon everything was in place, and they began the long, patient process of sifting through information as it came in, looking for the anomalies or openings that might yield leads to a hidden life.

19

Another Monday without visitors to the prison. He was spending more time in the library these days, helping the librarian, Bryan, with an ongoing project to transfer all their records onto the new computer system. Bookish and gentle, the librarian seemed an unlikely employee of a prison, and they got on well. Today Brock mentioned that he'd once known a former Belmarsh inmate by the name of Jarrod Causley, and was surprised when Bryan nodded and said, 'Yes, I know.'

'How come?'

'I've kept in touch with him, off and on. When you got arrested, he told me you'd been the one who arrested him. He thought it was kind of funny you being in the same position now.'

'I'll bet he did.'

'He wasn't like gloating or anything. Just said it was poetic justice, him having been innocent.' Bryan sounded a little defensive, Brock thought.

'Is that what he told you?'

'Yeah.' Bryan busied himself with his papers. 'I'd better get these filed away.'

'So how's Jarrod doing these days?'

'Great, really well. He's got a job in a public library and enjoying it. Amazing, really, how he's been able to readjust after fourteen years inside.'

'That's good to hear. You must have helped him lay the groundwork for that.'

'Yes, he did an external degree while he was here. He was very focused, very determined to put the past behind him.'

'That was an arts degree, was it?'

'Yes, majoring in English literature.'

'Twentieth century?'

'Yes, why?'

'Oh, I was just thinking that I should get down to some serious reading. I thought I might have a go at Orwell, maybe. Did Jarrod read Orwell?'

Bryan frowned. 'Probably. *Animal Farm* . . .'

'How about *Burmese Days*? Did he read that one?'

Bryan looked puzzled. 'It's not one of his popular books. I don't know if we've got it. Look it up.' He picked up his papers and moved away.

Brock knew that it was there because he'd borrowed it himself. He tried to find out from the library computer who else had borrowed it in the past, but wasn't able to access the information.

~

At six thirty that evening Kathy arrived back in her flat and set about preparing a vegetarian curry—cooking therapy— while she listened to the team reporting in on Jarrod. He had worked until five at the library, filled two shopping bags with groceries at the nearby Sainsbury's and then caught a Piccadilly line train to the Manor House stop at Woodberry Down, a couple of miles east of Hampstead Heath. From there it was a short walk to his two-bedroom flat on the sixth floor of a new block. Kathy knew that Jarrod had paid just under a million pounds for it, no mortgage, ten months before, and that it had absorbed the major part of his share of the brothers' inheritance from their parents' estate.

As she kneaded the dough for the coriander and onion flatbreads she'd decided to try making, Kathy listened to Jarrod chatting on his phone to a woman he'd met on the web. They seemed to be in the early days of a relationship, and Jarrod sounded very relaxed and confident, talking about the view from his living room window out over the landscaped water basins of the East and West reservoirs. Kathy knew that view because it was on the screen of the laptop sitting on her kitchen table, copied from the estate agent's website.

Her phone rang, a call from John to say goodbye. He was all packed, ready to leave early the next morning. Things were going well at Suzanne's, he said, where the weekend's events seemed to have had a galvanising effect on Stewart, who was now actually taking part in mealtime conversations, and offering to wash up.

Kathy laughed. 'That is a miracle.'

'Yeah. Maybe it's the realisation that he may have to appear as a witness in a court of law and it might be good to have a few friends around. Poor guy's still a bit broken up over Inga from Riga though. Any developments your end?'

'Yes, too early to say, but I'm hopeful.'

'Good. About the manuscript, I've had an email from one of my PhD students back in Montreal who's been working on it for me. His area is stylometrics, analysing texts through the frequency and pattern of words. He looked at Orwell for me, to compare with *The Promised Land*. With such a small sample of just two pages he can't say anything definite, but he tells me the indications aren't promising. I'll go over it with him when I get back, but he thinks it's probably a fake.'

'Is that right? But what about Weiner's experts?'

'Yes. We don't know what methods they used, do we? Though I know Mortimer Hartley isn't a great believer in computational models such as we use. But as I say, our sample is too small to give a definite answer. We really need a much bigger chunk, preferably the whole novel.'

'Little chance of that I'm afraid.'

They discussed their plans for the evening. John was taking the household out for a last meal at a local Indian, and Kathy told him she was also having a curry.

'Great minds,' he said, a little wistfully. 'I wish . . .'

He hesitated and Kathy said, 'Yes? What do you wish?'

'I wish I could be there with you. I miss you, Kathy.' Then he added, 'Am I out of line?'

For a moment she didn't know how to reply, but then she said, 'No, not at all. I wish you were here too. We've had so little time to get acquainted again.'

They were silent for a moment, then he said, 'I'll come back to London as soon as I can.'

After she'd hung up Kathy turned back to her cooking, so deep in thought that she almost missed the start of another conversation on Jarrod's phone, this time with a man.

'Hi, Jarrod.'

'Hello, mate. How are you?' Kathy registered how intimate, almost seductive, Jarrod's voice had become.

'Good, good. Saw your old friend again today.'

'Oh yes? And what was the great detective up to then?'

'You'll never guess.'

'Go on, surprise me.'

'He came into the library and just happened to mention that he knew an old inmate called Jarrod Causley.'

'Did he now?'

'Yes. So I told him I knew you, and he started asking me all these questions.'

'Like what?'

'He asked how you were doing now. I told him you were doing well, working in a public library. That was all right, wasn't it?'

'Sure. What else did he ask about?'

'What you'd studied while you were inside. That's all.'

'That's all? You sure?'

'He asked me about books you read. He was interested in George Orwell.'

'Orwell? *Nineteen Eighty-Four?*'

'No, another one. *Burmese Days.*'

'You sure?'

'Of course I'm sure.'

There was silence on the line until finally the caller said, 'Jarrod? You okay?'

'Yeah. I've gotta go.' Jarrod's voice had changed, become brisk, forceful. 'I'll be in touch.'

The line went dead, and immediately Kathy got on her phone and called the car that was waiting outside Jarrod's apartment block. 'I think he's on the move.'

She shrugged on her coat, grabbed her bag and phone, all the time listening on an earphone to the reports from the watchers. Jarrod had emerged from his block wearing a dark jacket and cap and was running in a westerly direction through the rain.

'He's reached the main road, Green Lanes, the bus stop on the northbound side. He's checking the cars going by. I'm driving past him now, Foxtrot Two. Over to you.'

The second car reported a few minutes later. 'He's boarded an N29 double-decker northbound. I'm following.'

Kathy crossed the river and headed north but soon got caught up in heavy traffic made worse by the rain, now a deluge. She sat, tapping her hands in frustration on the steering wheel in time to the steady sweep of the windscreen wipers, as she listened to the equally slow progress of Jarrod's bus up the A105, through Haringey and Turnpike Lane. Finally there was an urgent, 'He's got off. Wood Green Mall. Repeat, Wood Green Mall.'

The lead car had passed the bus stop and turned into a side street beyond, while the second car was stuck in the traffic a hundred yards behind. The result was a delay of a couple of minutes before their passengers reached the mall entrance in pursuit. They reported no sign of Jarrod in the ground-floor mall and one of the police took the escalators to the upper level while the other went into the big Primark store. When she couldn't find him there, she went next door to the market and food hall, where she finally caught sight of him, buying cheese at one of the stalls. He seemed in no hurry now, she reported, strolling from counter to counter, and he was still there half an hour later when Kathy turned into the car park.

She joined the officer who pointed him out, discussing something with a fishmonger. Watching him now, and remembering his previous urgency, Kathy asked when the markets closed.

The officer checked her watch. 'Still another hour,' she said.

Kathy felt she was missing something. It occurred to her that Jarrod hadn't used his phone since he abruptly cut off the call with Bryan, and she asked one of the stallholders if there was a public phone nearby. He pointed it out, at the entrance to the markets. Kathy took a note of its number and requested a search for calls made in the previous hour. She didn't have long to wait for the answer: only one call had been made, in the minutes immediately after Jarrod arrived in the mall, to a mobile number. Kathy requested a location and was told it was currently at an address in Islington, in inner north-east London. She returned to her car and told one of the surveillance crews to follow her there.

On the way, they were informed that there was no longer a signal from the mobile. As she approached the Islington address Kathy heard the sirens and saw the glow in the night sky, and as she turned into the narrow street of terrace houses she saw a fire brigade ladder silhouetted in the rain against a burning roof.

What with the jam of emergency vehicles and the milling

crowd of residents and bystanders, it took a while to establish that the fire had occurred in the attic flat at the end of a terrace row, and thanks to the swift arrival of the fire brigade had been confined to the top floor, which was completely gutted, though lower floors were badly damaged by water from the hoses. The flat was being rented by a young man known to neighbours as Robert Leonard, who had been living there for over a year. Two people identified him as the man in the police picture of Dean Causley. There was no sign of him at the scene. It was Alfarsi who later pointed out that Robert Sean Leonard and Ethan Hawke had played roommates in the movie *Dead Poets Society*.

Kathy ordered the team at Wood Green to detain Jarrod for questioning at the nearby police custody centre and it was there, an hour later, that she finally came face to face with the elder of the two Causley brothers. She didn't expect to get much more from him than one or two statements that she might later use against him, as well as a first impression of his personality. For a few minutes before going in she watched him on a monitor, seated with arms folded, staring unblinking at the door.

'Jarrod.' She smiled at him as she came into the room. 'I'm Detective Chief Inspector Kathy Kolla and this is Detective Sergeant Andrew Alfarsi.'

She took a seat and looked around the room. 'They've done this place up since I was last here. Sorry to break into your evening, but I need your urgent assistance. We're anxious to contact your brother Dean and we're hoping you can help us.'

She gave him another smile and he just stared back at her.

'Can you tell us how to contact him?'

He took his time to answer with one word, 'Why?', loading the word with contempt.

'There was a fire in a flat in Islington earlier this evening where we understand he was staying, and we're concerned for his safety. So how do we contact him?'

'I can't help you.'

'But surely you've been in touch with him, haven't you?'

Jarrod didn't open his mouth, his eyes fixed on Kathy's.

'When did you last speak to Dean?'

Again no response.

'Why are you being so obstructive? I asked you a simple question—when did you last speak to your brother? Why don't you want to give me an answer? Have you two been up to something?'

Jarrod didn't appear to move a muscle, but his gaze underwent a subtle malignant transformation.

Kathy said, 'I'll have to remind you that you're still on probation, Jarrod. This uncooperative attitude will not go down well with your probation board.'

He finally unfolded his arms and leaned forward across the table towards Kathy, who sensed Alfarsi shift at her side. 'I have no idea where my brother is,' Jarrod said. 'I know nothing of any fire. I can't help you.'

'Very well. I have a warrant here to search your home. You'll remain here while we do that. It may take some time.'

~

It was almost midnight when they finished, and it would have taken longer in any other apartment. But Jarrod had retained a prison inmate's economy of possessions; he would have been able to pack almost everything into a single suitcase. All but the clothes, which seemed to have been his one indulgence, along with the huge TV screen. Strangely, for a librarian who had recently gone through an arts degree program, there were no books and hardly any paper at all. The construction of the modern building left little room for concealed places, and these—the backs of fitted cupboards, skirting boards, architraves, plumbing cavities—were quickly checked. They found nothing. Their only satisfaction was to leave a number of electronic bugs inside the wall sockets. Kathy phoned the Wood Green custody centre and told them to let Jarrod go.

20

The week passed in a kind of suspended frenzy as Kathy tried without success to break into Jarrod's silence. She interviewed him a second and a third time, now in the presence of his solicitor, who advised him to answer none of her questions. She also interviewed the Belmarsh prison librarian, Bryan, whom she suspected of having a closer relationship with Jarrod than he claimed. Bryan protested that he had given him no more than prison gossip about Brock, with whom Jarrod seemed to be obsessed, although he had never heard Jarrod utter threats against Brock or hint in any way that he might be responsible for Brock being in prison.

Meanwhile, forensics examined every charred fragment from the Islington fire and were unable to find anything significant, or extract anything of value from the molten lumps of electronic equipment found there. A general alert was put out for Dean Causley and Kathy's team interviewed dozens of people in the neighbourhood, trying to build up a picture of his life. He came across as an isolated, friendless hermit who only went out into the immediate area for supplies. His close neighbours complained about his loud music late at night and his electronic equipment tripping fuses in the ancient wiring in the block.

When these more direct approaches yielded nothing, Kathy widened the searches, pulling in more people to help. Dozens of calls from the public of sightings of Dean had to be followed up and people who might have been on friendly terms with him while he was in prison were interviewed. Original witnesses from the time of the first two Heath murders were also spoken to again and shown pictures of the Causley boys and asked if they remembered seeing them back then. Nobody did.

By Friday she was running out of inspiration and becoming reconciled to the idea that this wasn't going to be easy. Under pressure from Torrens over the lack of hard evidence, she was forced to return detectives to other jobs and wind down the Causley investigation.

That evening she phoned John, now back in Montreal. He had no more information about *The Promised Land*, and had heard nothing further of Sir Mortimer Hartley. Listening to his voice, Kathy realised how much she missed him, and after she rang off, and to avoid dwelling on this, she forced herself to take a closer look at Donna Priest's book *Psychopaths*, in the hope that it might give her some new insight into the Causleys. She reached the end without learning anything new and, disappointed, put it down and got up to go to bed. In the shower, her mind still preoccupied with the two brothers, she remembered Priest's claim to have found out more about them than she had been able to put in the book. She wrapped a towel around herself and checked her phone for the author's number.

Donna seemed delighted to hear that Kathy had been reading her book.

'I thought it was very interesting,' Kathy said, trying to sound enthusiastic.

'But? It sounds like you've got a missing "but" in that sentence, Kathy.'

'Well, your research was very thorough, and I just wondered what you might have left out, maybe from shortage of space.'

'Ah yes. Not so much because of space, more to do with Charlie's lawyers—they were nervous about some of the things I couldn't prove, such as the possible link to the drowning of the girl in Majorca. Anything special you're after?'

'We'd like to talk to Dean, but he's disappeared. Any ideas?'

'Interesting. Any particular reason you want to talk to him? Or shouldn't I ask?'

'Best not.'

'Well . . . there was the aunt and uncle in Devon. Have you checked with them?'

Kathy took a note of their names. 'Anything else?'

Donna hummed. 'Not really. There was one thing, but I shouldn't really tell you. I promised their mother . . .'

Kathy waited while she made up her mind. Then, 'Long after I wrote the book, about three years ago, I got a call from their mother, Linda Causley. I was surprised, because she'd been pretty hostile towards me when I was interviewing people for the book, insisting the boys were innocent right to the end. But now her husband had recently died, and she was in poor health herself and probably knew she didn't have long either. She asked if I'd call and see her in Purley, so I agreed and got a train down there. She gave me tea and cake and we talked about this and that until finally she came to the point. When he died, she'd gone through her husband's papers and come across an envelope addressed to her. Inside was a note from him telling her he'd found the enclosed packet of Polaroid snapshots. The pictures had been taken by her boys, showing them taking turns to hurt and finally drown little Chloe. She felt it was discovering these photographs that had finished her husband off. "He couldn't live with it," she said, "and neither can I."'

Donna took a deep breath, then went on, 'She asked me to take them. If the boys came out of jail reformed characters, then I should burn them. But if they hadn't changed I should use them to have them locked away forever.'

Kathy said, 'You've got them, these photographs?'

'No. They were horrible. I didn't want to touch them. I told her it was too great a responsibility and I couldn't do it. I told her to give them to the police, but I don't think she did. She asked me not to tell anyone else about the pictures, and she died a few months later. I don't know what happened to them.'

Kathy said, 'But the police searched the house during the original investigation, didn't they? Why didn't they find the photos then?'

'They weren't in the house. They were in the garden. Linda took me out there and showed me—all that shrubbery and herbaceous borders. An old azalea bush had died and when her husband dug it up he found the packet, wrapped up in plastic and tape, buried in its roots.'

~

Sunday afternoon and the prison was quiet, a busy day for visitors. Brock remembered his early childhood, when his grandfather had insisted on taking the whole family on Sunday afternoons to the cemetery to look at the graves of their departed relatives. Now they come to the jail, he thought. Progress.

He noticed Charlie Pettigrew come out into the exercise yard to stretch his legs. He seemed different, Brock thought, his stride more confident.

'Hello, Brock,' he called, and gave him a wave. 'Can I join you?'

'Be my guest.' Brock shifted over on the bench. 'You're looking brighter today.'

'Yes, well, I'm feeling brighter. I had a revelation last night.'

'Really?'

'Yes. My new cellmate woke me—very green he is, very anxious. He was having a nightmare, calling out in his sleep.' Charlie did a vivid imitation of the terrified voice: '*Oh no! Don't, please! No, no, no!*'

'Disturbing for you,' Brock said.

'Strangely not. I remembered how I'd been when I first arrived, just like that, frightened of every sudden movement, every raised voice. And then it occurred to me that I'd been like that ever since I was a boy. Oh, of course I learned to hide it, to put on adult manners and pretend I was on top of everything. But I wasn't, not really. I knew I was a failure, a fraud hiding in the intimidating shadows of my father and grandfather, pretending to be proudly continuing their great tradition at Golden Press, but in reality watching it slowly die around me.

'Then disaster struck. In my panic to achieve just one real success I got myself caught up with *The Promised Land*, and landed myself in here. And I lay there in the dark and I thought, "All your life, Charlie boy, you've been terrified of this, of being exposed as a total failure. And now you've reached the bottom. It doesn't get any worse than this, and you know what? You can handle it. Yes, you can. From now on, for what's left of your miserable life, you can hold your head up and say, I can handle it."'

'Well,' Brock said, 'that's the spirit, Charlie.' He held out his hand. 'Congratulations. I admire you for that.'

Charlie ducked his head, embarrassed, but took Brock's hand. 'Thanks. I just have to keep remembering that things can't get any worse. From now on it's only got to get better.'

~

As soon as she got to work on Monday morning, Kathy retrieved the scene of crime team's report on the Islington fire. They had checked the top-floor apartment thoroughly, worked painstakingly through all the sodden debris and ashes to confirm that accelerants had been used to cause the intense fire, and made up a probable list of all the equipment that had been packed into the small rooms. They'd searched the small garden at the back of the block but hadn't dug it up, and neither had her own people. She set about organising it, and accompanied the team out there.

They set to work with a backhoe and shovels beneath the dark ruin of the end terrace, its walls blackened, its shattered roof and chimney like a rotted tooth against the sky, its lower floors abandoned from water and debris damage. Kathy directed them to uproot the shrubs and break up the small area of paving. They uncovered the foundations of a wartime air-raid shelter beneath what passed for a rockery. But no hidden evidence.

The team leader, checking his watch, came to her. 'There's nothing here, boss.'

Kathy hesitated. Just because they'd buried incriminating material in a garden once didn't make it an MO. Yet without hard evidence the police case was circumstantial. 'One more sweep,' she said.

And finally, crawling over every inch of the place, they found what she was looking for, a tiny Toshiba 32-gigabyte SD card from a digital camera in its protective plastic case, hidden inside a slot cut into the side of a timber post in the back fence.

When she returned to the Box, Kathy waited while forensic technicians scanned and checked the card for DNA and prints before giving it to her. She inserted it into a computer and saw that it contained five video files. Word had gone around the office and everyone had abandoned their desks and were clustered beside her as she opened the first file.

The camera panned across a parkland scene lit by a silvery morning light, and came to rest on the figure of Jarrod

Causley, standing beside a small lake. He glowered at the camera, breath condensing in the cold air, and rubbed his hands before pulling on a pair of latex gloves. He was wearing dark blue overalls and a cap. There was a bag at his feet, and from it he pulled out a hammer which he brandished at the camera, then pulled a document from the bag, a folded map.

There was a break to another scene, a copse of trees from which a figure emerged, running down a path towards the camera. Kathy recognised Andrea Giannopoulos, dressed in the track pants and singlet in which she was later found. She slowed as she approached Jarrod, who was standing in the middle of the path, studying the map. They exchanged a few words. The sound was muffled, the words hard to make out. Then Andrea turned towards the camera, seeing the other person for the first time. She looked puzzled, her feet still taking little steps as she jogged on the spot. Jarrod moved behind her, dropped the map to the ground, revealing the hammer in his hand. As Andrea began to move off he swung it in an arc to hit the side of her head. She staggered but didn't fall and he pounced on her, bringing her down and starting to pound her face, again and again. The camera moved in, observing his savage attack. At one point he jerked back as a jet of blood squirted into his eyes. He looked angry as he wiped at it with his sleeve, then returned to his work. When he was finally satisfied, he sat back on his haunches, breath steaming from his nostrils like smoke.

The clip came to an abrupt end. The room was silent, everyone staring at the blank screen.

Kathy didn't feel shock; just disgust, and a helpless pity for Andrea.

She took a deep breath and clicked on the second file.

It began with a long-distance shot of a woman striding alone up a grassy slope—Parliament Hill, Kathy guessed. At the top, she stopped to chat for a moment to a dog-walker, then moved on. The scene changed to an area of thick bushes where a gloved and hooded figure was pulling on a surgical mask and plastic goggles. Kathy caught a glimpse of his face, Dean Causley this time, and she registered his care with the preparations, learning from the first murder, insulating himself against what was to follow. He bent to a bag to get the hammer and a green towel.

The attack happened in a sudden flurry of movement, but it seemed to go wrong. Caroline Jarvis was more heavily built than Andrea Giannopoulos, and she managed to swing an arm to knock Dean off balance before he could hit her with the hammer. Once again the poor sound quality, rather as if it had been recorded underwater, gave the scene a sinister eeriness. Caroline turned and began to run and the image became chaotic as Jarrod must have joined in to bring her down. Then her face filled the screen, and her mouth formed an inaudible scream that was abruptly cut off as the hammer slammed down on her nose.

She was dragged into the bushes beside the pond and Dean hit her a couple more times, then looked up, breathing heavily, and Jarrod urged him to do more, do it properly.

When it was over, there was a further scene of Dean arranging the crime scene, several times corrected by impatient instructions from his older brother. He tugged the necklace from Caroline's neck and slipped it into a plastic pouch. From another pouch he took out a wad of tissue and wiped it carefully on her bag. And from a third pouch he took something barely visible and placed it in the bloody pulp of her face.

Kathy froze the picture and reran the scene. Someone said, 'What's he doing?' and she answered, 'The dog's hair. I think he's planting the dog's hair.' And thought, So how did they get hold of that?

The third file began with the Causleys waiting at the back door of Charles Pettigrew's house. Jarrod, wearing a backpack, knocked on the door. It was opened by Uzma Jamali, who waved them in, making some comment about their overalls. Kathy wondered if the tech people would be able to do something with the sound, which was almost inaudible. Uzma led them inside to the study and showed them Pettigrew sitting asleep in the armchair, a thick manuscript on his lap. They returned to the hall and climbed the stairs, Uzma leading, while Jarrod slipped off his backpack and drew out the hammer.

The murder of the judge, Sir Roger Walcott, took up the fourth video: Jarrod pulling on a mask and gloves outside the judge's hotel room, barging in when he responded to the knock and a blur of action as they subdued him. Finally the camera panned around the bathroom, with Walcott now slumped, strangled, on the marble tiles. Dean was on his knees nearby, tapping on the judge's laptop, while the head and shoulders of a teddy bear were visible in a bag lying on the floor nearby.

'Now Elena and Brock,' Kathy said at last, and reluctantly clicked the final file, knowing what they were about to see. The only surprise was the spirited way in which Elena challenged Jarrod when he told her to make the call to Brock to cancel their meeting, as if she already didn't trust him. They were standing in the car park next to Suzanne's red Merc, and when she noticed Dean filming them she turned and began gesturing at him. That was her mistake, for behind her Jarrod had drawn out Brock's knife. He reached forward and took hold of her hair and rammed the knife into her back. Her mouth opened in astonishment, her body arching out as Jarrod stabbed her twice more, then let her drop to the ground.

Kathy felt drained. Behind her Alfarsi was saying how lucky the brothers had been. 'Anyone could have driven into that car park and seen them,' he insisted. 'Or standing at the back of Pettigrew's house, or in the corridor of Walcott's hotel. They were just bloody lucky.'

But also clever, Kathy thought. She imagined how long it would have taken to work it all out, to arrange all the other details that hadn't been recorded—the grooming of Uzma and Elena, the stalking of Andrea and Caroline and Walcott, the baiting of Pettigrew and Brock, the hacking of computers, the forging of the manuscript. And she imagined the long nights in prison cells when Jarrod had thought the whole elaborate plan through.

'Scene of crime will have to study these,' she said. 'See where we should have caught them out. There are lots of lessons here.'

Then she got to her feet. 'Let's get Jarrod.'

21

Brock was packing his few belongings into a plastic bag when Danny returned to their cell. Danny said, 'You going to lunch, mate?'

'Yes,' Brock said. 'I think I'll have half-a-dozen oysters followed by beer-battered fish and triple-fried chips, washed down by a bottle of red or maybe just a couple of pints of best. Maybe finish off with a helping of tiramisu. Very partial to tiramisu. Accompanied by a glass or two of muscat.'

'Yeah, that'll be the day.'

'It is the day.' Brock held up his bag. 'I'm leaving you, Danny.'

'What?'

'They finally worked out that I'm innocent, just like I told you.'

'Blimey.'

Brock held out his hand and shook Danny's. 'Good luck, old son.'

He found Charlie Pettigrew down in the reception suite, gathering up the things that had been taken from him when he arrived, three months before.

'Didn't I tell you, Brock?' Charlie beamed. 'Things can only get better.' He pointed at the door. 'A new life awaits.'

'So where are you going to celebrate?'

'Oh, ideally the Strand Hotel, Rangoon, but failing that I'll just go home and open a bottle of 1949 Cheval Blanc my father set aside. It was the driest vintage since 1893. Lay a few ghosts to rest. Want to join me?'

'I'd love to, but I think my friends have plans.'

'Ah, I'll drink a toast to you. God bless.'

Brock watched him walk out the door and into the big wide world.

Kathy was waiting for him outside. He was astonished to see a hint of tears in her eyes as she hugged him and opened the car door for him, as if he were an invalid.

'I only went to jail,' he protested. 'I didn't have a triple bypass or anything.'

She shook her head, and he suddenly realised how hard she must have worked to make this possible.

They drove to Kathy's flat, where Suzanne, Stewart and Miranda had gathered. She parked in her basement slot and they took the lift smoothly up to the twelfth floor, and Brock entered her flat to a hero's welcome, Suzanne weeping, and the two youngsters hanging back in a kind of awe, as if expecting him to be covered in scars and bruises. Champagne was opened, everyone given a glass, a toast proposed and cries of 'Speech, speech!'

'I have no words,' Brock said, 'to express my joy at being here, and especially with my two wonderful grandchildren—if you will allow me to call you that—Stewart and Miranda.'

They stared at him for a moment, then, as one, they moved forward and he wrapped them in his arms.

Later, as everyone relaxed, Kathy phoned John to tell him the good news. He was overjoyed, and congratulated Kathy on pulling it off. Then he told her that he also had news. Just that morning he'd heard an item of breaking news from New York. One of the big five publishing houses, PDB, had announced that, after an intense bidding war, they had purchased the rights to publish George Orwell's previously unknown final novel, *The Promised Land*, for a seven-figure sum. At a press conference a representative of PDB introduced the world Orwell expert, Sir Mortimer Hartley, who had authenticated the manuscript. He said that this brilliant last work formed the third part of a 'dystopian trilogy', comprising *Animal Farm*, *Nineteen Eighty-Four* and now *The Promised Land*, and showed Orwell at the height of his literary powers in the final year of his life. A first print run of two million hardback copies had been ordered.

'I wonder if someone will write the manuscript's story,' Kathy said. 'I'll bet it's more exciting than the novel.'

~

In his study in Hampstead, by the light of his old desk lamp, Charlie Pettigrew slowly drew the cork out of the Château

Cheval Blanc 1949, Saint-Émilion, red bordeaux which had been laid down by his grandfather on the day of Orwell's death. Its current value was around fifteen hundred pounds, he knew, and he poured it carefully into his grandfather's favourite decanter, a gift from Evelyn Waugh. When everything was as it should be, he poured a glass, sniffed it appreciatively and raised it in a toast to the ghosts of the house. In response, he heard a creak outside in the hall and he smiled, wondering which particular ghost had stirred—his grandfather, perhaps, or father, or maybe Orwell himself. Then the study door swung open and he saw a pale shape standing there. And it was only when the apparition moved forward into the room that he saw the hammer held in its raised hand.

22

The next day Kathy hadn't been at work long before she got a frantic call from Zack on the far side of the floor.

'Boss, you've got to see this. Dean Causley wants to talk to you.'

She hurried to his desk and was confronted by the magnified image on the big screen of Dean's face, which was pressed close up to the camera, colourless in a harsh electric light.

'Ah, there you are,' he snarled.

'Hello, Dean. I'm glad you've called. I want to talk to you.'

'No, you want to listen!'

He moved suddenly out of shot to reveal the scene behind him, of a figure sitting slumped on a chair, bound with rope. With a scrape and a wobble of the light the camera moved closer, then Dean stepped into view again and lifted the figure's bowed head. Kathy recognised Charlie Pettigrew, the left side of his head grossly bruised and swollen.

She took a deep breath. 'Charlie, can you hear me?' She saw the lips move, but heard nothing.

Dean's voice snarled, 'Come on, Charlie.' He gave Pettigrew's face a vicious slap. 'Talk to the lady!'

Charlie raised his head and looked directly at the camera with his one good eye. He whispered, voice hoarse, 'Yes . . . can hear you . . . no idea where we are.'

Dean stuck his face in front of the lens again. 'Now listen. You release my brother Jarrod and put him in a taxi and when he's far away and absolutely sure he's not been followed he'll call me and then I'll let Charlie go. And if Jarrod doesn't call me by midday, I'll bash Charlie's head in a bit more with this hammer. Fair enough?'

Behind the computer Zack was holding up a piece of paper with a message scribbled on it for Kathy to see: *CAN'T TRACE HIM.*

'Yes, I see,' Kathy said. 'But I'm afraid it's not as simple as that, Dean. Look, I can arrange for you to talk to Jarrod. Would you like that?'

'Don't waste my time, bitch!' Dean screamed. 'Tell you what, I'll be generous. I'll give you fifteen minutes to make the arrangements. I'll call you back at eight forty-two exactly. You be there.' The screen went blank.

Kathy turned to Zack. 'What do you mean you can't trace him?'

'He's hiding his computer's IP address by going through a VPN, a virtual private network. We can't locate him, boss. He could be anywhere.'

She stared back at the screen. 'What can we do?'

'I don't know.'

'Well, find someone who does. Phil? We need a negotiator in here. Ten minutes.'

The action manager jumped to his feet. 'Yes, boss.'

Kathy was trying to sort through the blizzard of thoughts going through her head. 'Peter, get a local patrol car to Pettigrew's house, try to find out what happened. See if they can get any idea of when Dean grabbed him. The rest of you, I need ideas.'

She turned to her phone and put an urgent call through to Commander Torrens's number. He promised her priority assistance. A team of controllers would be made available immediately to coordinate searches across the capital once they had any indication of Dean Causley's whereabouts. 'Sir,' Kathy said, 'if he snatched Pettigrew last night he could be in Glasgow by now.' Torrens then said he would authorise a request for assistance from the National Cyber Security Centre to help locate Dean Causley's transmissions. 'Keep him talking, Kathy. Play for time.'

She rang off, wondering how she was supposed to do that. She went over to Zack and told him about possible NCSC assistance. 'We need to delay things, Zack, slow things down so we can have time to organise and react. Can you interfere with his signal?'

'How do you mean?'

'Make it look as if it's a bad signal, or his computer's playing up or something, so we can cut the conversation before he gives us another deadline. But it mustn't look as if we're responsible.'

'Blimey, that's dangerous, isn't it?'

'Yes, well, any other bright ideas?'

He shook his head. 'I'll get on to it.'

Over on the other side of the room Judy Birch and Peter Sidonis were staring at still images taken from the recording of the conversation with Dean.

'We're getting these enhanced,' Judy said. 'But we think that the pattern in the background is brickwork, yes?'

Kathy stared. Maybe it was, but what help was that? She said something encouraging and moved on.

The minutes ticked by. At eight forty a police negotiator burst into the room, out of breath. Kathy sat him down at Zack's desk and began to give him a rapid briefing while Zack fiddled with the cables on the back of his computer.

At eight forty-two precisely the screen came alive with Dean Causley's face. 'Who the fuck are you?'

'Hello, Dean. My name is Bill Wallace. I'm a police negotiator and I'm here—'

'Go away. Put Kolla on.'

'I have the authority to talk to you, Dean, and hopefully resolve our problem. The first thing we need to establish—'

Dean pressed his face close to the camera so that his mouth filled the screen. 'GO AWAY!' he screamed.

The negotiator turned to Kathy, who nodded and took his place. 'Hello, Dean. You'd really be better talking to Bill. He has the authority—'

'HAVE YOU RELEASED JARROD? YES OR NO?'

'It's not quite as easy as that. A car is on its way to Belmarsh right now to pick him up, but there's a problem. The prison is in lockdown this morning. There's been a fire.'

'BOLLOCKS!'

'It's true. If you turn on the BBC news, you'll probably pick up the report. Listen, I ...' Kathy made a hidden hand signal to Zack and immediately a crackle of static flared across the screen. 'Hello? Dean? Are you there?' The screen returned to normal. Dean had stepped back, looking puzzled. Kathy said, 'Can you see me all right? I lost you there for a moment.'

'I'm here,' he said impatiently.

'Okay, good, so what we're planning ...' She signalled for another burst of static. 'Hello? Lost you again.' She made a cutting motion with her hand and Zac broke the connection altogether. Kathy took a deep breath.

Bill the negotiator was looking confused. 'You didn't mention the fire to me.'

'I just made it up, Bill.'

'And the interference?'

Kathy pointed at Zack.

'Oh.' He was looking worried. 'This isn't how we like to do it. We need to engage with him.'

'You're the expert, Bill, but my orders are to play for time until we can get ourselves organised. When he comes back on, you go ahead and engage with him.'

Phil ran over with a message from Hampstead, where police had found the back door of Pettigrew's house standing open. Inside they discovered signs of a struggle, a glass decanter in one room lying smashed on the floor in a puddle of wine and a side table upset. An antique carriage clock had fallen off the table and lay nearby, its hands stopped at seven twenty-three. There were bloodstains on the hall floor. Kathy ordered a scene of crime team to the house and an urgent search of CCTV cameras in the area.

'If that was seven twenty-three last night,' she said, 'he's had over twelve hours to get ahead of us. He could be anywhere.'

They reconnected Zack's computer after ten minutes and almost immediately Dean appeared. 'What are you playing at?'

'I don't know what's going on, Dean. The trouble seems to be at your end. Are you in a basement or something?'

'Ha ha.'

'Here's Bill again, Dean. He's got something important to tell you.'

'Yes, hello, Dean. In a situation like this we need to—'

'Fuck off. Tell you what, we'll ask Charlie what he thinks. Come on, Charlie, tell her—tell Kolla what I'll do to you if she mucks me around.'

Charlie slowly raised his head again, blinking one eye at the light, and said, 'Please, Kathy ...' He hesitated for a moment, then went on, every word a painful effort. 'Take no notice ... of this little prick ... he's barely capable of stringing a cogent sentence ...'

He was interrupted by a roar from Dean, who launched himself at the seated man and sent him crashing backwards, the wooden chair shattering beneath him as Dean laid into him with blows and savage kicks. Kathy watched, helpless, as the beating continued. Finally Dean straightened and came back to the camera, gasping from the exertion, and pressed close to the lens. 'Tell me you'll free Jarrod, or I'll finish him off right now.'

'All right, all right,' Kathy said. 'We'll do it.'

'Fuckin' right you will.'

Dean's face slid away, leaving the image of Charlie's body curled on the floor among the broken pieces of the chair.

Kathy stared at the screen and whispered, 'What the hell can we do?'

She noticed a small movement, and bent closer to check. There it was again, Charlie's right arm. He was trying to untangle himself from the rope, no longer binding him to the broken chair. The others clustered around, watching. Charlie was trying to raise himself up. He collapsed, then tried again, agonisingly slowly, pushing himself into a crawling position. He scrabbled among the broken frame of the chair, then heaved himself upright and lurched towards the camera and passed out of view.

'What was that in his hand?' Zack murmured.

Kathy thought it was a piece of chair leg.

The silence was broken by a howl, a groan, and then silence once again.

'Blimey,' Zack whispered. 'The bastard's killed him.'

~

More staff arrived, including several tech people to help Zack. Minutes passed—fifteen, thirty, an hour—and the scene on the computer monitor remained silent and unchanging. Probably Dean has fled, Kathy reasoned. She imagined Charlie lying on the cold concrete floor, broken and bleeding, his life seeping away while they fumbled for clues.

A report came in of three vehicles identified from CCTV near Pettigrew's house as possible subjects; they were being tracked from cameras on a wider and wider perimeter across the city. Then one trail faded, and another, and finally the third was lost. Their numbers were urgently circulated. One of them, a white van, was reported stolen.

Zack called Kathy over to another monitor, where he had been working with Judy Birch. He showed Kathy detailed images of the background to Dean's transmissions that he had enhanced.

'I was right,' Judy said. 'It is brickwork.'

'Okay.' Kathy tried to sound enthusiastic.

'You see the colour?' Zack said.

'Ye-es. Sort of yellow.'

'Exactly!' Judy almost shouted. 'London stock bricks!'

'Ah.' Kathy got it. Most of the buildings in London up to the end of the nineteenth century used London stock bricks made from the distinctive local yellow clay. 'Can we trust the colour?'

Zack explained how he'd made adjustments to arrive at what he believed was a faithful hue.

'So they're most likely still in London.'

'Yes. And something else ...' Zack changed to another image. 'There, the pattern of the brickwork changes towards the top, do you see? It's curved, like a vault. And it looks old.'

'So, a basement? A cellar? In an old building in the London area.' Kathy nodded and called Sidonis over. He would circulate the information to the borough operational commands who would organise searches in their areas. But Kathy knew how slim the chances of success would be. Most of the cellars and basements would be unknown to the local police. What they were looking for might be beneath a house, a row of old shops, a warehouse, anywhere. 'Tell them to concentrate on disused buildings, old ones, Peter—Victorian.'

She turned back to Zack and asked him to run the recordings through again from the beginning. When they reached

the end of the third clip, with the howl when Pettigrew staggered out of view, Zack made to halt the recording, but Kathy
stopped him.

'There's nothing more,' he said.

'What about sound? Is there any background noise?'

She leaned closer to the computer as he turned up the
sound. They had been so focused on Dean and Pettigrew's
voices that everything else had been filtered out, but now,
in the silence, they agreed that there was a faint background
rumble.

'A truck?' Zack suggested.

'No,' Judy said, 'it's going on too long. Machinery, maybe.'

The sound gradually faded away. They held their breaths,
and then it began again, a distant rumble, rising and then fading
away after about twenty seconds. They waited, then, after a
longer interval, it happened again.

'Trains,' Kathy said. 'It's next to a railway line.'

'Or under it,' Judy urged. 'A railway viaduct?'

There was silence for a moment, then they all said 'Yes'
at once.

When the railway companies first brought their lines into
London, they marched over the crowded inner-city districts
on great brick viaducts. Now those vaulted spaces were filled
by workshops, the odd café or club, or were just derelict voids.

Kathy called to Peter to concentrate on brick railway
viaducts.

'Any bright ideas?' she said.

Alfarsi said, 'My money would be on the Deptford line
into London Bridge.' Others came up with different ideas,
and Kathy sent them off to lead the search in those areas.

Zack went to consult with other IT experts while Kathy stayed watching the screen. It was agonising, waiting for the image to suddenly erupt into movement, or some sound to disturb the soft background rumbling or, perhaps worst of all, for nothing to happen, which would mean that Charlie Pettigrew was now lying dead in some forgotten corner of the city.

It was Alfarsi's call that finally broke the tension. His guess had been right. The stolen white van had been spotted, covered in a tarpaulin, beside a long run of disused railway viaduct not far from the Den, the Millwall football stadium in South London.

Kathy jumped in a car and they raced across the river and down to South Bermondsey. Two ambulances were already at the scene, along with Alfarsi's searchers in their blue overalls clustered around a doorway formed in a rusting corrugated-iron sheet wall that filled one of the archways.

Alfarsi came to her as she ran over.

'They're both still alive—just,' he said. 'Both unconscious. Pettigrew's got a head wound along with lots of other things. Causley's lost a lot of blood. Looks like Pettigrew rammed the chair leg through his stomach.' Alfarsi shook his head in wonder. 'Didn't think he had it in him.'

'No,' Kathy said. 'It was probably the first time in his life that he really lost his temper.'

23

Spring was on the cusp of summer when the Causley boys were brought to trial. In view of the overwhelming graphic evidence against them they had decided to plead guilty to the multiple murders with which they were charged. Charlie Pettigrew was in the visitors' benches for the sentencing, with Donna Priest by his side. Together they watched the brothers receive whole life orders—life sentences without the possibility of parole.

Later, outside the Old Bailey, they watched the brothers' lawyer declare that they would appeal against the sentence.

'Where's the nearest pub?' Charlie said. He was still walking with a stick.

'The Magpie and Stump,' Donna said, pointing. 'That way.'

They turned to go but were intercepted by Kathy, who said how glad she was to see them both, and asked Charlie how his leg was doing now.

'Much, much better, though I'll probably set off alarms when I next go through airport security. We're going to have a celebratory drink. Will you join us?'

'I'd love to,' Kathy said, 'but I'm afraid I have to get back to work.'

'Oh dear, another time then.'

Donna said, 'Actually, Kathy, I was wanting to get in touch with you. There's something I need to talk to you about. May I give you a ring to explain?'

'Of course.' Kathy gave her the number and they said goodbye.

~

Donna called her that evening and got straight to the point. 'You're probably thinking I need help with a book or something, but it isn't that. I have something that I very much need you to see, something that could be highly relevant if the Causleys appeal.'

Kathy was puzzled. 'What, new evidence?'

'Yes, and absolutely crucial to a full understanding of their crimes.'

'Well, in that case, yes, of course, I must see it. Will you come to my office?'

'No, I can't do that. I'm afraid I must ask you to come to my home.'

Kathy was about to object when Donna added, 'It's really

quite important and I can guarantee you won't be disappointed by what I have to show you.'

'That sounds very mysterious.'

'It would mean a little trip out of the city to Surrey. Do you know Godalming?'

'No, I don't think I've ever been there.'

'It's a lovely little town and I'm sure you won't regret your trouble. I know you must have a very busy schedule, but how about this weekend? Make it an outing, come for lunch?' She sounded very anxious.

'Well, I—'

'I can promise that it will be worth your while.'

Kathy said, 'Can't you tell me something about what you want to show me?'

'Please, trust me.'

Kathy hesitated, thinking how dull her weekends had been lately, and said, 'All right. Sunday.'

'Excellent!' Donna's mood had abruptly changed. 'And if you take the train we can open a nice bottle of wine with lunch! Just the two of us, okay?'

Kathy hung up, wondering if she'd made a mistake. She sensed something uncomfortably obsessive about Donna, behind the matronly mask.

~

The author was waiting for her as the train drew in to Godalming station. It was a beautiful sunny day, the air fresh, the countryside green and bountiful beneath a cobalt blue sky. They took a short walking tour of the town along the winding high street to the curious little Pepperpot building in the centre, then on along Church Street to the parish church. Donna led the way down a small lane nearby, to a cottage whose garden was bursting with spring flowers. A winding brick path took them to the front door. There was a name on the door, and Kathy looked at it in surprise: *The Promised Land*. Donna laughed at her expression. 'Yes, I thought you'd appreciate that. Mind your head. The doors are a bit low.'

She took Kathy into a comfortable room that seemed to function as both a sitting room and a study, completely lined with books. At one end, with a window looking out over another garden to a wood beyond, was a table with a computer and reference books—*The New Shorter Oxford*, Fowler's, Roget's, Butterworth's *Police Law*, *A Practical Guide to the Police and Criminal Evidence Act*, *The Oxford Companion to English Literature*.

'This is exactly how I imagine a writer's den,' Kathy said. 'How long have you been here?'

'Take a seat, Kathy. I'll get us a glass of wine and tell you the story. Oh, and while I'm getting it, have a look at this.' She handed Kathy a hardback book with an image of an antique map on the cover, and the title, *The Promised Land*. 'Have you seen it already?'

'No, I haven't.'

'It's just been released. I got this yesterday from Waterstones.'

She fetched two large glasses of wine. 'What do you think? Impressive, isn't it? With an effusive introduction by Mortimer Hartley. See his comments on the back cover: *A masterpiece . . . a milestone of twentieth-century literature . . . a work of genius.*' Donna laughed. 'Poor Sir Mortimer. I fear he'll come to regret those words. Anyway, this copy is for you, Kathy, and I hope you don't mind, but I've written a little dedication inside.'

Kathy turned to the title page and read Donna's words: *To Kathy, Scotland Yard's finest, from a fellow traveller on this epic journey to The Promised Land, Donna Priest.*

'Thank you, Donna. I really appreciate it.' But Kathy sensed something inappropriately excited, even slightly hysterical, in Donna's manner that made it hard to follow her train of thought and was beginning to worry her.

'I believe you will, Kathy! Yes, yes! Anyway, you asked how long I've been here. Twenty-six years it is now. Before that I worked in the City, and in the early eighties I was working for a firm of stockbrokers in Threadneedle Street—very traditional, very old school. Then, in 1986, Margaret Thatcher deregulated the financial markets and initiated the Big Bang—you remember? Of course you don't, you would have been barely a teenager, yes? Anyway, soon we were caught up in the whirlwind and within a year our business was completely transformed and my life became very hectic and very exciting. I was good at my job; I made deals—intricate, complicated arrangements tailored precisely to my clients' needs. By 1989, on my forty-second birthday, I was making a serious amount of money and was offered a position in New York to make even more. Instead I decided to get out and do what I'd always wanted to do—become a writer. I'd already secretly written two novels which had got nowhere with publishers, and I decided it was time to get serious. People thought I was crazy, but I bought this place and moved out here to the depths of wildest Surrey to embark on what I felt to be my true life's work. Fresh from my experiences in the City, I decided to write a contemporary thriller set in the money markets, which I called *The Big Gang*. The first publisher I sent it to snapped it up. Somehow it seemed to catch the mood of the time and it got great reviews and sold reasonably well. The second book was okay but not such a big success, and the third sold even less. Then my publisher was gobbled up by a bigger conglomerate and all the people I'd known there vanished. The new editor reviewed my sales figures and said I was "on the downward curve", and refused to look at my fourth book.

'Eventually, after a number of refusals, I did get a publisher for it, a less prestigious one, and I stayed with them for a couple more books before they decided that was enough. By this time, I'd been a professional author for ten years and I wasn't sure where I was going. Looking for inspiration I decided to sit in on the Causley brothers' trial, which was probably the most notorious case in that year, 1999. I was surprised to recognise the foreman of the jury as one of the publishers who had turned me down a few years before, Charles Pettigrew, and it gave me an idea. I found the whole trial and the people involved—the victim, the killers, the lawyers, the detective Brock—quite compelling, especially when the jury took so long to come to a verdict. So when it was over I approached Charlie with my proposal to write a true-crime book around the Causley case. I was lucky in that he had found it a pretty overwhelming experience, and liked the idea of somehow capturing it in print. That was how I changed to writing non-fiction, and since then Golden Press have published three of my books. Here, let me top you up. Am I boring you?'

'Not at all. It's really interesting to get the . . .' she fumbled for a moment for the word, '. . . the inside story on someone else's career.'

'Well, it's not exactly dazzling, Kathy. My old colleagues in the City would fall about laughing if they knew how little I've made out of it—less in twenty-six years as a writer than I made in one year in Threadneedle Street. But I can't complain about that. No one asked me to do this, and it's a common enough story, the mid-list writer who just doesn't take off. I know that Charlie has been wanting to terminate our relationship for some time but has never quite worked up the courage to tell me. And in my own terms I've been a failure—I wanted to write fiction. My true-crime books were interesting to do— the research, the character studies—but for me they weren't the creative works of the imagination that I wanted to write.

'But look, I'm going on too long. Let's have some lunch. I've bought a quiche from a lovely little patisserie in Church Street—I think I really would starve to death if they went out of business. Would that suit you, Kathy? I've got some salad as well. Bring your glass through to the kitchen.'

As Kathy followed her through she had a strong sense that something here was not quite right. Donna's story had been told with an odd fervour, almost desperation, that Kathy couldn't interpret. And then there was that nameplate on the front door, *The Promised Land*. It hadn't looked new to her. In fact, it had seemed quite weathered, as if it could have been there for twenty-six years.

It was hot in the kitchen, from the sun shining through the window and the Aga in which the quiche was warming. Donna took another bottle from the fridge and topped up their glasses, spilling some wine in the process. 'It's nice to have company,' she said. 'It can be a very solitary life, writing. The opposite of yours, Kathy, I imagine, constantly surrounded by people in a state of crisis, yes?'

'It can be like that. Sometimes it's good to shut the door of my flat and just be on my own.'

'No partner, Kathy? Is that because of your work?'

'Sounds like I'm one of your character studies.'

'Sorry! Can't help myself. I've never been married. There was someone ... at the end of my time in the City we expanded to offices in Canary Wharf, and a new man joined the firm. We worked closely together and became quite fond of each other, but I decided that I had to sacrifice that so I could focus on my writing. More fool me, I suppose.'

She put on some oven gloves, took the quiche from the Aga and laid it on the pine kitchen table. 'How's that?' She handed a slice to Kathy. 'Help yourself to salad. Is it my imagination or are you looking a little apprehensive?'

Kathy met her eyes. 'You said it was urgent that I come, Donna. Why was that? Is it about *The Promised Land*?'

Donna held her look for a moment, then gave a tight little smile. 'Ah, that's perceptive of you. But please, do eat up while it's warm. You must forgive me if I sound anxious. I just ... have to get this right, and ... I have dizzy spells.'

Donna began to eat, and Kathy followed suit, giving her time to come to the point, whatever it was. She was feeling the heat in the small kitchen, and felt a little dizzy herself. She tried to remember how many glasses they'd drunk. Alcohol always seemed to have more impact during the day, she thought, rather than at night.

Finally Donna put down her knife and fork and said, her voice suddenly firm, 'What really upset me, what I just could not tolerate, was that they never took me seriously. Even with that successful first book, they patronised me, as if I was just some silly woman indulging a hobby. All of them did, Charlie most of all. What I was doing was basically trivial in his eyes, not *real* literature like that written by the great authors his father and grandfather knew—Waugh and Maugham and Orwell and the rest. They didn't take me *seriously*, Kathy. That really pissed me off. In the City I had managed more wealth and more complexity in a week than they would see in a lifetime, but *they* patronised *me*. With their sense of privilege and their lazy judgements, they refused to take me seriously. But they bloody well will now.'

She was gasping and gulped a glass of water. She took a deep breath and continued more slowly. 'I mentioned I had something to give you. If you've had enough to eat, let's go back to the living room. It's cooler there.'

Kathy got carefully to her feet and followed her, wondering at how tired she felt. The last eight months had really stretched her, but still.

'Take that comfortable chair, Kathy.'

She sat and watched Donna go to a roll-top desk and take out a thick package that she brought over. 'Here, this is for you.'

Kathy opened the package and took out a weighty folder. On the front was a title: *The Promised Land*. She opened it and saw the familiar typewritten text of the manuscript, with its scribbled note at the top. She looked more closely and said, 'This isn't a photocopy, is it?'

'No. It's the original, written on that typewriter over there.' Donna pointed to an ancient machine sitting on the roll-top desk.

Kathy felt a dull shock, like a slap on the head, the sense that she had somehow completely missed the point of a long and elaborate story. Trying to deny this to herself, she said doubtfully, 'By you?'

'Yes, Kathy, *by me*. I finished it about a year ago. It took me four years, what with all the Orwell research and so on. I began thinking about it when I learned that Dean Causley had been released from prison.'

This was crazy, surely. And yet the document in her hands was undeniably the original. 'You're saying Sir Mortimer Hartley has authenticated a fake?'

'Yes. Serves him right, pompous old fart. But no, that's not fair, because actually he's absolutely correct; it *is* a masterpiece. It's just that nobody would have said that if my name had been on the cover instead of Eric Blair's.'

Kathy struggled to find flaws in this bizarre claim. 'Orwell's diary in the National Archives . . . you altered it, did you?'

'Oh, you know about that? I had to be careful not to overdo it, but it was such great fun. If you go back through their records, you'll see when I was there. I used my real name.'

Kathy swallowed, her throat dry. 'Careless of us not to check.'

'Not at all. You had a much more important problem to solve—the Heath murders.'

A moment's silence, then, 'I'm almost afraid to ask.'

Donna chuckled and disappeared for a moment, returning with their refilled glasses.

Kathy said, 'I think I've had enough.'

'Well, real authors of genius who write milestones of literature are invariably notorious drunks and right now I need all
the help I can get to go through with this. So cheers.' She
sat down with a sigh. 'The other thing that really annoyed
me, apart from not being taken seriously, was that they didn't
believe I could really tell a good story, either because I relied
too heavily on plot, or else not enough. That publisher who
turned down my fourth book told me that I'd failed to think
up *a killer plot.* Well, I sure as hell have now.'

She got to her feet, went back to the desk and returned
with a second fat folder which she handed to Kathy, who read
the label on the front: *The Killer Plot, by Donna Priest.*

'Don't read it now. I'll summarise it for you. Talented but
unrecognised author devises a spectacular plot in which two
vicious killers, recently released from prison, take revenge
on the four key people who locked them up. She explains
her plan to the two killers, who love it, and together they
resolve to make it a reality. At first the killers want to simply
murder the four, but the author points out how obvious that
would be, how they'd be back in jail in hours. She has something much more subtle, more complex in mind. The four
must suffer as the brothers have suffered—disgrace, humili-
ation and incarceration—and their families must suffer too.
The killers aren't sure about that (they're not really very
bright), and finally they reach a compromise—they will
murder the pompous judge who sentenced them, and,
because they enjoy murdering women, the wife of the pros-
ecuting council, and then go along with the author's plans
for the rest. Frankly, they have no interest or understanding

of her larger themes. The author adjusts her planning and the story begins.

'However, when writing fiction, the characters sometimes act in ways the author didn't anticipate, and further adjustments and improvisations in the plot have to be made as it develops. So too with the real-life version. For example, the obliteration of the features of the three Heath murder victims was intended to make it impossible for the police to identify "Shari Mitra", but unfortunately Uzma made herself known to Charlie's cleaner Nadia, which she wasn't supposed to do, and then clever old Brock followed that up and discovered who she really was. This entailed a rapid adjustment in the plot and a second trip to India by the author to obtain forged birth and other certificates to form a connection between Amar Dasgupta and Uzma Jamali's birth family, to convince the experts that the provenance of the manuscript was valid.

'I could go on, but you get the picture. The whole story is set out in that folder, Kathy. I killed those people, and sent Charlie and Brock to jail. I did it. The Causley boys were just my instruments.' She got to her feet and said, 'Excuse me a moment.'

Kathy felt strangely remote, her mind labouring to take this in. She believed Donna, and wondered if she intended to kill her too. Certainly she felt barely able to move or resist.

Donna returned with a bottle of pills and swallowed a couple with a gulp of wine. 'Sorry, headache. Where were we?'

Kathy said, 'Why Andrea Giannopoulos? Why did she have to die?'

'To establish the initial momentum of the plot. It was a random choice, to throw you off the scent of the true story to come. And her death was used to plant the idea of pools of water as a significant motif in the story, harking back to the death of Chloe Honnery. The same with Caroline Jarvis's death. The brothers liked that, not realising that I would use it to implicate them.'

'Jarrod Causley has never mentioned you.'

'No, he doesn't believe I was anything more than an irritating but helpful old biddy, giving him a few tips and ironing out a few problems. He's very arrogant. He probably thinks by now that it was all his own idea.'

Kathy fought to clear her head. This was madness, surely? Donna was playing some sort of literary game with her. 'You're not really serious about all this?'

'Oh yes.'

'You killed Andrea Giannopoulos just to establish background . . . ?'

'To be perfectly honest, neither she nor Caroline Jarvis were very nice people, both very spoilt and self-obsessed. And we all have to die sometime. I felt worse about the two girls, Shari and Elena, struggling to make their way in the world against all the odds. When we finally found Shari working in the kebab shop, and discovered how intelligent and educated she was, I couldn't believe my luck. She was just perfect for the part—but then, when I got to know her better, briefing her on the role she had to play, I grew rather fond of her, and it was a real effort to harden my heart. But the plot had to come first—the killer plot—and it was vital that the stakes had to be of the highest. And then Elena Vasile, her flatmate, got wind of what we were doing and demanded a share of the action, and so I used her to groom Stewart Chambers and entrap Brock.'

'I wouldn't have taken you for a cruel person.'

Donna's voice hardened. 'No, well, maybe when you finally confront your own death you become a little more ruthless, Kathy, and a little more impatient with people who are wasting their lives. I hope I've given Charlie a big enough shock to stop him going on wasting his.'

'You were very ...' Kathy struggled to form her words, '... clever ... with the forensics.'

'I'm a crime writer, Kathy. I know far more about killing people than any real-life murderer.'

'The dog hair. I should have realised ...'

'Yes, I thought afterwards that was probably a bit over the top. I got it from the dog basket in Charlie's office, of course, along with the tissues in the wastepaper basket. He had a cold that day.'

'My aunt and uncle in Sheffield ...'

'Research, Kathy. When I discovered you would be the senior investigating officer, I found out everything I could about you. I never met your relatives, but I almost feel I did, I know you so well. And I was so glad it was you, Kathy; a woman after my own heart, I think, determined, a fighter against a biased world. I was so glad that it was you to whom I could make my confession.'

'But ... what did you mean about confronting ...?' Kathy began, but then couldn't remember where she was going with that. She felt a flutter of panic and tried to get to her feet, but felt Donna's hand on her shoulder, pushing her firmly back. She saw something in Donna's other hand—a syringe, a needle—and tried to cry out. It was the last thing she remembered.

24

It was dark when she woke. At first she had no idea where she was, but then she made out the shelves of books, the desk by the darkened window. She forced herself out of the chair, stumbled to the doorway and pressed a light switch.

'Donna?'

There was no response in the silent house.

She made her way to the kitchen, ran a glass of water under the tap, took a deep drink and looked around. No one there. She went down the tiny hallway to an open door leading to a bedroom. There she saw Donna lying on the bed. 'Donna?'

She switched on the bedside light and repeated the name, but Donna didn't stir. Kathy felt her throat and could find no pulse. When she took the other woman's hand, it was cold and stiff with rigor mortis.

Still feeling shaky, she sat on the edge of the bed, wondering how much of what she remembered was real or a dream. Then she saw the empty syringe lying on the bedside table.

She got to her feet, intending to go to find her bag and phone, when she noticed a sheet of paper on the bed beside Donna's body, with her name on it. She picked it up and read the handwritten note.

Kathy,

In the living room you will find a black travel bag which I now give to you along with its contents. Inside you will find the following:
- *the original manuscript of my work of fiction* The Promised Land *by Eric Blair*
- *the hardback copy of* The Promised Land *fresh from New York, which I gave you*
- *the file marked* The Killer Plot, *by Donna Priest, being my journal of the true-crime case of the Hampstead murders, which sets out in detail everything that I did*
- *my last will and testament, in which you will see that I name you as my sole beneficiary and owner of my house, its contents and all my other assets to do with as you will. Use them to compensate the victims if you so choose, and mop up the damage I caused. It's entirely up to you.*

Kathy, I am relying on you. Don't let them blame my tumour. That sentence you couldn't finish—yes, I am confronting my own death, and have been for some time. The cancer is slow-growing but insidious and inoperable, a nasty little octopus sending out its tentacles to become more and more entangled with my brain. It cannot be treated with surgery or chemotherapy, and radiotherapy is very difficult. I underwent one course and it cost me three months' work and I'm not going through that again. I get head-aches, periods of dizziness and nausea, but I am NOT deranged. In fact, I seem to become more focused, more clear-headed as time goes on. A death sentence certainly concentrates the mind and drives one to action, but I am completely sane and utterly rational. I knew exactly what I was doing.

And now I'm going to take my pills and go to sleep and find peace. It has been a privilege to cross swords with you. Please don't feel too angry with me.

Donna

25

From the train station Brock walked through Hampstead to Charlie Pettigrew's house. Large gin and tonics seemed to be the order of this hot summer's day, and they sipped them as Charlie gave Brock the guided tour.

'I'm planning a few changes,' Charlie explained. 'Modernise the kitchen for a start, and clear out some of the old junk. Grandfather's taste in furniture was pretty ropey, even for those days. But I've been so busy I haven't had time to get on to it.'

'Work?' Brock asked.

'God yes, haven't had a moment. We're rushing to get *The Killer Plot* into print, of course. Donna's text is very clean, hardly needs editing, but the lawyers are worried about some of the passages. No compromise, I say. We'll publish and be damned. And if someone sues us that'll only increase publicity and improve sales. There's a huge reading public out there hungry for this.

'And then there's all the other business that's come in. We've been inundated by approaches from agents and authors wanting to publish with Golden Press. Angela and I have taken on two new editors to cope with it, and some of the material is very promising indeed. I tell you, Golden Press is undergoing a renaissance, Brock, and so am I, all thanks to Donna Priest. Have you been following the social media clamour about her? Rock star status. And then that *Panorama* program on the BBC. Well, now, if you've finished your gin I suggest we stroll across the Heath for lunch. I've reserved a table at the Flask in Highgate.'

They set off, Pettigrew careful to set the alarm and double-lock the front door. He brandished his walking stick in the direction of Hampstead Heath and they made their way into the wooded perimeter, heavily shaded now by dense green foliage. Soon they came across the first of the eccentric figures that the Heath seemed to be home to, a small woman of inde-terminate age, heavily rugged up in what looked like a Native American blanket, being pulled along by six small dogs. They emerged into the open Parliament Hill Fields, where children were flying kites, and walked up to the high point with its distant views out across the city.

'And how about *The Promised Land*?' Brock asked. 'Any idea what's happened to that?'

Charlie laughed. 'Spectacular! PDB wavered for a while after the story broke that it was a fake, but the demand for the book only increased. Mortimer Hartley tried to stop it and get them to withdraw his introductory essay, but they'd already printed their two million hardbacks and PDB refused. That essay only made the novel more scandalously attractive, and all they did was insert a frontispiece explaining the context, as if everybody didn't already know it. They say poor old Hartley's a broken man, but then he'll have the consolation of his share of the royalties to ease his embarrassment.'

Charlie was interrupted by an elderly man with an ancient Highland terrier. He wanted to know if they'd seen a certain letter published in that day's *Sunday Times* concerning the migration of swallows. 'It's a disgrace,' he said, shaking his finger at them. 'An utter disgrace.'

They were saved by a phalanx of runners who distracted the old man and allowed Brock and Pettigrew to walk on towards Number One Pond and Highgate.

'But how about yourself, Brock? Have you made a full recovery from your time in Belmarsh?'

'Oh yes. I see the world afresh, with bright new colours.'

'I hope your former employers have given you a grovelling apology?'

'Not quite, but they have offered me a job.'

'Really? Will you take it?'

'Yes, retirement didn't agree with me. They call it a "consultancy" and hope it will shut me up and stop me suing them for wrongful arrest. They imagine that I'll sit on my restored laurels and stay well away from the pointy end, but I have other ideas.'

'Really? Detective work?'

'That's what I am, Charlie, a detective.'

They reached the Flask and took their pints out to a table in the courtyard of the eighteenth-century pub.

'This place has its own ghosts,' Pettigrew said. 'The high-wayman Dick Turpin hid down there in the cellar, and Karl Marx used to drop in for a tipple, so they say. I propose a toast to ghosts, and to one in particular—Donna Priest.'

'That's very forgiving of you, Charlie,' Brock said, 'considering she planned to kill the two of us.'

'What?'

'Did you ever see her talking to a lifer called Arnold on her visits to Belmarsh?'

'Yes, I remember him. I think she said something about including him in her next book. I tried to keep well clear of him—they say he's a real psychopath.'

'Well, Kathy told me the other day that he's informed the prison authorities that she promised to take care of his dear old mum if he murdered us both. And he'd have done it too. It would have been part of her pact with the Causley boys, to wipe the slate clean, all four of us who put them inside—Jarvis, Walcott, you and me.'

'Good God.' Pettigrew had gone very pale. 'But Jarvis killed himself, didn't he?'

'Kathy says they're reviewing the forensic evidence. It seems Jarrod Causley made a trip up to Scotland at the time Jarvis was there. We were just lucky that Kathy cornered the Causleys when she did and got us out in time, otherwise ...' Brock took a deep draw on his beer. 'Ah, that's good. No, it's Kathy we should be drinking a toast to, Charlie. Without her we'd both be ghosts.'

They raised their glasses in silent thanks.

Pettigrew said, 'What's she going to do with Donna's house in Godalming?'

'I believe she's talking to some literary organisation about turning it into a kind of retreat for budding authors.'

'Oh, that's a good idea.'

'Is it? I should have thought there are enough budding authors in the world without giving them any more encouragement.'

Pettigrew laughed. 'You don't mean that.'

'Yes, I do. Imagination without responsibility. Look what it did to Donna Priest. She should have stuck to Threadneedle Street.'

'No, no, no,' Pettigrew protested. 'It's essential, the unfettered exploration of ideas, of imaginary worlds of the mind . . .'

They continued arguing about this for some time, until their roast Hampshire topside beef arrived, when they stopped talking and concentrated on the more important business of lunch.